CW01390768

THE
EDGE OF
SOLITUDE

Also by Katie Hale

My Name Is Monster
White Ghosts

THE EDGE OF SOLITUDE

KATIE HALE

CANONGATE

First published in Great Britain in 2024
by Canongate Books Ltd, 14 High Street, Edinburgh EH1 1TE

canongate.co.uk

1

Copyright © Katie Hale, 2024

The right of Katie Hale to be identified as the
author of this work has been asserted by her in accordance
with the Copyright, Designs and Patents Act 1988

The excerpt on p. 23 quotes the Antarctic Treaty (The Antarctic Treaty
Secretariat [ATS], 1959). Excerpts from Ernest Shackleton's *Diary of the
Quest Expedition, 1921–22*, appear by permission of the University of
Cambridge, Scott Polar Research Institute

Every effort has been made to trace copyright holders and obtain
their permission for the use of copyright material. The publisher
apologises for any errors or omissions and would be grateful if notified
of any corrections that should be incorporated in future reprints
or editions of this book.

British Library Cataloguing-in-Publication Data
A catalogue record for this book is available on
request from the British Library

ISBN 978 1 80530 169 1

Typeset in Goudy by Palimpsest Book Production Ltd,
Falkirk, Stirlingshire

Printed and bound in Great Britain by CPI Group (UK) Ltd,
Croydon CR0 4YY

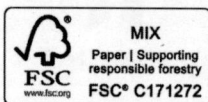

MIX
Paper | Supporting
responsible forestry
FSC
www.fsc.org
FSC® C171272

for Loren,
in lockdowns & lock-ins

'In the darkening twilight I saw
a lone star hover: gem like above the bay'
Ernest Shackleton,
Diary of the Quest Expedition, 1921–22

THE BEAGLE
CHANNEL

Let's start with the whales, shall we? Humpbacks, both of them, a mother shielding her calf, drift-net scars across her back white like spiderwebs. There are the whales, and above them, there is me. Half dizzy from too much air, I lean out over the railings as we hold our course along the darkening channel. Below the shadow of the mountains, in the oil-slick slipstream of the ship, are the whales. I watch as they follow their own breaths to the surface.

'Ms Cunningham?'

If we start with the whales, we also have to start with the man: stoic, metallic, giving nothing away. He does not look at the whales, or the mountains, or the sky lit blue and gold at the back of them. He's dressed all in black, a touch of grey peppering his temples, and so still, so indistinguishable from the painted ship, I'd already forgotten he was there.

From across the water comes the ring and clatter of minerals being docked, of consumer goods being loaded in their place. Underneath them, a barrage of warning calls, echoing like the cries of frantic birds. The whole northern shore is a castle of concrete docks and sidings, jetties that bristle out into the water. Against the backdrop of blue mountains, lit drones circle the shipping containers like fireflies. I'm close enough to make out the IntuTech logo plastered across the containers' corrugated sides, far enough that the dock workers are thumb-smears as they dodge the swinging mechanical arms.

When I was last here fifty years ago, I was told they called this place the End of the World.

'Ms Cunningham.'

'Yes?' It comes out snippily – as in, 'Yes, yes, what now?' Probably I've crossed too many time zones. I can feel the lag in my bones, in my gut, in the soreness where my ribs press against the railings. Around me, everything feels loud and disgustingly slick: the frenzy of the port, the man in his black uniform, the sleek drive of the icebreaker along the channel, like a solid hand pushing through a HoloPlayer's projection. To cover it, I point to where the whales nudge among food wrappers and yellow foam. 'Look.'

'A fairly common sight down here.' He says this with a shrug – impossible to tell whether he's talking about the rubbish or the whales. 'I came out to tell you dinner will be an hour.'

'Thank you.'

'In case you'd like to freshen up.'

Meaning: you really ought to freshen up. I resist the urge to sniff my armpits.

'One of the staff will unpack for you later. For now, the dress code is informal. The ship is heated using intuition tech,' he adds, 'so you should be warm enough.' So typical of a man, to see an older woman and assume she's vulnerable, to imagine she needs reminding to take care of herself, to wrap up warm. I look again at the grey around his temples. He can barely be twenty years younger than me. I'm only seventy-five, for god's sake, and I know how to put on a fucking coat.

As it happens, I am cold. I tell him I'll stay out a bit longer, though, to watch the humpbacks and to spite him. Besides, I've been on ships before; spending time on deck is the only way to counteract the claustrophobia. I try to remember if it was this cold fifty years ago. Probably it was colder.

'Cabin number three,' he tells me. 'One deck down via the main staircase. The communal areas are all marked. When you're ready,' he adds, with a smile that vanishes into the tunnels of his eyes. Then he leaves, and the deck is empty.

Once, there would have been others, a crowd of us, clutching our welcome drinks, lapping up the billionaire's hospitality while we networked for all we were worth. Then, later, a shift, as I became not just part of the crowd but its centre. Before the whole Helsinki affair, I would have revelled in the theatre of it all – would have swept, fashionably late, right into the thick of it, drip-feeding words like precious coins, my glass held slightly to the side so a server could fill it without interrupting my flow, the others radial around me. At my elbow, the occasional reverent touch.

Tonight, there will be none of these things. *An exclusive.* That's what AJ told me on the vid. No journalists or vid-makers to impress. No rivals clinging to my every word like a covering of rime. Only me. Only the work.

I message AJ to let him know I'm safely on board. Not that he cares about my safety. In an effort towards professionalism, I send him a photo from the deck: Tierra del Fuego; Isla Navarino; darkening peaks catch the setting sun, spin the light like a party trick. Out of shot, the metal wharfs rust into the sea. Loaded ships groan their way in from the Southern Ocean. All along the northern shore, automated cargo trucks pull off from the jetties, sound their horns along the narrow road to the airfield. Groups of sea-migrant workers cling to the rear doors, hitching a ride back to the shanty towns of Ushuaia. I wave, but nobody waves back.

*

Ushuaia. Nestled at the toe of the South American continent, it's the world's most southerly city. Among the locals, it's known as *fin del mundo, principio de todo*. At least, it used to be, fifty years ago. At least, that was what they told me last time I was here.

5

Fin del mundo, principio de todo. The end of the world, the beginning of everything.

Back then, I suppose, a journey south was always a beginning. Something hopeful. The Antarctic Treaty just about held. It was still possible to imagine Antarctica as somewhere pristine, a new page, a fresh start.

Except that words rarely have just one meaning. I should know – I've built my whole career on their slippery definitions – and as well as 'end', '*fin*' can also mean 'aim' or 'goal'. Not just an end, but an end-to-work-towards. The objective that justifies everything to come before it.

What is the goal of the world? Beginnings. To begin again.

*

So let's start instead with the ship.

Sleek and dusk-blue, she pushes along the channel, her name, *Lone Star*, emblazoned at her prow. Her soundscape includes: slither of hull through calm water; the soft *pfff pfff* of whale breath; my own ragged breath as I lean out to catch the spray of the humpbacks.

Above, halyards clink against their masts, light and musical against the clang of buoys and distant frenzy of machines. With her sails unfurled and the wind driving her on across the waves, this ship must be magnificent, spindrift catching the light like fireworks.

For now, though, the sails are dormant, bound up against the spars and full of uncaught potential. The *Lone Star* is a hybrid ship – built for eco-travel as well as for convenience – but this is a business trip, with no time for the whims of the wind. The electric engine thrums up through the deck and into the soles of my feet, up through my calves, my pelvis, into my stomach. The ship has barely a roll and already I'm feeling queasy.

The gins on the jet feel like hours ago. I need another drink before dinner and the presentation. This was always my habit:

6

arriving just a fraction late. As Bree used to say, a shepherd doesn't spend the whole time with her flock. Important for there to be some mystery for the sheep, for them to wonder what happens beyond the four stone walls of their field. That way, your arrival becomes an event. That way, when you come with the butchering knife, they will cluster around you, bleating.

*

We could begin years earlier. Decades, even. After all, where does one story end and another begin? *The end of the world is the beginning of everything.* But for now, let's start with the call from AJ a week before, and the invitation from the billionaire. (This is what I've been calling him in all my articles, though nobody knows exactly what he's worth. Part of his cultivated mystery. For all I know, 'billionaire' could be an understatement.)

'A miracle,' AJ told me on the vid, talking nineteen to the dozen as usual, always frantic, always slapdash, always chasing some uncatchable zeitgeist. 'Ten days of luxury at the cutting edge of conservation. And his people asked for you personally.'

I sat by the window in my crumbling Edinburgh flat, and stared at the grey rain sheeting across the Firth, at the old red bridge left to rust into it. My vid flashed up a warning: water rising again in the city. I swept it off the screen.

Out of shot, I picked at my cuticles, listened to AJ gushing as though I was his favourite client. 'This'll be the remaking of you, Cunningham. No more of those little columns on backwater sites – a chance to put the past behind you, get you back in the right circles.'

Clarification: that isn't why I agreed to come on the trip. Not when I shut off the vid to AJ a week ago. Not when I boarded the plane from Edinburgh, when it lifted me up above the sleet, through the almost-constant cloud. And not now. Conservation, not reputation.

I've heard the rumours that surround the billionaire. After all my research, I may be more familiar with them than most: whispers that rustle like the passing of old money, folded into bills. Whispers like the small flutterings of hope, trapped and panicked, the only things left once all the horrors have lacerated the world. Bree always did say hope was the worst thing to come out of that damn box.

It occurs to me only now, telling you this, that I should have asked AJ for a more specific brief. That, beyond gaining ten days' exclusive access to the billionaire's conservation project, I have no idea what is expected of me, what I am expected to write. Has it really been so long since I've been offered legitimate work, that I've forgotten how to ask the necessary questions? Only now does it strike me how rashly I boarded the public airbus in Edinburgh, then the smaller private jet from Buenos Aires down to Ushuaia, and then the ship. How this unchecked zeal may have been my first mistake.

*

Cabin number three is bigger than I expected – a far cry from when I first made this journey, in a cramped two-bunker that smelled of endurance and stale breath. Here, as I cross the threshold from the corridor, soft music trickles from hidden speakers: a low female voice, which I recognise as the start of my relaxation tracklist from home, winkled out and transferred to the ship's systems. The cabin is all polished-wood floor and pale furnishings, a bed wide enough to lose myself in, dusk-blue cushions with a lone star embroidered on them in silver. Half the floor is taken up by a plush white rug.

The only nod to our destination is a painting, which occupies most of the wall above the headboard: a blue and white icescape, impressionistic, and in the foreground, a single sun-sculpted berg. Ballsy, to frame a painting of an iceberg on a ship. The brush-strokes are fat and hurried, an opulence of paint. Even without knowing its provenance, it's obvious this is not art but Art – curated and intellectualised, the kind sold at public auctions or exclusive galleries, bought as a future investment. I lean in closer, and the lights above the painting brighten in response. When I look for an artist's signature, I draw a blank.

Someone – the man from the deck, maybe – has delivered my bag to the rack beside the bed. Draped over it is a dusk-blue parka, the same blue as the cushions, the same blue as the ship. It's downy, soft, with a lavish halo of faux-fur around the hood, and a corporate logo on the breast: an iceberg in calm water, its secret bulk made visible below the surface. The IntuTech branding sits just below. From the upper sleeve glint the silver words PLAN B.

I start to undress and the air controls raise the temperature. The lighting above the mirror brightens and disperses to create a more flattering wash. Intuition tech. I shouldn't have expected anything else – of course the billionaire wants to show off his company's most lucrative invention. I wonder whether he's on board, whether he'll fly out to meet us at the conservation site, or whether he'll be absent altogether, and have some put-upon assistant handle the entire thing. I tell the music to stop playing and the cabin lapses into the quiet whirr of the moving ship. Still, I get the feeling the walls are watching, learning my behaviours, assimilating me into the system.

In the small en suite, the sink fills itself to let me wash away the long haul from Edinburgh. I've always run water slightly too hot for comfort – I like the almost-hurt of it, the way it brings my blood to the surface and makes my skin tingle – and the cabin's technology apparently knows this. When I wash the fug from my underarms, the water sears and I gasp. It smells unusual. Sharp. Something nostalgic about it, a smell of childhood. It reminds me of when Ross was a baby, when he suffered from skin rashes and the only place that stopped him bawling was the medical spa in Beacon Hill. I cup the water to my face, let it run down over my neck and collarbone, let it drip from my chin back into the basin.

Clean, that's it. That's the smell. I leave the plug in to reuse the water before bed.

The dress code might be informal, but after hours of travelling in them, my clothes feel both damp and crusty, and anyway, informal dress codes are for amateurs. I dig in my bag for the black suit dress I used to wear for the book launches and parties of casual acquaintances, or for difficult meetings with hard-to-crack politicians. I like its businesslike elegance, and the way I can still fit into it years later. Smart but impersonal, a chic armour. It's the dress I wore to Bree's funeral.

I zip myself in and set my feet hip-width apart, the way Bree taught me to. I do that exercise she used to do with her class, thinking myself into my bones till I can feel each of my vertebrae, till I can stack them one by one, building myself taller, my shoulder blades rolling back, my head drawn up by that balletic length of string until I'm ready to face whatever formalities the evening might bring.

Till I'm almost ready.

The lights in the cabin are still bright. They know my final ritual, and wait for me to perform it. I can almost feel the IntuTech holding its breath. Gathering data. Passing judgement.

I find the circuit break behind a small panel above the door. My stomach muscles pull and my calves shake as I stretch up to turn it off; the IntuTech powers down and the lights flicker off, plunging the cabin into twilight. Then the manual system boots up, and I can turn the lights back on at the switch. Less convenient, perhaps, but also less invasive. It's one thing using IntuTech at home, just one data point among billions – another letting it read me in the web of its creator. I imagine the systems, already searching for my missing data, already registering my cabin as an absence.

Unobserved, I knock back a miniature of whisky, blink away the burn. There are four miniatures in total, lined up against the driftwood mirror the way the nicer hotels used to leave little bottles of shampoo. When I tell myself I'll ration them, I almost believe it.

*

The dining room is at the stern of the ship: crystal light fittings, an antique mahogany table resting heavily in the centre of a rich wool carpet. Style from the last century on a ship from the next, which I suppose is what it means to be super-rich, to be unconstrained by time or fashion. Two waiters, gold-liveried and poised in attendance, stand on either side of the door. Other than them, the room is empty. The table is set for ten. 'Am I in the right place?'

'Yes, ma'am.' One of the waiters hands me a flute of champagne, gold-edged, a delicate stem. He has gap teeth which his breath whistles through when he speaks and curly hair which flops forward to cover his temples. A nice face. The sort which might just give away his employer's secrets, if I press the right buttons.

'This is beautiful.' I smile at him as I gesture out at the channel, but he only nods. I try not to fidget with the stem of my glass. 'Have you worked here long?'

'Yes, ma'am.' He says this in the same tone, as though agreeing with a statement instead of answering a question. 'If you'd just like to wait.'

I try to catch the eye of the second waiter, but he's staring resolutely ahead, so I turn away to sip my champagne beside the curving picture window, looking out on the Beagle Channel. The whales are long gone, the water dark and dead. Only a cargo ship lumbers towards Ushuaia, lights blazing like its own fanfare. The champagne, like the water in the cabin, is sharp: a fizz so subtle it's cruel – and as the ship sways, my feet sink into the carpet. In the world of money, it seems, every texture can be taken to the extreme.

I'm aware of the waiters behind me, watching, but I keep my back to them. I've been playing this game long enough, I know

11

how it works. It's always the staff who keep tabs on the guests, who report their movements back to the boss. Damned if I'm going to give them anything. At least, nothing they haven't already gleaned from the IntuTech before I turned it off. I notice the low relaxation music from the cabin has followed me.

'Good, you're here.'

A petite dark-haired woman – spike-heeled, suit sharp enough to cut through the bullshit – takes a glass without looking at the waiter. Her voice is clipped, as though she's speaking with her lips too close together, and the doors click shut behind her. At her arrival, the music changes, slides almost seamlessly into something the technology thinks we will both appreciate: still low and soulful, but duller, somehow, a persistent, headachy beat. It isn't a song I recognise.

'Spectacular, isn't it?' Her gesture takes in the room, the view, the champagne. Whichever she means, the answer is yes. 'Maretta – project director.' When I shake her proffered hand, her grip is firm but fleeting, a thought snatched back. 'I spoke with your agent on the vid.'

Shit. The only person AJ mentioned was the billionaire, and, like an amateur, I hadn't asked. I smile. 'Yes, of course. Ivy Cunningham.'

When she says, 'It's wonderful to have you on board, Ms Cunningham,' her thin lips suggest she isn't fooled in the slightest. 'Shall we sit?'

We position ourselves across from each other at one end of the enormous table, like an interview, or a duel, and the waiters click into life as though somebody has flicked a switch. They disappear through the swing door into the kitchen, re-emerging with their quick-change act of platters: fruit; warm, floury bread; cold-cut meats. My fingers have left smeary prints on the highly polished wood, which I see the gap-toothed waiter notice. I try to wipe them away in the guise of unfolding my napkin from its elaborate swan.

Maretta indicates to begin. The other place settings are still unoccupied.

'Are we expecting anyone else?'

'Sky won't be joining us till later,' she says. 'We start to lose connection once we're out of the channel, and then only old-school sat-tech works till we reach the Peninsula. A man like him – he needs to make the most of every moment.'

'I see.' So the billionaire is on board after all. As the second waiter pours us each a glass from a fresh bottle of wine, I try to push aside the nagging doubt: if he's here, why hasn't he already shown himself, eager, rushing forward to meet me? I'm still only halfway through my champagne, but I resist the urge to neck the rest. Instead, I take a restrained sip, draw it through my teeth and around my palate like a connoisseur. The chill spikes up into my skull, rings against the dull beats of the music.

'The forecast is for a fairly calm crossing – unusual even at this time of year. We should reach Antarctic waters in around thirty-six hours.' Maretta reaches for her water glass, holds it out to be filled. 'The water is local to Tierra del Fuego,' she tells me. 'Bottled at source. Filtered, of course, but otherwise untreated.' Like the man on deck, she speaks as though she's reading from a card. I've met her type before, efficient and unimaginative, a human spreadsheet. Easy to break, but rarely worth the effort. 'All the food is sourced locally, too. Cooked from fresh by our chef. As I'm sure you're aware, Sky's a huge advocate for tradi-tional small-scale farming.'

Over the past few years, I've written quite a number of articles about him, which of course this woman – Maretta – must know. Just as the billionaire himself must know. You get a sense, as a journalist, of when a feature hits its mark. It isn't about whether your subject responds or whether they don't – it's about *how* they do it; how they don't. The slightest indicator can betray them.

When I first wrote about the billionaire, it wasn't personal. It was shortly after Helsinki, and I was publishing anywhere that would take me, targeting any companies and CEOs that caught my interest: those who made a big song and dance about their environmental credentials, all the while undercutting them for the sake of the bottom line. Greenwashing, they used to call it. Almost everyone was culpable; I merely cast my pebbles into the water to see which would make a splash.

Some of my targets lashed out in response. Most ignored me, the way they must have ignored a thousand other accusations. With the billionaire, it was neither. Only an offhand comment in an interview. Another journalist asked him about the accusations – in general terms, they didn't mention me by name – and he responded with this small back-of-the-throat noise, a gesture as if brushing away a fly. There was something about it – the noise, the gesture, the casual dismissal – that felt curated. At the kitchen table, I paused the vid, replayed the moment over and over, and saw the fleeting fury scored across his brow.

After that, I ignored all those other targets, focused all my energies on him. An obsession, maybe, but we all have to chase after something, and what opponent could be more worthy than the richest man on the planet?

I sat at the kitchen table in the big empty house outside Boston, and later in my Edinburgh flat, delving through forums and news bytes, interviews and wild conspiracy theories. For someone so prominent, I came up against a lot of unknowns: deliberate obfuscation of his net worth, of which companies he owns or has a hand in, of his background, his personal life. What small discrepancies I did find, I published as best I could, on small sites run by sweaty men who tried to crawl under the radar of the IntuNet. I don't know if the billionaire ever read anything else I wrote. He was never asked about it again, or if he was, I never saw it. But I carried on casting out pebbles, hoping one would find its mark and that, at least for a moment, I might make him ripple.

And now here I am. On his ship, delivered right into his inner circle.

'Yes,' I tell Maretta. 'I am aware.'

Still, she launches into a run-down of projects I've already researched with a fine-tooth comb: his Eat Where You Are campaign; the Manhattan Sea Wall; the Sydney Recovery Project; desalination patents; patents for Ark Ships and air filters; a legal battle with Taiga over the Sahara Barricade; guilting PacifiCorp into expanding their coral farm. What she leaves out, I notice, are the whispers of his famous Chiller technology, the whispers of Plan B.

'Yes,' I say again. 'And what about the impact of his more profitable ventures?'

Her eyes cloud over as she says, 'That isn't really my department.' She looks pained at the thought of being shut out of any aspect of her boss's life. As if to prove she can, she gives me a potted history of the billionaire's rise to wealth: his founding of Cirrus Holdings thirty years ago; the company's invention of intuition tech; their pioneering of its predictive capabilities, and the widespread incorporation of the IntuTech branding by other firms around the globe.

I already know all this as well, but it's easier to let her talk, to sip my champagne without worrying about having to reply.

'Did you know this whole ship is run on IntuTech? It can read windspeed and swell and a thousand other data points. We keep a small skeleton crew, of course, just a handful in case of emergency. And for aesthetic purposes.' She nods to the two waiters in their garish livery. 'Sky's a big believer in style, Ms Cunningham. But essentially, the Lone Star is her own navigator – isn't that marvellous?'

I make a noncommittal noise and take another sip. It feels strangely claustrophobic, being on a ship with so few people and yet surrounded by so much space. The bruise-coloured edges of the Beagle Channel slip past through the windows, and I try to take comfort in the knowledge that we are, at least for now, contained by land.

'I'm a huge fan, you know.' Maretta says this in the same dispassionate voice. For a moment, I think she's still talking about the billionaire, and I wonder if this is simply professional hero worship or whether she might be in love with him. Then I realise she means me. She says, 'I saw the famous photo of you when I was a kid. It stayed with me.'

I don't remember the last time someone expressed that kind of admiration. I try to work out where to look, and settle on a single grape at the edge of my plate, thinly sliced into a five-fingered spread. I tell her, 'You're too young to be a fan.'

Maretta smiles and accepts the compliment, and indicates again that I should begin.

The food is good – thin strips of cured pork that melt against the roof of my mouth. Apple that has been grown outside rather than in a polytunnel. It tastes the way fruit tasted when I was young, like the wind that tested it and the rain that swelled it and the sun that ripened it off. It tastes so good I almost resent it.

Once, when Ross was very small, we took him to a heritage garden, the kind with overpriced entry and headsets spieling information about how food used to be grown. In the walled orchard, he ran from tree to loaded tree, fascinated to see the fruit growing in the open air. As Bree lifted him up, as she held him so he could stretch an eager hand towards a pear, as she comforted him when it snapped from the branch, I captured it all on the vid.

To break the silence, I ask, 'How did you end up working here?'

'I was head-hunted.' For the first time, I see Maretta's eyes shine, but it's muted, like fish scales out of water. 'I'd made a name for myself with one of Sky's rivals.'

'PacifiCorp?'

'Taiga. I headed up the tree-planting project north of the Sahara – but it was never going to be big enough to stop the expansion. A PR stunt.'

'And this isn't?' For a second, I'm worried I've crossed a line. Up until now, she hasn't even mentioned the Antarctic conservation project – though it is, of course, the reason we're all here.

She pulls back her shoulders, arranges her cutlery neatly on her plate. 'You'll have to wait for the presentation.'

I deliberately take my time with my last few mouthfuls, savouring each one longer to show that I can make her wait just as easily. It's a childish game, but one I'm good at. Even finished, I leave my own cutlery askance.

The waiters clear the plates, their movements tilting, as though we're in rough seas instead of the calm waters of the channel. As they retreat through the swing doors to the kitchen, Maretta says, 'You know I met you once before?' Her voice is casual, but there's something forced about it, as if afraid of betraying something underneath. I start to apologise, to say I've met a lot of people and maybe her face will come back to me, but she cuts me off. 'You wouldn't remember. I was a child, after the earthquakes in Buenos Aires. You headed the campaign for a green regeneration of the barrios, do you remember? Trying to stop big businesses coming in and charging twice as much for housing that was half as safe. I'd been living on a roll-mat in a temporary shelter for almost a year while the politicians argued back and forth.'

'God . . .'

'When the government eventually signed off on it, we all lined the street – all the quake orphans – cheering and waving as you walked past. You stopped and spoke to people – you probably don't remember. You shook my hand.'

I remember the project – not just Buenos Aires, but in cities across Argentina, across most of South America – fighting to put community, education and environmental stability at the heart of all the rebuilds. Bree used to joke that I was angling for them to name a housing complex after me, but now here is Maretta, living proof that my system worked.

She says, 'I used to want to be just like you. Rallying people around you, fighting to take on big businesses.'

The waiters return bearing plates, which they set down with a flourish. The man with the floppy hair and gap teeth announces it as Patagonian lamb: four pink coins of it, like fingerprints beside an arrangement of vibrant green vegetables. 'And now you're working for the richest man in the world.'

'Yes.'

'Why?'

'Everyone deserves a second chance, don't you think? An opportunity for redemption?' As she picks up her fork, it catches the light, and for a second becomes a blaze, a beacon flaring in the dark, and I can't decide if it's a celebration or a warning. 'I'm here for the same reason as you. To save the world.'

To avoid answering, I try the lamb, and with it I can taste the farm, the grass it fed on, the rich cultivated soil of its pasture, the chill wind blown up from the south. What must it do to a person, to eat like this all the time? To bring the whole inter-connected world inside your body with every mouthful? I wonder about the billionaire, what sense of ownership this must give him over the earth.

The crystal lighting dances in the wine glasses, slips between shades of white and red like costumes, each glass a new taste, a fresh unpronounceable vintage. By the time dessert arrives, I can't distinguish the sway of the ship from my own internal roll, the beat of the music from my heart banging up into the base of my skull. Somewhere above my head, clarity peals a high musical note, just out of reach. Belatedly, I tell her, 'You know there's more than one way to save the world.'

*

Maretta points in the direction of the lounge and then excuses herself, so I make my own tentative way towards the front of the ship. Through the wide glass doors, the room is lit like a stage set, all leather chairs and hardwood furniture, a bar glittering with rows of bottles, the spirits inside them shining like old-fashioned bulbs: a gentlemen's club from the early twentieth century, deep burgundy blinds pulled down to block out the night. The only break to this illusion is the back wall – a mosaic of jagged mirror, shards that send their reflections back haphazard and unpredictable. In the pieces, the lounge is disjointed from itself, and perhaps it's this which throws me, because it isn't till I tumble through the door that I realise the lounge is already occupied: a man, sitting in the shadows at the edge of the room, his face lit from below by his vid screen.

At my arrival, he starts, and stuffs the vid into a pocket. Then he smiles a slow, spidery smile. He stands, gestures me in.

'Sorry, I didn't mean to interrupt.'

'Not interrupting.'

He's pale from screen-exposure, his eye sockets tinted purple. When I look into his face, it's like those old plastic bags that fill themselves with ocean currents, that still wash up on beaches whole continents from where they started. A sadness, impossible to look away from – a part of him I've never noticed, not in all the times I've seen his face on the vid. Not in all the hours of footage I've consumed. All of a sudden, I'm hit by the physical reality of him. No longer an idea on a screen, but a body. Someone with ideas and wants and consequences. Until this moment, I've never quite thought of him as human.

His eyes are cliché-blue, and vice-like; they know how to hold a gaze. His lips twitch under a thin moustache. 'You'll be the journalist?'

'I'm sorry?'

(Stop, I think, saying sorry.)

All my sniping IntuNet comments and accusatory articles

19

tumble through me, and I feel breathless, like a child waiting for approval. I'm disconnected from my own body; the digital version of my life is catching up to the physical, overlaying it but not quite touching – like a badly aligned hologram. I push my mind back into my vertebrae, remind myself to stand tall. 'I don't think we've been introduced,' I say, as if that's better, as if either of us needs an introduction. Even the cable knit of his jumper looks expensive.

'No.' His movements are jagged, all long pauses, frenzied starts, a daddy long legs skittering up a wall. His fingers weave over one another in a nervous pattern and there's a bounce in the balls of his feet, as if he's on the verge of launching into speech.

'Ivy Cunningham.' I hold out a hand for him to shake, and this is good: starting again, defining the parameters of our new real-world interaction. 'Environmental activist.'

'Also journalist.'

'When it suits me.'

'Clearly,' he says, 'it's been a few years since it suited you well.'

He says this casually, a throwaway remark, but the words hit me like a high-speed train – and this is maybe my second mistake: that I let it show in my face.

And my third: in trying to avoid his gaze, I glance towards the mirror and see pieces of my fractured body scattered across it – physical, digital, none of my features quite settled – and the vertigo knocks me sideways.

And my fourth: that I'm still holding out my hand, unshaken, like a desperate intern at an interview. The back of my neck is damp, the dress clingy and restrictive. When he takes my hand, I have to hold myself back from thanking him.

His grip is too soft, a shudder. A tactical move, perhaps, designed to put people on edge from the outset. Out of habit, I listen for a trace of Australia in his voice, but even here, away from the interviewers and vid cameras, I can't find one, his accent clipped carefully back into something belonging to an English country manor. 'Sky,' he says, with a coldness I can only assume is borne of all my articles – so perhaps he has read more of them after all. 'Also an environmental activist, of a kind.'

Sky. I wrote about this once, for a small gutter-press site: this single-name culture that's taking over young people, this abandoning of family names – like astronauts, unclipping their tethers to float loose from the mothership, drifting through space with no hope of return. It makes me want to hold on tight.

'And as it happens,' he says, 'a journalist is what I need – otherwise you wouldn't be here.' He indicates the back of the room, where a second man hovers moth-like behind the projector light of a HoloPlayer. In shadow, yes, but still it unnerves me not to have noticed him till he was pointed out to me. Losing my edge. The man nods, carries on syncing up a data chip. 'Sharma,' the billionaire tells me, 'is my head of security. My right-hand man.'

The man glances up. 'We've met.'

As he turns, his face catches the HoloPlayer glare. The man from the deck. This is the second time I've forgotten him. I try to cover it with a 'yes, of course', but I suspect that once again I may have overdone it. Mercifully, this is the moment Maretta arrives, bearing a slender document case and a smart professional smile.

The billionaire judders on the balls of his feet as he indicates for me to sit. Always moving. Always weaving a web of his body. Maretta and the man behind the HoloPlayer are so still they could have been sculpted from ice. 'Now we can begin.'

The leather chair looks hard and cold, but when I sink into it, it's an effort not to loll. Important to still look poised, even if you're out of your depth and off your tits.

Not, I tell myself, that I'm either of those things. I wouldn't want you thinking that. But it must be testament to how far I've flown that day, that it takes time for the implications of what he's said to percolate down through my brain.

That what he needs right now is a journalist – and yet, by his own admission, I haven't published a major article in years. Which begs the question: why has he chosen me?

The head of security – Sharma – finishes setting up the data chip and hands us each a whisky. In my dazed state, I expect there to be another gold-liveried waiter – till I remember what Maretta said about a skeleton crew, and the ship largely running herself. I can't help but wonder how much of this is about efficiency and the billionaire's pride in his most successful invention, and how much is about the privacy afforded by a smaller staff. It stands to reason that the man who created intuition tech must be hyper-aware of the power of information, and understandably cautious about who he gives it to.

I set aside my drink, at least for now. As Sharma tells the lights to dim, Maretta opens her document case and offers me a paper fact sheet, with the heading PLAN B. 'Just a bit of information for you to read at your leisure,' she says. She perches on the edge of her chair, legs crossed at the ankle, the perfect performance of attentiveness. The billionaire leans one elbow on the armrest, brushes his thumb across the bristles under his chin, and nods to Sharma, who brings up the vid controls.

An old photograph appears on the screen – colourised, though it's difficult to tell. There's so much white in it, so much skeletal dark. A sailing ship, caught fast in jagged sea ice, tilted, mast askance, rigging all at war with itself. The ice has risen up around the hull like a pale fist. In the foreground, a team of sled dogs slumps on the pack ice.

The *Endurance*, photographed during her final days. I recognise the picture. It's one of Frank Hurley's, the photographer on Shackleton's ill-fated Antarctic voyage.

Once, Antarctica was a place of exploration. Of human endeavour and scientific research.

A female voice surrounds us, artificial, its accent unplaceable. The image begins to animate itself. As the ice creaks around the

22

ship, and the dogs shift anxiously on their leads, the image expands, projects itself beyond the screen as a hologram, plunges us into its monochrome world. Around us, jagged hulks of ice encase the chairs, the elegant wooden tables, the lamps with their coloured glass shades. Ice formations nearly two centuries old turn our faces grey-white, so when I glance over at Maretta and the billionaire, they look cross-hatched and unfamiliar. Only Sharma, behind the HoloPlayer's projection, stands in shadow.

It was a place protected by international treaty: 'in the interest of all mankind that Antarctica should continue for ever to be used exclusively for peaceful purposes, and should not become the scene or object of international discord'.

For over eighty years, this treaty held true.

The old photograph melts into open water, which laps at the armchair castors and table feet under an artificial blue sky. From the screen, a corporate drill ship sheens the ocean with oil, giving me the urge to pull my feet up out of it.

Then, the discovery of minerals. Oil. Precious metals. As the Lidenbrock drill method in the Arctic began to enable cheaper extraction from below the ice, so the eyes of the corporations turned south. National claims on Antarctic soil, which had lain dormant for decades, were re-established, and then disputed. First came the fisheries. Then the mines, the pipelines, the fossil fuel extraction. Finally, the factories and processing plants. In barely more than a decade, the planet's last great wilderness had disappeared.

Emperor penguins starving on bare rock. An abandoned chick. Whales cut bloody by propellors. Funnels of smoke coiling above a keening leopard seal.

Some of the footage is recent, and some from the early days of Antarctic industry. I recognise a couple of clips from our own expedition fifty years ago, up-teched to fit the HoloPlayer.

With the exploitation came the beginning of the thaw – a drastic change that will continue for thousands of years, with catastrophic consequences felt around the world.

Enclosed by the drawn blinds of the ship's lounge, the holographic sea ice retreats. Glaciers calve from the bar stools into the sea, as we are bombarded by news clips: the Thames flood barriers burst; typhoons squall along tropical beaches; a wildfire rips up North America.

As the ice continues to melt, the earth darkens, absorbing more of the sun's rays and raising the global temperature. These changes – long seen in the Arctic – begin to be felt at the opposite end of the globe, making weather patterns increasingly unpredictable. Every year, more lives and livelihoods are lost.

A change in the music. A swelling major key, the kind that fills the space behind the sternum, expands the heart.

But there is hope. While we may have failed to prevent the onset of change in much of the Antarctic continent, there is now a way to restore it.

In place of the carpet, pristine snow sparkles under a pale sky, free of vapour trails. The image pulls back to reveal the edge of an ice sheet that glitters in the sun, expanding out and out for miles. I always thought I'd come back to Antarctica sooner, but there was so much life that got in the way. My breath catches, and I can't tell if these are tears or if my eyes are watering from the brightness.

Here at our Antarctic conservation site, Cirrus Holdings' patented Chiller technology uses IntuTech to give the earth what she needs: to recapture our past for the present age, to create natural investment in our future.

Today, unlike before, there is a Plan B.

The ice twinkles, glints, then falters. Plunges us into darkness. The steady passage of the ship thrums up through the chair.

*

'You can really do it?'

'We can really do it.'

'Why?'

24

'Why wouldn't we?'

'No, I mean— ' The clear cold peal above my head is a jangle, now. I try not to look at my reflection in the fractured mirror. 'Why you?'

Maretta says, 'Antarctica used to be this planet's balance, the plumb weight at the bottom of the world.' She glances at her boss for permission, then adds, 'The Plan B site is just the prototype. An experiment, if you will, in conservation. If it succeeds, we could begin to lower global temperatures, stabilise weather systems and oceanic currents, and reduce climate poverty on an unprecedented scale. It all starts with the ice. With Plan B.' Her face glazes over as she speaks.

The billionaire spreads his arms wide, his eyes crackling like firewood. His open palms say, Because we can.

*

After the nostalgic glow of the lounge, the deck is dark and exposed. At the heavy PlastiGlass door, I realise I should have gone back to my cabin for a coat. This dress might be armour, but it won't protect me from the cold.

Like so much else on this ship, the door to the deck sports the IntuTech symbol. Probably it has already read the outside temperature, already scanned me to decide if I should be allowed to pass. Dressed as I am, the light blinks red. Still, drink always makes me brazen. I project an old vid photo of myself in a coat, to trick it into letting me out, and am surprised when it works. I vow not to stay out for long, to sleep it off and be better in the morning.

The water is louder at night, an immersive slosh, slosh, which washes over my skin like the icy hologram. On the shore, wharf lights flicker like stories to lure a traveller from the path. If I squint, I can just make out the outlines of mountains against the sky, visible only as an absence of stars.

I lean on the railings. Alone on deck, breathing the vast air with barely a trace of chemical on the breeze, it feels like my own private conversation with the world. Up until this exact moment, I hadn't realised how much I'd let Edinburgh pen me in: its towering buildings and slim winter light, its lower warren of basements always flooded, now, blocking so many of the routes out.

And I'd hidden myself away in that Edinburgh flat for four years. Four years, writing articles for increasingly less salubrious outlets, letting bloody AJ make me feel irrelevant. Not his fault, of course – just a symptom of his careless generation. Neither of us would ever have chosen to work with the other, but he took over Patrice's client list when she retired. I suppose you could say he inherited me, like a dented fob watch whose value he didn't understand. This was already five years after Helsinki, but I still remember how, in that first conversation, he said, 'I'm so sorry about what happened,' and then in the same breath, 'You should write a book about it. You know, individual and environmental guilt – an exposé on personal and eco-trauma, get public opinion back on your side.' And I flat-out told him, 'I will never, ever write about that,' and shortly afterwards, he had to take another call, and it was four years before I heard from him again.

I send a VidNote to Ross. The small square pans the channel from the deck: nothing but framed night.

'Sorry it's so late. It's Ivy.' My voice feels lost in the darkness and I wonder whether he'll be able to hear me over the sound of the water. 'Mum.'

I raise the vid, try to capture the soft lighting on the sails. In the corner of the frame, the red starboard light is a warning spike through the dark.

'Last time I made this journey,' I say, 'you were just getting ready to be born. Remember? Course you don't. Sorry. But the stories – we told you the stories often enough.'

It's quiet for a moment, apart from the water. No sound from the shore. Somewhere, a distant bird calls, too far away, too quiet for the vid to pick it up.

I finish the way I always do: 'Miss you.'

*

Back in the cabin, I turn the lights to a low, soothing yellow. Somebody has drawn the curtains to prevent bird strikes, and my clothes have been unpacked and steamed, hung up or folded away into the drawers. No way of knowing if this is a generous act of hospitality or an excuse to search my luggage. As if the baggage scanner on the dockside hadn't been enough.

When I go to wash, I discover the water has been let out of the bathroom sink. Clearly here, the normal rules about water usage don't apply – yet another extreme offered by the world of the rich. Extricated from my dress, I dab fresh water on my forehead, the back of my neck, my collarbone, underarms, back, as far as I can reach. The water comes out cold, now, with no intuition tech to tell it to heat to my desired temperature. I press the washcloth to the bottom of my ribs, which cuts through the swimming feeling in my head.

The bed has been turned down and my sleepsuit laid out on the pillow. In a way I'm used to it, this insistence on keeping the staff out of sight, everything happening behind the scenes. But knowing there are so few of them . . . How many is a skeleton crew? Ten? Five? I've met two already – four if you count Sharma and Maretta – surely there must be more? The person who unpacked my bags at least – though I was out on deck long enough, any of them would have had the opportunity to come into my cabin and do it between their other duties. It's unnerving: a feeling of isolation with the ocean stretching out ahead of us. When I close my eyes, the only sounds are the creaking ship, the engine humming up from below, and a faint rattle from something loose behind the painting above the bed.

I sit on the edge of the mattress, push into the tops of my thighs to try to release the muscle-ache. Softer, since I moved to Edinburgh – or before that maybe, since Helsinki.

Some of my body, of course, is artificial. Protein shots. Streamlined nips and tucks around the chin and lower ribcage. An accentuated jaw. What was it Bree said to me once – just because someone's had to work for something, doesn't mean it isn't real? And I've worked damn hard on this body. Not that I want to look young, exactly. Despite what your average health column says, there's a power in looking my age – because underneath it all, there's still a lifetime of fight and determination. I feel it when I press my finger into the soft top of my thigh, like restless geology just below the surface.

*

Moments like this, I remember the hotel in Helsinki.

What always comes first is my luggage, teetering on that gleaming chrome trolley. I remember tipping the porter – generously – for bringing it to the room. This image is all shine, all polite professional smile. Then suddenly I am alone, barefoot on the soft false fibres of the rug. Everything is shades of cream and dusky pink, a blousy pattern of flowers. When I inhale, the air is a vintage rose garden.

Sometimes, I will remember standing by the window, the skyline all solar-panelled roofs and the last light reflected off the water. Sometimes, I will remember calling Bree.

*

But first I want to tell you about another room, another act of being alone – because it is an act, a performance perfected through long rehearsal. I learned this on the field trip I went on as a student, my first time in Antarctica – or anywhere, really – accompanying the professor to the research base at the South Pole.

28

The professor was my dissertation supervisor, and this was a media trip – on-location filming for a new simulation based around his research – but to cut down production expenses, he had billed it to the department as fieldwork and, somehow, got away with it. To fit in with the university's Opportunity Outreach policy, this meant he had to take a student, so he took me. Mostly, my opportunity involved bringing him mugs of instant coffee between shooting, and so other than being sent a brief safety guide to read two weeks before, I received no training for this trip. Perhaps this was supposed to be the professor's job, or maybe they just assumed I wouldn't need it. We had a large team, and I had no real responsibility. We would almost always be in the relative safety of the base.

But the professor worked short hours by demand, which left plenty of free time for me to wander indoors, to practise feeling awestruck and lonely in equal measure – so maybe this is where we start the story after all, with my young and impressionable wonder.

When I try to remember who I was back then, I find myself difficult to pin down. Other people's gazes often slid over me, so I suppose it's only natural my own gaze should slide over me, too. I was a final-year undergraduate who frequented the library more than the bars. I liked the atmosphere, the muffled voices of the books, the fact that nothing was expected of me here.

Later, I would learn to judge other people's expectations, to exceed them or to defy them altogether. Back then, if I had a reputation, it was by accident. If people assumed I was clever, it was only because I was too shy to contradict them.

The trip to the research base was, unsurprisingly, the furthest I'd ever been from home – by approximately nine thousand miles. A bus and two clattering trains delivered me from my student flat in Edinburgh to the middle of Oxford, then a grease-smelling taxi out to the military airport, where I met up with the professor, who'd been ferried along the same journey but by private car. Then there was a long, near-empty flight to the Falkland Islands – grassy and windswept, where the air snatched my breath and gave it, laughing, to the wide-open sky – before a military aircraft for the transfer south.

Somewhere over the Southern Ocean, the journey must have caught up with me and, despite the jolting turbulence and the jet-engine roar, I fell asleep. Later, I was told I slept through our pit-stop at a British base on the coast: through our landing, our refuelling and our taking off again. The professor laughed and told me I slept like the dead, then gave raucous impressions of all the engine noises that had failed to wake me. My first touch-down in Antarctica, and I'd missed it – typical of me, in those days, to not appreciate the momentousness of an occasion till it had already passed me by.

So my first view of the continent wasn't distant shores or huge slabs of pack ice drifting north, but the plateau. The great icy level, which stretches from the Transantarctic Mountains to the South Pole and then beyond, right towards the eastern edge of the continent. From the belly of the dull-grey plane, I stared out through the tiny window at the featureless white world below: an unthinkable expanse of ice, engulfing the plane with its glare.

When I'd first seen the plane, at the airport on the Falkland Islands, I'd thought it was too dark and hulking, too full of its own serious mission – where was the elegance, the sleek lift of adventure? But as I looked out at the endless plateau below, with only our own small shadow to break the brilliant white, I understood. Antarctica was hostile – a place not designed for human habitation, and ready to remind us of it at any moment. I remember thinking, no wonder we've come here in a craft that looks ready for battle.

When we landed at the Pole, the base also looked like a military operation – but if the plane was a foot soldier, then the base was the whole multi-legioned strategy. A vast silver structure, on hydraulic legs to raise it above the snow, it was a masterpiece of architecture and engineering, a seminar on international co-operation in the days when such things still existed.

As I shivered at the edge of the runway, skidoos and electric caterpillar trucks wove across the ice in a choreographed dance I hadn't learned the steps to. Workers, fat with cold-weather gear, unloaded supplies from the hold of the plane. Stacked beside them were the crates and boxes for reloading, the waste and baggage to be flown back. My backpack dug into my shoulders and I felt myself shrinking. On the Falklands, when I'd shivered from the wind, the professor had laughed and said, 'You're not cold, not yet.' Now, my cheeks were raw with it. I breathed in and the air seared the inside of my throat till my eyes watered and stung.

And yet.

The snow crumped under my boots. Whenever I moved, my windproof jacket rustled like a whisper, beckoning me on. I exhaled and diamonds hung in the air in front of my face.

While the professor was shown to his own quarters, I was delivered to a shared bunk room, scruffy with other people's strewn possessions, dim through the drawn-down blind. I tried to call my parents. No answer – but then, in those days, comms back home were always being taken out by the storms. I left a quick message to let them know I'd arrived, then simply stood. In the middle of the room, with my bag at my feet, I breathed the thickly processed air, listened to the station's unfamiliar clanks and bustles and whirrs. When I crossed the two steps to the window to pull up the blind, I had to screw up my eyes against the glare, and when I opened them, I opened them slowly, cautiously, letting myself adjust. I remember thinking I ought to be wearing sunglasses. I remember thinking I didn't care. I opened my eyes and let the light in.

I watched a plane taxi to the end of the runway. Not the military bulk we'd arrived in, but a smaller, high-winged craft. A six-seater maybe, a skinny red cross against the white. When it reached the end, it turned, paused, then began to accelerate, hurtling towards take-off. I imagined the thunder of wheels from the inside, the moment of commitment, when it hung in the balance like a held breath, and then the lift, pushing off into the clear blue.

The plane shrank, winked, and was swallowed by the glare.

I lifted my bag onto the only unruffled bunk and spread my hands across the mattress. It was cold, an illusion of damp from lack of use. I let myself focus on the physical contact, the feel of worn cotton under my fingers. I was here, I told myself. I existed. For now, that was enough.

*

Since that first trip, it's become something of a ritual: to take time in each new space, to do nothing, to claim it for my own.

Which brings us back to the *Lone Star* and cabin number three, and me sitting on the bed in my underwear, my shoulders sagging from drink, my head nodding closer to my chest. I'm tempted to crawl under the covers like this, but there's more of a swell now, not quite open ocean, but approaching it. The rattle from the painting above the bed is louder. Insistent. It cuts through any thoughts of sleep, till I force myself to get up, to clamber onto the bed, feet apart for balance, to feel around the edge of the frame for whatever is making the noise. A loose fixing, perhaps. Some kind of protrusion I might be able to muffle with a sock.

I reach up, run my fingers along the indent between the frame and the back of the painting, and something drops onto the pillow.

An old-fashioned data chip. Or more precisely, a pass-chip. A physical decrypter for online data – like the ones office workers used to use to give themselves back-door access to secure files on the IntuNet. The kind of thing which was always getting left accidentally on trains and causing a national scandal, before they brought in the new ones with the tracking tech, and then most of the trains stopped running anyway.

I weigh the chip in my hand. It's dull and cumbersome, the

size of a molar. I'd forgotten how heavy these pass-chips used to be. Judging from the soldering, this one has had to be adapted to make it compatible with modern vids. The rattling has stopped.

Instinct tells me I'm not supposed to have it. Grey and conscious of its own doctored ugliness, it's the antithesis of the billionaire's sleek expensive branding, and I want to know who hid it, whether they plan to come back for it. I catch myself thinking about those scams you read about on the IntuNet: pass-chips given out as freebies, only for them to burrow into your software, to root out bank details, security passwords, voting numbers. Not that I'd expect to find that here, obviously, but then, I didn't expect to find a pass-chip at all. And beneath my reservations, there's that old curiosity – an embedded journalistic habit, despite what I told the billionaire, impossible to shake off – that urge to shove something over the edge just to count how far it will fall.

I clip the pass-chip into the port on my vid, then turn the screen so it projects onto the wall.

A loading wheel – blue, trying to link to the IntuNet, trying to unlock the online files. The loading wheel turns.

Connecting . . .

I open up the vid's coding, shut off its extraneous systems to see if I can boost its search for a signal.

Connecting . . .

Connecting . . .

It's a long time since I've done anything to manipulate technology like that, and I enjoy it. It feels like digging for something: a flame still kindling under damp earth. The wheel spins on the wall above the bed, around and around, a dog chasing its own tail.

Connection lost.

I remember what Maretta said about losing signal, and unplug the chip: metal casing warm now from working to connect; fat bead of soldering smooth and incongruous. I turn it between my fingers, as though just by holding it I can force it to give up its secrets. After a moment, I tuck it into the toe of my left shoe for safekeeping, and change into my sleepsuit.

I expect to lie awake, turning the evening over and over in my head – the possibilities of the pass-chip, the billionaire's conservation project, the exclusive scoop – but drink and the journey tug at me like a current, and I think instead of the humpbacks: mother and calf, their own connected unit among the endless dark of the waves. As I drift into sleep, I feel the change in the swell. We're leaving the safety of the channel, now, pushing off from protective land, out into the rocky waters ahead.

LET'S START
WITH BREE

Before I go any further, I want to tell you about the humpback whale:

The humpback sings. This is common knowledge, and her music is the soundtrack to meditative therapies the world over. Less well-known is that her melody is a record of where she's going and where she's been. As she travels, she weaves each new place into her song. This is a form of belonging.

When the humpback nurses her calf, it's with milk drawn from her own fat reserves. In the process of feeding, she can lose up to a third of her body weight, can give this much of herself over to her young.

The humpback whale can bellow or she can whisper. The bellow enables her to call to other whales across great distances, to sing out against the loneliness of the ocean. The whisper is protective, a bond only between her and her calf.

Half a century ago, I read all this online, scrolling in the dead hours in our thin-walled Boston apartment. While Ross fed crabbily from the bottle, I hummed old lullabies, listened to Bree sleep-breathing in the next room.

*

An activist – that's how I described myself to the billionaire. A person who takes action, who inspires action in others.

Over the years, plenty of people have asked me how I first became involved in activism, and over the years I've given many different answers: I was radicalised as a student; or, it was through learning about climate collapse in school; or, every night I'd sit with my parents as they talked me through the news.

I suppose I've always cared about the planet in an abstract sort of way. I was aware from a young age that it needed saving – impossible not to be aware of it, growing up in the '20s and '30s, with their storms and temperature spikes and the wall-to-wall footage of people displaced by them – and, yes, I was desperate for somebody to step in and save it. I just never thought that somebody might be me. Yes, I signed petitions. Yes, I went on protests. Yes, I stood outside Parliament with my classmates and chanted slogans while we brandished our hand-daubed signs.

'Our future!' we yelled. 'Give us back our planet!'

'One world, one chance to save it!'

'What do we want? Green policies! When do we want them? Five years ago!'

Back then, everything was an exclamation, and nothing was ever truly said till we'd made ourselves hoarse saying it. We wore down shoes with our marching, skipping school in order to feel like we were doing *something*, because we were teenagers and what else was there we could do?

Mostly, though, I protested the same way I did everything else – the way I watched the latest films or followed the eating habits of celebrities, or kept a hidden folder of bikini-clad models on my phone. It was just what everyone did, and though I'd never admit it in interviews later on, I marched and chanted just to fit in.

Then, in my final year of school, I entered a Scotland-wide young essayist competition and won.

It was a piece about powerlessness and inertia – felt, I argued, by so many of my generation. *Small Icebergs, Drifting*, I called it, in the manner of pretentious teenagers everywhere – but still, the judges praised it for its raw honesty, its bleakness, its so-called voice-of-a-generation sincerity. I had my photo taken with the iconic red span of the Forth Rail Bridge in the background, and articles about me were posted on the Edinburgh news sites. The woman at our local café gave me a free coffee and told me I was a star in the making. At school, in assembly, I was hauled up to the front, where the head shook my hand and announced in a booming voice how proud they all were, and how they'd always known I'd do great things – which was when half my year group noticed for the first time that I existed. Just a few weeks after that, I had my first kiss, with a beautiful red-haired girl from the year above, whose name I don't remember, but who led me round the back of a pizza restaurant, to an alley next to the bins, and held my face as she called me *iconic*.

When asked, I always used to say this essay was the moment I realised my words could make a difference. But in my head, all these things – the coffee, the school assembly, the kiss – have always been inextricably linked, and what I mainly realised was that activism didn't just have to be about *the cause*, but that the cause could do something for me in return.

Once, to Bree and only Bree, I said, 'Maybe I just liked being thought of as a hero.' And Bree handed me a glass of wine so red it would stain my lips and said, 'A hero? Or *the* hero? Anyway, it doesn't mean you can't do good for others at the same time.'

It was only years later, when it was too late to ask, that I wondered if this was the same reason Bree became a teacher, that combination of altruism and ego, and if this was why she was always so quick to understand.

*

I first met Bree in a church hall outside Boston, reached via ancient train and two feet of snow. The rails had contracted in a snap freeze, the trains running late, so by the time I arrived, the setting sun glowed red between the buildings. My one pair of professional shoes had soaked through to my feet, so I was forced to give my talk in a pair of borrowed heels, which pinched at the toes but were too big everywhere else. The only way to stop them slipping off was to root myself to the stage, and halfway through speaking my legs cramped and I had to grip the podium to stay balanced.

Those were the old days, before I'd learned to use clothes as a weapon. Back then, I thought all I needed to be was 'presentable': respectable square-toed court shoes with a low heel, shapeless monochrome suits bought off the rack while shopping for groceries. Even then, there was always something of fieldwork about me, as though I was only ever two steps away from water-proof overtrousers and an army-surplus coat.

The problem, I think, was not the solid oblong of my body, but that I failed to appreciate it – and so instead of accentuating my shape, I tried to dress in spite of it. Back then, I was always so afraid of being laughed at. Perhaps all young people are. I hadn't yet realised that being invisible is far, far worse.

It was Bree who taught me how to use an outfit. Of course it was. 'What you wear,' she said, 'is your last line of defence, and your first line of attack.'

In years to come, there would be bold colours, asymmetrical lines, and what Bree referred to as 'statement pieces'. In the future, I would learn the value of time and space to prepare myself – the change of outfit, the last-minute retouching of make-up, a final crisping of lapels. By which time, of course, I would have other people to do all those things for me.

But not yet. In that church hall outside Boston, I hadn't yet honed the performance, hadn't worked out how to persuade people onto my side. I stood with my cramping legs and projected holographic images from my phone. I spoke about Antarctica as though my brief few days making cups of instant coffee at the South Pole made me an expert. 'All we can do,' I read from my pre-written script, 'is look forward. We can't undo the damage caused by the older generation.' And I looked up at a hall filled with the older generation.

During the interval, teenagers from the high school sold raffle tickets while their parents served weak coffee and vinegary white wine. I found myself on the sidelines as the conversations carried on around me, a tide of thawing bodies and performative philanthropy.

'Talk about guilting.'

These were the first words Bree ever said to me, her voice lilting, liquid, filling the shape of my ear. Guilt/gilt/guillotine. The cutting glitter of accusation. A burnished double-edged blade. I don't remember if I understood her, then, or if I only filled in what she said in retrospect.

She offered me an olive branch and a plate of someone's homemade cookies, and in return she took all my remaining powers of speech. She was like one of those photographs of ballet dancers, taken mid-leap, all that movement, all that definition, captured in a single frame – always flowing through a world that was lucky just to catch her. I've never believed in love at first sight, but worship-at first sight happens all the time, and Bree was impossible not to revere. She was the only Black woman in a sea of white. I remember noticing this and thinking I shouldn't, then thinking perhaps it would be worse if I didn't.

'You know,' she said, 'if you flatter people, you're more likely to get them on your side.' Traces of a Southern drawl, ironed out. She smiled as I tried to think of something – anything – to say, and told me, 'I liked your talk.'

And suddenly, she was the brightest thing in the room, a bug zapper on a summer porch and my flight path long out of control. Around the mouthful of cookie I already felt self-conscious for taking, I managed to ask, 'Are you a speaker?'

'Not exactly.'

'Only slightly?'

She laughed, which I remember thinking was generous of her, then said, 'I'm here with the choir. I teach elementary school.'

'Oh.'

'Oh?'

'No, I didn't mean it like that, I meant— ' Panic now, as I fought to backtrack. I scrabbled through every possible inflection of the word 'oh', trying to find one that would sound less judgemental, less dismissive. *Oh* of surprise, *oh* of disbelief – neither of those would do. *Oh* of curiosity, of tell-me-more-about-your-ohhh-so-interesting job. No.

The irony is that, even if I didn't sound it, I was actually impressed. Back then, I thought anyone who could hold the attention of a room must be some kind of god. Later, I tried to explain that I hadn't expected her to do something so apparently ordinary, something where I understood what the job entailed. There may have been admiration in teaching elementary school, but there was no mystery. At least, I didn't believe there was. Not back then.

She took back the plate of cookies. 'There's more than one way to save the world.'

For the rest of the evening, I sat at the back of the hall, afraid to cross my legs in case my borrowed shoes slopped off and clattered on the scuffed wooden floor. The second half began with Bree's choir singing a medley of gospel songs interspersed with contemporary hits. The children opened their eyes and mouths wide, joyful and desperate as they let out their torrent of sound. When they finished and Bree turned to thank the audience, I felt as though she was thanking me, specifically me, for the attention I'd given her children. I watched as she led them off-stage, as they filed back into the front two rows. I kept watching her through the other performances, through the poet from the next town who recited with his eyes closed and swayed to his own rhythms, through the Christian rock group slamming down 'God So Loved the World' and 'Our Heaven is Right Here in Massachusetts', through the announcement of the evening's total donations to aid climate refugees, and through the thunder of self-congratulatory applause.

Afterwards, as she zipped the children into their brightly coloured winter coats and packed them off towards their parents, I told her, 'I wanted to apologise.'

'Did you?'

'Yes.'

Two boys were squabbling over a stolen half-cookie. As she separated them, she said, 'Go on then.'

'Go on . . .?' It struck me for the first time, then, how there was such a thing as an inadequate apology, and how simply setting the stage for one wasn't enough. I took a breath and said, 'I'm sorry. You don't look like a teacher.'

'What does a teacher look like?'

'I don't know.' I aimed for what I hoped was a nonchalant shrug. 'Less beautiful.'

While a small ponytailed girl tugged at her sleeve, she appraised me. Then she smiled with just one corner of her mouth and said, 'Give me a moment.'

I waited till the children and their parents had been dispersed, then Bree grabbed her own coat and beckoned me out of the door.

Back in my own damp shoes and the still-falling snow, I walked with her towards the station. Remembering what she'd said about flattery, I told her, 'The children were great.'

'They *did* great – not the same thing.' Snowflakes caught in her hair and hung there, unmelting, and when we passed beneath the streetlights they shone like jewels in the blue light.

'The way they followed your direction, though – it was incredible. Like you were pulling them out of themselves.'

'See?' she said. 'You're learning.'

On the platform, she touched her cheek to mine, warm against my cold one, and slipped something into my pocket. 'Call me,' she said. 'If you can bear to.'

When I unfolded the paper on the train, I saw that alongside her number, she'd written her name – and only then did I realise I'd forgotten to ask it. I messaged her before I'd left the false blue lights of the town behind.

*

To begin with, it was all tentative back-and-forth. She asked about my research travels, how my writing was going (at that time, badly), and whether I was getting platforms. In return, I was careful to ask thoughtful-sounding questions about her teaching.

In those days, I was living mostly on a research scholarship, which had brought me to the States to explore the role of journalism in the climate crisis. In my chaotic Boston flat, surfaces were piled high with old print newspapers borrowed from the archives, and with dishes I hadn't got around to washing up, so they congealed and mouldered among the used coffee cups from the artisan roastery on the corner. This was where I immersed myself, typing away between the research library and my living room, just six blocks from the edge of the flood-risk zone. Then I met Bree, and for days after, I only left the flat to get more coffee, battling through the unseasonal snow to caffeinate myself so I could keep on messaging her into the night. How she made it through her classes that week, I never knew.

In the first couple of days, we covered jobs, food (highly appreciated), politics (left-leaning, both of us), hobbies, pet peeves and books. On the third day, we talked about family. (*My mom died three years ago*, she told me. I replied, *Oh god, I'm so sorry*. She said, *Then my sister followed me to Boston*. When I said, *I'm sorry about that, too*, she messaged back, *Why the hell would you be sorry?*)

By the end of the fourth day, things had turned confessional, and by the end of the fifth, we agreed that it was too much, that we needed to see each other face-to-face.

And so, a week after we first met, Bree picked me up at the station in her battered old electric car, and drove us out to a trailhead on the edge of the woods. Cold flensed the air from our throats as we laced on snow boots to follow the virgin path through the trees, our skin a-tingle under the high pale sky. As we set off into the wood, the icy ground creaked and cracked underfoot, and we spoke in stilted whispers. Trees towered overhead, branches still lurid with moss. Slimy snow-capped fungi listened from the trunks.

We rounded a bend and something moved. A shift in the snow. As our eyes refocused, a gap between trees became a single white-tailed deer. Then a family of deer. Then a whole herd, startled still, their black eyes round and staring. I grabbed Bree's arm – to warn her, maybe, or just to feel connected. Me. Bree. The deer. The forest. The whole precarious winter. For a moment we were all one single nervous unit, as my fingertips sang against Bree's coat sleeve through my gloves, as the blood beat a tattoo inside my head.

Then, as if there had been some hidden signal, the deer spooked, flashed away between the trees. We spoke more freely after that, our nerves also taking flight, till the past week of intimacy gushed through. We left the main trail, branched out onto a smaller path, which, Bree said, she knew like the back of her hand. I wondered if she'd brought other women here, if this was her go-to first date and if so, whether it was some kind of test. I felt an enormous pressure to appreciate this rare and unspoiled landscape, to show her I was experiencing it in *the right way*.

While I tried to formulate insightful observations about the forest, Bree asked, 'So you're ambitious, right? That's what I got from you the other night. You want to be *somebody*.'

I stumbled, kicked myself against a buried root.

'You good?' she said.

'Fine.'

We walked in silence for a while, listening to the soft *phut phut* of snow dropping from the branches, landing in the drifts, till she said, 'You didn't answer the question.'

'Sorry.'

A pause. 'And?'

'If being *a somebody* means I have a platform,' I started, then stopped. I started again: 'I suppose – if it means people listen, if it means I can wake people up to the cause . . .'

Bree looked straight through me and said, 'Sure, that too.' Then she kissed me.

That's how I remember it, although our whole life, Bree swore I kissed her first. Which may have been true – that I felt so *seen*, by her, so *understood*, that the desire overtook me. I don't remember it like that, but with hindsight, it may have been the case. What I do remember is how she kissed me after, how she pushed me back against a tree so the snow clumped in my hood, down the back of my neck. I remember how she was all rush, all cold hands and lips, all warm breath I couldn't get enough of. When she pulled back, I felt as though something vital had been tugged away.

'Here,' she said, breathless. 'I bought you this.' She clipped a silver chain around my wrist. Dangling from it was a single musical note.

'It's beautiful.'

'It's to remind you,' she said, 'of the first time we met.'

'Bad wine and self-congratulation?'

'That there's more than one way to save the world.'

I lifted it to look more closely, and the musical note gleamed in the snow-light. Glinted. 'Now who's guilting who?' I asked her – but I loved the feeling of conspiracy, the reference to our own brief history, the proof that we'd already come up against misunderstandings and resolved them.

She kissed me again and I felt myself pushed back against the stubbled bark of the tree. For a moment we were all teeth and breath, and when she unzipped my coat, when she pushed past the elastic of my leggings, when her teeth nipped at my stomach, my pelvis, the soft inside of my thigh, I heard my voice scatter, following the deer like shadows between the trees. I remember grabbing at a branch and the bracelet flashing like a guillotine. I

46

remember droplets flung from the budding twigs, reflecting its silver in their faux-glass worlds.

*

It's a lie, of course. Falling in love with somebody. A piece of propaganda created to keep society in line. If you love someone, the lie says, you'll work hard to provide for them. You'll spend money on buying them expensive gifts, allow yourself to be manipulated in the name of *love*. Like everything else, it's a capitalist tool.

Besides, it's never the other person you fall in love with. At best, it's yourself, the version that emerges when that other person is with you – a morality tale to convince us we're less selfish as a species. At worst, it's just a kind of gratitude – a comfort blanket to cling to through the longest nights, to make us feel we're not alone.

Despite that first frenzied week, it took time for us to find our ground. We circled one another, always returning to the same points and then away again. A kiss. A hand held in public. Dinner and a sim, a night together, but always with the unanswered question of breakfast. It made me think of those charity donation wells you used to find in supermarkets – waist-high and wide, with a clear plastic dome over the top. The kind where you pushed a coin through a slot in the side, to spiral downwards, its own gravity drawing it into tighter and tighter orbits till it dropped through the hole at the centre and was lost. I mentioned this once to Bree, who said, 'I have literally no idea what you're talking about.'

I told her, 'If you put two coins in at the same time, sometimes they would crash into each other. Mostly not, though. You had to get it just right – the speed, the timing, the exact moment of release.'

'So what you're saying . . .?'

'What I'm saying is I think our timing is right. I think we're on the same trajectory.'

'Romantic.'

'It is,' I insisted, while trying not to sound like I was stamping my foot.

Bree looked at me hard. 'If you wanted a metaphor involving orbit, you could've gone with stars. Planets, moons, comets. Something cosmic, you know? You're a writer, Ivy. Nobody wants to be compared to a plastic chute for dimes.'

'I thought this was more relatable.'

'Oh honey.' Bree laughed and pulled me close, spread her fingers down the waistband at the back of my jeans. 'I don't need relatable. No great romance was ever won by being relatable.'

Bree often called me out over words in this way, often used them to unpick arguments, or to push me further. Up until I met her, I'd only been using 'guilting' as a verb. As in, 'to guilt someone'. As in, to make a person feel guilty, to make them acknowledge something they've done wrong.

As a noun, 'guilting' was Bree's word. A guilting, she said, was a form of acknowledgement. Something physical you wear to own your wrongdoing. A bracelet or a sticker, perhaps. A way of admitting you've done something you shouldn't. 'So a symbol?' I asked, 'Like a badge of pride?'

'No.' Mostly, she said, it was a teaching tool. A way of resolving conflict in the classroom, of getting the children to admit they'd done something wrong. 'It's the first step toward making them take responsibility. What better way is there to acknowledge something than to display it on your body?'

I nodded as if I understood.

Back then, I was always earnest. Too earnest. I believed the world would bequeath me a single noble cause, and that I would spend my whole life fighting it. I hadn't yet realised that casting such a narrow net was a sure route to failure. It was Bree who taught me this too. In the classroom, she told me, things were always moving – you couldn't let yourself get hung up on yesterday's problems, or you'd have no room to tackle the new ones today.

As in Bree's classroom, so in my career. I learned quickly when to throw my whole body into a fight, and when to step away. I learned to accept victories with grace, to recognise what had been achieved and not to push for what was unobtainable. I learned to move on, just at the apex of my success. At times during my career, other journalists have accused me of being fickle, unable or unwilling to commit. Usually when they were jealous, of course. Besides, it's impact that's important, not intent – and look at the impact I've had across the years.

Take the Ross Sea, for example. Last time I was here – last time I travelled to Antarctica – we were fighting to protect it from industrial damage. And we succeeded, after a fashion. Thanks to that expedition, it became the Ross Sea Protected Region, and the watching world applauded.

And yes, I could have continued to argue for greater protections. And yes, I could have led the same campaign for other parts of Antarctica. But where was the prestige in that? By that point, the fight had its own momentum and didn't need me. I could always return to the campaign if I wanted to – and I would, decades later, in Helsinki, to lend my voice in support of the Antarctic Industry Cap.

But back then there were other fights. From the Ross Sea, I moved on to argue against the continued felling of the Amazon rainforest – and secured a conservation order on almost half of it. I campaigned against soil depletion across Northern America, until the United States government agreed to fund a strategic patterning of deep-rooted prairie grasses across the Midwest. When I fought for the rights of displaced people in the South Pacific, three major corporations bonded together to create temporary camps from their converted container ships.

I celebrated each of these wins in turn – all high-profile, all under the gaze of the world's media. I never stuck around long enough to see each glittering success dim into a long, slow struggle for more. What would have been the point? By then I was a name, a personality, a force driving each campaign to the apex of its parabolic curve, and I needed to spread my influence accordingly.

There were always other fights to attach myself to. Always new areas where I could impact policy. Always more governments and corporations to guilt.

*

'Can I ask you something personal?'

We were lounging on Bree's sofa under an old throw, legs intertwined, sweat drying on our skin. The snow-melt had flooded the railway tracks back to Boston, so I'd been stuck there unexpectedly. We'd drawn the curtains against the grey and the sound of dripping, so our only light came from the muted screen in the corner, a hologram of a flickering fire to lend the room what Bree called 'ski-cabin chic'. My fingers still glistened from being inside her as she said, 'How much more personal d'you think it's gonna get?'

'Emotionally personal, though,' I said. 'Something deep.'

'Sure.'

I pointed to the silver chain around her neck. The pendants were two halves of a broken heart, hooked onto the chain so they could never quite meet. 'Is that a guilting?'

She rubbed at them. 'My first.'

'What are they for?'

'OK, that is more personal.'

'Sorry.'

'Don't be. I always tell the kids it's because once I was mean to my mom, and I wear it to remind myself to be kinder to people.'

'And is it?'

She pulled the throw further up, tucked it under her chin. 'When I came out to her,' she said, 'one afternoon back in high school, we were sitting in the kitchen, and I'd made her a coffee. Some expensive blend, on the stove the way she liked. It was just the two of us. My sister was with a friend, Daddy was out at work

50

– I hadn't told him yet, but I figured he already knew, or guessed maybe, he was better at those things than my mom. Anyway, I remember giving her this coffee in her favourite cup – putting it down on the tablecloth like it was the Holy Grail – and I sat across from her and got myself all psyched up. I don't know what I was nervous about exactly, it wasn't like I thought she'd disown me. But she was a traditionalist, my mom, church-goer even when it wasn't fashionable. And it's just, it's a thing, isn't it? Coming out to your parents. It's a rite of passage.'

I nodded – although since my dad had walked in on me with my tongue down another girl's throat in the cloakroom after the leavers' prom, I'd been allowed to skip that particular milestone.

'Anyway, I sat across from her, and obviously something big was about to go down because she just sat there, staring at me, not even drinking her coffee. I think she thought I was pregnant. It was that kind of town, and I guess she thought, Here we go. So I told her. I just . . . came out with it. Literally, I guess. I literally came out. I said, By the way, Mom, I'm a lesbian – I thought you should know.'

'What did she say?'

'Nothing.'

'Nothing at all?'

'Sat there, staring into her coffee like she could drown her sorrows in it. So I waited and when she still didn't say anything, I told her that's who I was and if she wasn't OK with it she could fuck off.'

I whistled.

'You know what she said?' She put on an imitation of her mum's voice, all high with elongated vowels: '*Don't curse, Bree.* Just that. Don't curse. Great big revelation and she's on about my *fucking* language.'

The artificial fire burned lower, the flames diminished to a sad red glow as they worked towards the end of the video. I spread my hand on Bree's leg. 'What did you do?'

'Cursed again. I gave her a volley of it, every forbidden word I knew – some I wasn't even sure what they meant, so I know my mom didn't. It was just language, one after another, till I was all out of words and out of breath and I stormed up to my room and slammed the door and wept.' She paused as the on-screen coals collapsed into the grate. 'I don't know how long after, maybe an hour, maybe less, Mom came up to see me. She stood by the bed and apologised. Said she'd been trying so hard to say the right thing, to think of something supportive, something – what's the word – *affirming* to say, she ended up saying fuck-all. She said the cursing thing was just a reflex, just her brain on autopilot.'

'So she was fine with it?'

'The first time I brought a girl home, she made her whole church give thanks that I'd finally found someone.'

'Wow.'

'Yeah.' Bree twirled the two halves of the silver heart around her finger. 'Anyway, that's the first one – for losing it with my mom when all she needed was some time. The second one's for feeling guilty about it.'

'I don't get it.'

'OK, so look.' She pulled the two half-heart pendants further apart to illustrate. 'The first half is for raging at her, right? It's my way of owning up to that mistake.'

'Sure.'

'Well the other half is to remind myself I shouldn't have felt guilty about it. Sure, I lost my temper – but I was a teenager, a teenager trying to figure out who the hell I was. You've been there, right? It's up to other people to learn to handle who I am, not me. Except— ' Bree's leg twitched, as though she wanted to pull herself back from me. Then she stilled. Sighed. 'Except I never apologised to her. I let her feel guilty, and I never once apologised for thinking the worst of her. And now it's too late, and I can't not think about that.'

'But,' I said, 'isn't that the point of a guilting? To take it out of your life and onto your body? To own your mistakes to stop them owning you – to not have to feel guilty?'

On the screen, the video came to an end and looped back around to the beginning, as burnt-out logs remade themselves and dying embers leapt back into fresh yellow flames. Bree said, 'It's just a teaching aid, Ivy,' and when she looked up again, her eyes were bright with the newly rekindled fire. She traced a slow line, from the arch of my foot up the inside of my calf, and said, 'Enough now. Tell me again about Antarctica.'

BELOW FIFTY, THERE IS NO GOD

There was a terrible joke we used to tell, last time I crossed this stretch of water. It went: did you hear the one about the seasick sailors? They *waved* goodbye to their stomach contents.

It's the swell that wakes me, side to side, rocking, lurch dip surge in the gut. Sick. Rock. Sick. I try to centre my gravity to the middle of the mattress. Focus on where my body presses against the white cotton sheet. *You have to feel your way into it. You have to become an extension of the ship.* This is what they told me on the expedition fifty years ago, while I retched into the toilet bowl and mumbled slick-lipped to the indifferent ocean, 'But I'm on your fucking side.'

Again, I try the trick of inhabiting my spine, each nub filling its own shallow dip in the memory foam. Most likely, my bones are crumbling now – my mum was younger than this when hers started. I've meant to get checked, so many times, but it was always Bree who was organised with that sort of thing.

I sit up and plant my feet on the rug, push my weight into them, to connect through my soles instead of my back. I spread my toes into the thick white fibres, feel through to the hard wooden floor underneath. I take a breath and stand up.

A wave lurches me into the wall and I stagger towards the bathroom, where I cling to the edge of the sink.

*

Washed and dressed, I check the time and realise I must have slept through half the morning. I've missed breakfast, but in such rough waters, food might not be the best idea in any case. Perhaps 'rough waters' is an understatement. After all, the Drake Passage is infamous, the most dangerous stretch of ocean in the world. Between where the toe of South America curls down and the long finger of the Antarctic Peninsula lifts up towards it, the Pacific, Atlantic and Southern Oceans clash. There's an old saying: below 40° South, there is no law; below 50° South, there is no god – and we're already well below that. Here, the circumpolar current is forced through its narrowest gap, as all those waves that circle the planet – around and around with no land in their path to break them – concentrate themselves here, on us, on our little icebreaker rocking and plunging on the open ocean.

When I pull back the curtains, the horizon swings up and down so wildly my stomach churns, and I have to draw them to again. What I need is fresh air, but going on deck in this would be suicide. Besides, the IntuTech will certainly have locked the outside door for safety.

I ease myself back onto the bed and close my eyes, grit my teeth through the sickening roll. I think I must have fallen asleep, because the next thing I'm aware of is a soft knock at the door.

It takes a moment for me to lever myself back up, to cross the room gripping onto the furniture, to open the door. The corridor is empty, and again I have that hollow prickling feeling from the night before. Not even a retreating back. No sound of footsteps on the thick carpet. *Out of sight, out of mind.* On a tray on the floor is a plated assortment of food – the kind of wholesome non-synthetic fare it's so hard to find in a city, but which I would scour my vid for pictures of: breads, cheeses, olives, cold meats, a large slice of rich-looking chocolate cake, a bottle of water. Food which my home IntuTech knows I crave, which the crew must have accessed to prepare accordingly. Perhaps the waiter from last night, with his gap teeth and floppy hair. Perhaps I could pick his brains for a story after all.

I pull the tray inside with my foot, then carry it over to the desk. I eat the savoury offerings and drink half the water. I decide not to test my stomach with the cake.

While I eat, I pick up the fact sheet Maretta gave me the night before. Strange for them to give me information on paper, rather than through a data chip or file drop. But then, I suppose paper's harder to hack, and easier to destroy.

Once, the Antarctic was a place of exploration. Of human endeavour and scientific research.

The words are familiar, but at first I struggle to place them.

While we may have failed to save parts of the Antarctic continent, by combining IntuTech with Chiller technology to repurpose waste heat as energy, we now have a way to restore it. Today, unlike before, there is a Plan B.

I read the words over again. It's the same information as the info-vid, the same cleverly crafted expressions, trotted out in a different format. I grit my teeth. Even when I scan down the sheet, there's very little actual information. The occasional choice fact: number of off-site jobs created by the project (eighty-three), how long the site took to create (just over seven years), and how long it will take to become stable (another twelve). Nothing at all about the size of the conservation site, or its exact location. Nothing technical. No scientific data at all.

I put the sheet aside and dig out the pass-chip from my shoe to try again. On screen, the wheel turns and turns, then settles once more on NO CONNECTION.

When I was younger, it felt ridiculous that there would still be places, decades on, which managed to resist the call to connectivity. 'Off-grid', they used to call it, and I always pictured this grid as the graticules on a globe: the lines of latitude and longitude that snare the earth like a fishing net – as if being off this grid meant you'd somehow managed to slip the bounds of the earth's map altogether. A delicious non-place, a kind of freedom.

Now, the lack of connection is simply frustrating.

If only I could open up the pass-chip – not only learn what it holds, but perhaps get a clue as to whose it might be, or why they needed to hide it behind the painting in my cabin. What else might I be able to learn from someone like that?

I think again about the kind-faced waiter, consider how I might get him talking. A drink, maybe. A few careful questions. It's always the staff who harbour the biggest secrets. Maybe I'll find him in the dining room, then, setting up for dinner. Or perhaps the kitchen.

I open the second miniature of whisky, gulp it down in one. For courage. The heat sinks through my gut, and I feel something inside me calm. I stare into the icy blue depths of the painting above the bed, and sip the third whisky more slowly. There's something reassuring about the symmetry of this: the cold-coloured paintwork; the warm comfort of the drink.

Now there's only one miniature left, glowing amber beside the row of empties. I should have rationed them more carefully. I shouldn't have stayed so long within the four pressing walls of the cabin.

*

I take a circuitous route towards the dining room, turn prow-wards back along the corridor, lurching with the roll of the ship past numbered cabin doors. Sky's perhaps, or Maretta's or Sharma's, or the liveried waiters' – although perhaps the crew have their own separate quarters. Who knows what might be down in the bowels of the hull? How little I know about this ship, about what it holds. Each shut door is a small frustration. A challenge.

I check behind me – the corridor is clear – press my ear to door number six.

Nothing.

I press my ear to door after door, but there's only the ever-present hum of IntuTech, the vibration of the engine from below, the creak and draw of colossal waves. When I try a handle, it's locked.

I resist the temptation to kick out. What am I looking for anyway? Would I know it if I found it? I tell myself I would, that my journalistic instincts may be rusty, but given a chance, they will fizz like sparks across the surface of a lake. Someone may have left me a pass-chip – a route to hidden information – but in the absence of the connection needed to access it, I resolve to forge a route of my own.

Even though I can't see them, there must be cameras and sensors on the corridor, gathering data for the IntuTech. When I try the next cabin door, and the next, I do it surreptitiously, tumbling one by one into the handles as though tossed uncontrollably by the chaotic motion of the ship. My performance may not be enough to fool a human, but it should at least convince the algorithms.

But one after another, the cabins remain locked. Doors unyielding. It's become more than a challenge, now – a personal slight. A barrier to be overcome. I collapse into the door handles over and again, bruise my arm with my pretence at falling. The harder the ship refuses to give up its secrets, the more tender I become. Now a barrier, now a battle, between my will and the will of the ship, between my pain thresholds and the doors guarding whatever secrets they have to guard. I no longer care if anyone hears. I crash into the doors so aggressively that when the last one opens, suddenly and freely, my foot twists under me and I collapse onto the threshold, half in, half out of the room.

Pain sears through my ankle, up into my calf, and I chew on my knuckle to stop myself crying out. In my new stillness, the ship is quiet. Expectant. I grip my ankle, try to massage away the pain.

The cabin I've tumbled into is almost identical to my own – dark like mine, curtains drawn against the raging ocean. Tidier, perhaps. Everything away in its proper place. The room of someone who wants to give away as little about themselves as possible. Sky, perhaps. Or Sharma. When I try to stand, pain cuts up through me like a blade, and I collapse back onto the plush carpet. I try not to imagine being caught like this, snooping and in pain, towered over in judgement. But the corridor is still empty. For now, at least, I am safe, and I refuse to believe my ankle is punishment for my prying. The world doesn't work like that, not really, and besides, I can hardly be blamed for an unlocked door; I merely stumbled into it, and it opened of its own accord.

But there's little to see from the threshold. Expensive pale furniture. Faux-fur rug. A different iceberg on the wall, framed in impressionistic strokes. No miniatures of whisky on the little shelf; in their place, another smaller frame. Impossible to tell from here what it contains.

One quick final check of the empty corridor, then I pull myself across the floor, hands and knees, dragging my sore ankle behind me. Not very dignified, perhaps, but more dignified than being ignorant. More dignified than leaving an unlocked room without any questions answered. The old determination shivers through me, like grit between the teeth. I grab the edge of the desk to pull myself up, halfway, onto my knees. When I reach for the frame, I catch the edge of it and it clatters to the floor. Two pale faces peer out at me from the dark beneath the desk.

The picture is a photograph – edited, filtered and printed to look like an old-school Polaroid. It's the sort of photo we used to take and share online as teenagers: against a background of brightly painted buildings, a young couple press their cheeks together to pose for the camera. A selfie – the woman pouting heavy lips, the man serious, but with the beginnings of a smile, as though the camera has caught him by surprise. Unlike the rest of the immaculate room, the frame is marked by fingerprints: something picked up again and again, too often absent-mindedly handled to be wiped clean. A talisman, like the objects Ross used to clutch for comfort. His blanket. His carved wooden seal.

The colours in the photograph are all enhanced, so that the whole scene looks unrealistic. So much contrast that some of the features become lost in the shadows, in the over-exposed high-lights. Even despite this, the woman's angular face and deliberate stare are easily recognisable. Maretta. Or, no – someone related to her.

I look again, try to date the slick hair, painted-on eyebrows, false kiss for the camera edited out of all reality. Maretta's mother, perhaps. I look again at the man with his cutting jaw. Maretta's father.

I remember what Maretta told me over dinner – how she slept on a roll-mat in a temporary shelter after the earthquake destroyed her city. Were these two people – so young, once, so in love – still with her then? Or had she already lost them? In the white space beneath the image, someone has drawn a small love heart, purpling now where the ink has faded.

Time to return the photograph to its proper place, to see what else this room might hold. I roll my injured ankle until it clicks, and the pain dulls. Again, I pull myself up by the desk, but it's harder to put the frame back than it was to pull it down, and I have to pull myself up further, till I'm standing, supporting my weight with the desk. When I reach towards the shelf, I must trigger the IntuTech sensors, because suddenly music is playing. It's soft and melodic through the cabin speakers, but loud enough to make me jolt – pain in my ankle – and I force myself back through the cabin door, slam it shut behind me, every second step a searing squeeze up my leg.

It isn't till I'm halfway down the empty corridor that I realise the music was my own relaxation playlist. That the ship not only registered and recorded a trespass in what should have been an empty room, but that it registered the trespasser as me.

*

The dining room is empty and the doors to the kitchen are locked, the gap-toothed waiter nowhere to be seen. My heart is still beating hard from my subterfuge and near-discovery, but the strain to my ankle is easing. I take this easing as an endorsement of my search: somehow, before the day is out, I will discover something beyond the dry official wording of Maretta's information sheet. Surely, somewhere on this ship, there must be someone with a story I can winkle out.

In the lounge, I find the man. The billionaire's right-hand man. Sharma. He stands with his back to the door, a large wooden packing crate on the table in front of him. As I enter, he turns, nods, then goes to the bar. 'Coffee, Ms Cunningham?'

'Please.'

Outside the panoramic windows, there is only roiling blue in all directions, a furious sea and bland disinterested sky. Not even a cargo ship to break the lurching horizon. The packing crate is half-open, FRAGILE red-stamped across each of its faces. In the pieces of the mirrored wall, the sea pitches above and below the reflected sky. I stand with my back to it.

'Sharma, right?' I know, this time, that it's right, but I want him to see that I've made the effort. Names, after all, are the first step towards establishing a rapport, to uncovering the person below the professionalism.

'Yes. Cream?'

'No thanks.' I try to remember what the second step might be, what I used to say to start a conversation off. I used to be so good at this.

When the ship smacks against a wave, the jolt up through my

still-tender ankle tips me into one of the leather armchairs, and I try to arrange myself as though I'd intended to sit all along. As if to make a point, Sharma carries the coffee over without spilling a drop. He moves like the old fishermen I sometimes saw when we visited the seaside, growing up. Steady, a surety that comes from a lifetime of learning exactly where to place his feet. His centre of gravity is low. His body rolls with the ship. I can see how he must be good ballast for the billionaire's nervous energy.

The coffee smells fresh and bitter and I want to close my eyes and breathe it in.

'Do you mind if I . . .?' Sharma indicates the packing crate.

'No, no, carry on.'

He gives me a small smile like the one from last night, swallowed by his eyes, then turns and picks up an orange-handled screwdriver. He wedges the blade into the gap in the top of the crate, presses his palm against it and pushes down on the handle like a lever, till the wood splinters. Then he takes the screwdriver out, moves it a few centimetres along the split, and repeats. The nails pull loose with screams like a small animal being stepped on.

I anchor my feet flat on the carpet, my back against the back of the chair, and try to ignore the oceanic roll in my head, my shifting gut. I can feel the whiskies gurgling about in there, and I don't know whether the coffee will settle it or make it worse. 'What's inside?'

He works slowly, hypnotically. Insert, push, release – over and over, each lifting the lid by the smallest amount. 'I'll let Sky show you.'

I'm not sure whether I've been encouraged or rebuked. I don't remember conversation ever being this difficult before – but then, I was younger, more in practice. Maybe if I can get him talking about himself . . . People like to talk about themselves. We are, all of us, inherently selfish. I need you to understand that, if we're going to continue. 'How long have you worked for him?'

'Forever, pretty much.'

The coffee is rich and earthy, like the coffee I used to get from the artisan roasters, a block along from my Boston flat – and for a moment I'm back there, on the way home from a bar or sim-movie with Bree, vivid-eyed and struggling to keep our hands to ourselves, or on a bleary afternoon, surfacing from hours plugged into a screen, or early mornings, a jumper over my pyjamas, pushing Ross's chair back and forth over the rough-wood floor to try to get him, finally, to sleep.

I take another sip and bring myself back to the present. 'Where are you from, Sharma?' It's important to address people by name like this, to convince them of your attention.

He says, 'About.'

Perhaps he's signed a confidentiality clause as part of his employment. Or perhaps he just isn't interested in conversation.

The screwdriver jinks against his thumb and he drops it, a soft thud, on the carpet. He sucks the bubble of blood from his knuckle. Thickly, around his skin, he says, 'No name, just a number.'

'I'm sorry?'

'We never called it anything because there was never anywhere else for us to go.'

Not *about*, I realise. *A boat*.

He says, 'My mom and pa were originally from Fiji. I was born at sea.'

'On a ship?' I don't know why I interrupt him. As soon as I've said it, I want to snatch it back. He's talking, for god's sake. Every amateur knows the best way to keep someone talking is just to listen.

'You know the difference, between a boat and a ship?'

'You can put boats on a ship, but you can't put a ship on a boat.'

'Right.' That smile again, so flat it's almost a frown. 'Like lifeboats – boats that go on a ship. Later, when we moved onto the floating factory, we used to joke about how it had no lifeboats on it. Therefore, it must be a boat and not a ship.' He laughs, and I can't tell if I'm supposed to laugh with him. I take a gulp of coffee instead.

In a way, I suppose you could say the floating factories were my own personal victory. Arks, the news sites like to call them, as though they were hopeful, or as though they contained animals instead of sea-migrants – people whose only escape from the rising sea has been to find a way to float across it. As storm after storm battered the South Pacific and the displacement crisis deepened, I guilted the corporations into taking responsibility. Second only to that initial stance in the Ross Sea, the floating factories have probably been my most notable success, my greatest legacy: the conversion of dirty-fuel container ships into homes and employ-ment for countless displaced people. True, they were only ever supposed to be temporary – a sticking plaster while something more permanent was constructed – but isn't any progress better than none at all?

For those first few decades, there were petitions to allow these Arks to land. I added my name to them of course, but by that time I had moved on to campaign against soil erosion in the Midwest, and couldn't afford the time to get more heavily involved. To begin with, governments capitulated and said, Yes, of course, anything else would be unhumanitarian. Except, they said, it would be a shame for them to land somewhere so low on space, or housing, or jobs, or food, or water. Here, our system's under strain from other migrants, from disease, from our own displaced populations. Let them land, they said, but somewhere else. Then the corporations, who owned the Arks and enjoyed having such an easily exploitable workforce, applied their pressure, and soon the governments stopped saying even that.

'So how did you end up working for the richest man in the world?'

Sharma looks at me as though he doesn't understand.

'I mean, how did you get off the Ark?'

As though it's the most obvious thing in the world, he says, 'I got a promotion.'

'And that's when he recruited you?' My error, of course, is that I assume he must be grateful. Already, I've begun to colour in the creaking rust of his former home, the stink of brine and sewage from the hold, the leak of hunger and disease. Already, I can picture him stepping ashore, promoted, free, the drag of the ocean retreating from his heels. Bree always did say I had a white saviour problem.

'He didn't need to recruit me,' Sharma says. 'It was one of his corporations which owned the factory.'

I take another sip of coffee. 'Go on.'

'A lot of the boats are like that – the floating factories – they pass between owners with buyouts and mergers, a small component of much larger companies. Sea-migrants, we have a kind of religion, that each of us has our own current. Inevitable, like fate. We learn early how to drift, how to lie at the mercy of the tides.'

'Is that what you believe?'

'It brought me here, didn't it?' For a moment he's quiet, twirling the screwdriver tip against the top of the packing crate. 'No. You have to set your own course. If there's something you really want, I believe in working your whole damn life to make it happen.'

'You're ambitious.' He reminds me of myself, but when I start to smile, he shakes his head.

'Most of my homeland was underwater before I was born, my mom and pa moving up the mountain as their island was battered by bigger and bigger storms. But they wouldn't leave. Stuck to it, they said, till my mom was pregnant with my brother, a storm flattened the bure, and they didn't have the energy left to rebuild.'

'Which storm was it?'

'It didn't have a name. Not by then, not in that part of the world. It was just another storm, like all the others. My parents struggled out eleven days in the wreckage, before the rescue boats came to carry them away.' As he talks, he looks older. Like a lot of people who've known hardship, who've lived through rough weathers, his eyes are lined, shadowy. He takes a breath, pulls himself visibly taller. 'More coffee?'

I shake my head.

'It was a fishing vessel, the boat where I was born. Trawler nets, tube diving – anything so we could eat. Any surplus we sold to food corporations, but that wasn't often. We lived on top of each other, twelve families, all of us with no country to claim us. Just the sea.'

'That wasn't the Ark, though.'

'No – the floating factories didn't exist till a few years later.'

My *doing*, I want to say, and don't. No need to make him feel obligated. I take another sip of coffee and try to look nonchalant.

'I was twelve, maybe thirteen, by the time we joined. Me, my pa and my brother.' He must see the unasked question in my face, because he says, 'My mom died when I was small, tube diving for fish. The umbilical kinked, so her air ran out. Nobody's fault – just one of those things. That was one of my pa's favourite sayings. *Just one of those things.* He was good at drifting like that. When the corporations created the floating factories, he got us a place on the very first one. The Boat, we called it. The only one that mattered, after that.'

'What did the factory make?'

'All sorts. Tech parts, mostly, or the tech to make the parts. It wasn't like a factory you have on land, with one big production area. We lived and worked as a community, each family in its own converted container. Cottage industry, my pa called it. Something from an old history textbook about England. It became our kind of joke – people started calling our container The Cottage. When my brother was alive, he painted flowers around the entrance, from a picture he found on a sack of flour.'

'It sounds lovely.' Even before the words leave my mouth, I know they're wrong.

'You think?' His forehead clouds, lightning-flash across his eyes, before he blinks it away. 'My pa and brother got the sick – no point in a fancy medical name if you don't have the drugs to cure it. It wiped out half the Boat. *Just one of those things.*'

I shift in my seat and try not to look at the floor. The floating factories, I want to tell him, were still a success. They might not have been perfect, but at least they were better than the nothing that came before. Perhaps he's too young to remember properly. I clutch my cup and say, 'I'm sorry to hear that.'

He shrugs. 'After they died, I had nothing left to do but work. I levelled up and up, till I got myself guarding the factory runs, and so I was brought ashore. I've been guarding Sky ever since.' Sharma picks up the screwdriver and goes back to worrying at the packing crate, a soundtrack of splinter and screech. 'People like me, we make good security. When you grow up part ocean, you learn when to fight against the current, when to let yourself drift. You get a sense for the direction of the tide.'

*

By dinner, the waves have calmed enough that the goats' cheese tart doesn't make me want to hang my head over a toilet bowl. Maretta, typically, manages to eat without a single pastry flake drifting loose; I give up trying after the first few mouthfuls. I try not to watch her too closely, try not to think about her resemblance to the woman in the photograph, in case she sees me looking and I give myself away. All afternoon, I've been waiting for someone to realise that I was in her room. Waiting for a stern hand on my shoulder or disapproving glare – but perhaps nobody has noticed. Perhaps I'm just one unexamined data point among millions. Under the table, I find my finger tracing the faded heart from Maretta's photo against my leg. My fingertips are claggy with remembering the frame, the prints of its talismanic hold.

The billionaire is in more expensive knitwear. With the anti-quated furnishings and home-cooked food, he could have stepped out of a photograph documenting early polar exploration. The waiters are still in their gold livery. The gap-toothed man with floppy hair, the other with teeth that look bunched too close together. I watch him surreptitiously. His left ear is scarred from old piercings – presumably an aesthetic that didn't match his livery – and I want to be reckless and ask if it was his choice to remove them or his boss's. But after a day of fierce nausea, reck-less is the last thing I feel, so instead I watch both waiters' passive faces, their identical listing walks as they deliver the plates, as they pour glass after glass of crisp sharp wine.

'I was impressed with last night's presentation,' I say, following Bree's old adage about flattery. When this receives a gracious nod from the billionaire, I ask about the science behind it – what it takes to refreeze a tract of land and sea, how much the technology costs, how many years it took to develop.

Maretta starts to speak, but the billionaire cuts her off. 'It's important, don't you think, to see the conservation site first? Before it all gets crowded out by technicalities.'

Maretta goes back to cutting her potatoes. Her knife rings out against the plate. Perhaps his reticence is because of my articles; perhaps he's still loath to trust me with too much information, and if so, perhaps I should consider that a kind of victory. But his smile is biting and I don't have the nerve to ask.

Through the curving picture window, I watch a pair of birds circle in the wind, dipping in the lee of the enormous waves. Feathers the colour of soft charcoal, and with elongated wings. The light-mantled sooty albatross. Their dance is something between courtship and a duel, neither surrendering itself to the other. Against the wall, now, the two waiters stand guard in their gold livery. Their faces remain blank, but I like to think they, too, are watching the birds.

'There isn't enough marvel in the world anymore,' the billionaire says. 'Not enough opportunity for awe.' He speaks as though he's lived a great many lives, as though he's talking down through multiple generations. He is (I know from my kitchen-table research) only just fifty. He puts down his cutlery and sits forward in his chair, holds my gaze. This is a trick speakers use, to make the listener feel important. I know. I used it myself with Sharma just a few hours earlier. 'I want you to experience Plan B – to really experience it – totally fresh, before we put you to work.'

I watch the albatrosses twirl and turn. It reminds me of those early months with Bree – how we danced closer and then apart, neither of us leading, each following the circling patterns of the other. Drifting – though it was years before either of us realised how far. I down my own cutlery. 'About the work – nobody's been very specific about what's actually *required* . . .'

Maretta glances at her boss, then says, 'We want you to be the voice of the project – a feature, a diary piece, whatever you feel comfortable writing. We want you to represent Plan B to the world.'

'Your early work for the Foundation, the Pulitzer essay, your connection with the Twelve Nations . . . You're a journalist – sorry, environmental activist— ' The billionaire grins and holds out his glass. The piercing-scarred waiter steps forward to refill it. 'But the point is – the point is, you work with words. You know how to spin a story.'

'Not *spin*,' Maretta corrects. 'Tell.'

'Right,' he says. 'Besides, nothing's contractually binding. This trip is about winning you over, not buying your service. If we reach the site and you decide not to write for us, there are always alternatives.' He continues to watch me with his magnetic blue eyes, a faint smile as though he knows something I don't. 'We won't make you publish a single word.'

What kind of person, I want to ask, shells out on an exclusive PR trip without even demanding a payoff? The corner of his mouth twitches, but he gives nothing away. Outside, the albatrosses lift above the frame of the window, then circle back into view. They do this all without flapping their wings, the epitome of balance against the buffeting thermals.

I take a sip of bracing white wine, which turns into a gulp. 'Surely someone like you doesn't need my connections?' I'm aware I sound like I'm flattering, but it's hard not to when he's being so amenable.

'The distrust of multinationals . . . It's complicated. Political. There are always other voices spreading their different truths.'

'You have a history in this industry,' adds Maretta. 'We want to show the world you're on our side.'

Which is the moment everything clicks into place. This, I realise, is why they chose me. Not in spite of my articles about the billionaire, but because of them. To solve a problem, to smooth a rippled surface. A risky move, I'll give the billionaire that: inviting me into the fold, on a gamble I won't sink my teeth into his precious Antarctic conservation project, purely for the satisfaction of tearing him to shreds. I think of AJ on the vid – *this'll be the remaking of you, Cunningham* – and fortify myself with another sip of wine. And another, till the glass is empty. I tell them, 'I'd be honoured.' When I look again for the albatrosses, they've already drifted astern.

*

Albatrosses are supposed to mate for life – did you know that? But, like so many creatures, they play around while their partner's away on the waves.

Even after we got married, there were others – women I was never sure if Bree knew about, though I always told myself she must. During expeditions and retreats and summits, when Ross was growing up and Bree was home looking after him, I threw myself into them – a plethora of one-night stands that moved from the bar to the hotel bedroom and no further.

Coming home, I sometimes found fresh sheets on the bed and

the house blueing with incense, and wondered whether Bree had found others of her own. If she had, neither of us ever mentioned it. We drifted on our own wings, the distance between us growing infinitesimally wider, less navigable.

*

Here are some facts about the light-mantled sooty albatross.

Albatrosses are most often sighted far from land, drifting and wandering on the winds. They are the souls of sailors, lost at sea.

Despite the more recent superstition that it's bad luck to kill an albatross, their feathers were once prized as writing quills. In Māori culture, their wing bones were also traditionally used to make flutes, or kōauau, whose breathy voices were said to render the player captivating to women. They are birds which carry both words and music within their bodies.

The light-mantled sooty albatross flies to conserve energy. By letting herself soar, she can use less energy in flight than she would while sitting on a nest. She can travel thousands of miles, if the weather patterns are right, without any need to land. When I was down here with the Foundation, I only ever saw one albatross flap its wings, and only once.

*

Maretta excuses herself after dinner and says she has work to do. Her lipstick is unsmudged from eating, and I'm tempted to ask her if it's tattooed on. I've always distrusted people with no visible ruffles.

The gap-toothed waiter follows us to the lounge, where he and Sharma pull down the blinds, and the burgundy makes the room feel warmer, like a womb or a seedy night club. In the relative calm, even the shattered mirror on the back wall seems less threatening. The wooden crate on the table is open now, beige packing ready to spill from the top. The waiter pours two whiskies and, at a nod from the billionaire, leaves the decanter

74

on another table, away from whatever is marked as FRAGILE. When he makes to return to the bar, the billionaire waves him away. 'You too, Sharma – take the night off.'

A pause that crackles the air between them.

'We're in open ocean, Sharma. I'll be fine for tonight.'

'You're sure?' Sharma's eyes flick towards me.

'If we hit any icebergs, you can come and get me.'

Another glance in my direction. 'Let me know if you need anything.'

'Sure, sure.' The billionaire waves his hand and turns back to the box on the table. When we're alone, he says, 'There's something I've been wanting to show you.'

The chaotic roll of the ship is softer now, a lullaby rocking, though I still grip the back of a chair with one hand as I sip my whisky with the other, still plant my feet as he moves towards the open crate. Now it's just the two of us, I can't help but notice how he occupies space, both more and less of it than I expect him to. How stocky he is – isn't that what people always say about the super-rich? – on my eye-level, so that he reminds me of Ross as a teenager, before he outgrew me. Also like Ross, the billionaire is never still, every fidget pulling the edges of the room in towards him. When he reaches into the crate, it's like that experiment they make you do in school – the billionaire a magnet and me nothing but an upturned pot of iron filings. No wonder he's managed to amass such wealth, such influence. He reminds me of myself.

'Here.'

I put down the whisky as he presents me with the first object from the crate: a scrimshaw – a carved stump of sperm-whale tooth, the ivory yellowing at the point. The base is still rough where it was hacked from the whale's jaw, but otherwise it's smooth against my palm. On one side is an intricate design of interlocking hearts encircled by a wreath of flowers – a valentine, perhaps, created for the woman left on land. I try to imagine the hands carving away at the enamel over long nights, heavy needle scratching in chorus with a bilge of rats, the sailor reminiscing about his sweetheart as he rubbed lampblack into the grooves.

Carved on the other side is a whaler in full sail, the huge beast harpooned and bloated alongside. I say, 'I suppose that's one way to declare your love.'

'Scrimshaws are ten-a-penny – I just liked the design of it.'

I put it aside as he pulls out a small wooden box. Inside is a ship's compass, polished brass and heavy.

'Amundsen's,' he says, 'from the *Fram*. And this – look!' and he unwraps an old canvas harness: a wide body belt with crossed straps to go over the shoulders, a length of rope at the back for hauling the sledge. 'Imagine,' he says, 'when the only pulling power you had was your own. Imagine towing the whole weight of your ambitions, dragging them day after day across the ice.'

As I sip at my whisky and watch, he unearths a pair of snow-shoes like badly strung tennis rackets, an unopened yellow tin of Lipton's tea, packed for an expedition, a delicate white penguin egg. Each one is produced with more scattergun excitement than the last, his earlier coldness falling away in the face of his enthusiasm, till he's like a schoolchild showing off a class project, and his eyes are Ross's eyes, his gestures, Ross's gestures. I take the objects, hold them and admire each of them in turn.

'This one,' he says, shifting aside a layer of packing from the depths, 'this took me years to get my hands on.'

He pulls out a large wooden box. Inside, pillowed in air-bubbled packaging, is another box, grey cardboard, the edges foxed, labelled in a narrow, slanted hand. From inside this, from the custom-moulded cushioning, he reverently lifts a boot. A single boot. The right, calf-high in tough brown canvas, criss-crossed with straps. The sole and vamp are reinforced with hard brown leather, and the whole thing is stained, weather-battered, worn to a sheen. It's a boot that has been through hell.

'When I was a boy,' he says, 'I had this book – the old-fashioned kind, big and heavy, glossy pictures – all about Antarctica. The Heroic Age. I used to sit under the bed sheets and pretend I was off on an expedition, off with Scott, Amundsen, Shackleton. *The Boss.* This was one of his.'

'Shackleton's?'

'His actual boot, from the 1914–17 expedition. Here.' He passes it to me and I take the gentle weight of it in my hands. There's not much to it, this great article of history. It doesn't tingle to the touch. It smells of must and years of museum storage.

'You bought the wreck site in the Weddell Sea.' I remember something I read during my kitchen-table research, about his underwater conservation work. 'The *Endurance.* Shackleton's ship.'

'He was always my favourite,' he says. 'The way he pulled through, the way he got all his team home safely. No wonder they called him the Boss.'

When he speaks, the expedition flickers in his eyes, lighting his whole face. I used to tell Ross those same stories, of Shackleton's attempt to cross the Antarctic continent – something nobody had ever done before. Of the *Endurance* trapped in sea ice, hull buckling till she went under. Of the men drifting, finally finding refuge on inhospitable land, of Shackleton's treacherous fifteen-day voyage across open ocean in a tiny boat to find help. I used to watch Ross pull the duvet up under his chin as his eyes shone with adventure, with daring, with nostalgia for a bygone age.

Which explains the billionaire's tendency towards gentlemen's club décor and liveried waiters. Possibly it explains the entire Plan B project.

I say, 'He didn't though.'

'What?'

'Shackleton.' I hand back the boot and pour myself another whisky. 'It's what people always say about Shackleton, how he brought all his men home safely. It's why they always bang on about him at leadership courses.'

'A hero.'

'But he didn't, did he?' I can feel a wildness creeping into my speech so I take another sip, try to revert to facts. 'In 1914, Shackleton had two teams on the Imperial Trans-Antarctic Expedition: his own, which aimed to approach via the Weddell Sea and begin the crossing from there, and another one, which went round to the Ross Sea to make preparations for Shackleton's arrival on the other side of the continent.'

'Yes.'

'Three of the Ross Sea party died waiting for Shackleton to arrive across the ice.'

The billionaire waves a hand as though he can swat the fact like a fly, and it's there again: that fury scored across his brow, fleeting, then gone. 'Not part of the story.'

They are, I want to say, very much part of the story.

But his buzz from the artefacts is palpable, and this is, after all, his trip. Besides, I don't believe these deaths make Shackleton any less heroic. People like a story of survival – or mostly survival – against the odds. A successful failure, like the recent Mars missions or Apollo 13.

'Enough of that.' He reaches into the very bottom of the crate, extracts a wide cardboard box and places it on the table. 'This is what I really wanted to show you.' He repacks the other artefacts, tenderly, as though tucking a child in to sleep, then picks up the decanter. 'Pass me your glass.'

ALRIGHT – LET'S START WITH THE EXPEDITION

Looking back on the early days of mine and Bree's relationship – before the expedition to Antarctica, before Ross – it's a struggle to remember any decisive steps we might have taken. Everything seemed to just happen: evenings at Bree's, half-dozing while she sat naked at the desk and graded papers; weekends at my apartment in the city, spending full days in bed as rain battered the window and the storm sirens wailed six blocks away, living on leftovers whenever we remembered to eat. Occasionally, we would throw on clothes and wellies to run down to the food truck on the corner. Or else, on milder evenings, we would emerge, glamoured to the nines at Bree's instruction, to go to a wine bar to drink up each other's company in public, to let our desire build again. Stopping on the way home – light-headed, prolonging the moment of touch – we would sit, thirsty for one another, in the artificial light of an all-night café.

It was in these heady months that I first understood the power of denial, the fine line between patience and longing.

Bree in the stuttering shower, saying, Stand there, saying, Watch. Bree making me touch myself, then saying, Stop, let's go out – the electricity for the rest of the evening, every time I brushed against her, every time she ran a deliberate finger up my bare arm, down my spine, along the inside of my thigh under the table. This was how I learned the correlation between desire and control.

I remember Bree standing in my bedroom doorway, wrapped in a bedsheet and holding an unopened bottle of wine from the fridge, condensation gathering, dripping small releases on the bare floorboards. 'What do you love most about me?'

I don't remember what I said – her generous heart, or her knife-blade humour, or how frankly she would take me to task.

'No,' she said. 'About my body.'

'Remind me of the options?'

For the rest of my life, I'll remember Bree letting the sheet fall, how it cascaded over her skin, pooled itself at her feet, how the dust motes drifted in the late winter light. I said, 'I want the world with you.'

'That isn't an answer.'

And so I panicked, the way I always did when forced to make a decision. We were still early enough in our relationship that I thought every wrong answer might spin us out of orbit – and when I ran through the options, all of them felt wrong. Her eyes? A cliché. Her breasts? Too male-gazey. Her hair? Too fetishy. In the end, I settled on her collarbone.

'Why?'

Because sometimes it was more prominent, sometimes less, and I liked the inconsistency. Because of the two shallow hollows above it, which perfectly fit the pads of my thumbs. Because when Bree sat above me, her collarbone was the hard upper edge of a breastplate I longed to break through, and because sometimes when I touched her, her collarbone would lift in a beautiful moment of vulnerability.

I crossed over to her, ran my tongue along the raised edge of it and said, 'Because I can do this.'

*

When did we make the transition from honeymoon couple to functioning partnership? I don't remember exactly. Perhaps it was

after we moved in together – though even this happened by accident, as the mudslides made trains out of the city less and less
reliable, till the only way for us to see one another was for Bree
to drive her ancient electric car into town. With it, she brought
clothes, books, even ornaments, till she joked that she may as well
just move in and apply for a job in the city, which she then did.

The romance never truly fell away. (We would not, I was
determined, be one of *those couples*, whose most sensual moment
was pulling each other's clean socks from the Quik-Dry.) But
people can only sustain complete immersion in one another's
bodies for so long. In the end, work reasserts itself, and you have
to make good on some of those dreamy half-murmured promises.

Were we moving too quickly? Probably.

Would hindsight have stopped us? Of course not.

We got married. We researched artificial insemination. I
applied for expeditions on the other side of the world.

*

One thing that's always fascinated me about Antarctica is the
naming of things. Elsewhere, in landscapes less hostile to human
habitation, places are named in two ways. The first occurs gradually, through habit. You refer to a place by describing it, till
eventually the description sticks. Hill Top. River Crossing. Road's
End. A description passed down from mouth to mouth, an identity grown on the breath.

The second way is more violent. It is a staked claim, a desire
articulated and acted upon. *I name this place Elizabeth Town. I
name it Victoria Falls.* In Antarctica, where there is no indigenous
population, everything must be imported – the food, the technology, the people, the ambition, the names. In this way, I suppose,
the whole continent is artificial, every feature of the landscape
a decision made elsewhere.

The same was true of Ross's conception. It was never going
to happen accidentally – but the claim we staked there was not

to the earth, but to repetitive meetings at the clinic, to waiting rooms with hard chairs and hushed voices, to killing time between appointments under the decades-old flatscreen which flickered, earnestly, from the corner. Wildfires outside Frisco, typhoons across the South Pacific, climate-refuge camps struggling under too much waste and not enough water. When I let myself, it was easy to hate us for wanting to bring a child into all of this, let alone two (although by the time my turn came around, I was too busy with work to attend the appointments). In the clinic, I was always careful not to let any misgivings show on my face. There were already too many questions to contend with – questions posed by white-coated professionals from atop carefully steepled fingers. Did we understand the process might take several attempts? That it might not work at all? Did we accept that, as with every pregnancy, there would be risks?

And on to genetics. Were we aware that only one of us – Bree – would be the biological parent? Yes. That the donor would remain anonymous? Yes. Were we clear that this included medical records? That if the child were ever ill, if it were something hereditary, there would be no possibility of tracking down the father? Did we understand what this might mean in terms of treatment? Yes. Did we want to request a particular sex? Bear in mind, ladies (*ladies*, pronounced in that patronising tone, over-emphasis on the first syllable), that nothing is guaranteed. No, we said, we're happy with any gender.

'Normally,' the doctor said, 'I ask about the ethnicity of the donor, whether you have any preferences or stipulations, but in this case . . .'

Bree frowned. 'In this case?'

'Leave it, Bree.'

The doctor coughed. 'Some couples,' he started, then stopped. Started again. 'Some white couples – they often feel they don't have the necessary qualifications, that raising a mixed-race child comes with, well, complications. Identity complications, you understand – a case of a white parent never being fully able to understand their child's experience. That's why we offer a choice.'

Sure, I remember thinking. That's the reason.

Bree said, 'But not us? Do we not get offered that choice?'

The doctor looked to me for help. I saw Bree notice this.

'No,' I said, 'we don't have any preference.' Later, I wondered if Bree had seen this as a betrayal. The doctor smiled and said, 'Lovely,' then typed it into the system.

*

The day we found out it had worked was the day I learned I'd got the expedition job with the Foundation. When the acceptance came through, I messaged Bree at school to say I'd cook us a celebration dinner. She messaged back to say she'd bought a test.

That evening, we sat together on the edge of the bed, the way we'd done so many times already, neither of us speaking, focusing on each other's pulses through our clasped hands. The test sat innocuous on the bedside table. Neither of us looked until the timer on Bree's phone pinged. Then I leaned across and we both looked together.

It was such a small thing, that thin blue line against the white – like a lead in an ice shelf, the locked water opening up into the possibility of a journey.

'I suppose I ought to cancel the trip.' I fought to keep the bitterness from my voice, but it oozed out into the space between us. The opportunity of a lifetime – that's what I'd said in the interview. The chance to make the world a better place – and now for the sudden reality of an unborn child.

'Go,' Bree said, her palm flat against my cheek. 'You'll be home before I'm due.'

*

So I did the training, pushing myself through run after run of physical exercises. Rigorous, this time – a shock after what little

I'd received for the South Pole. As Bree grew wider, I grew leaner, fitter. I rehearsed routine procedures, learned the correct way to layer thermals and woollens and windproof outers. I learned how to perform advanced first aid, how to recognise the symptoms of frostbite and hypothermia, and the difference between dehydration, heart attack, stroke. Bree's world contracted to the classroom, the clinic, and the sofa in the Boston apartment, where she sat with her swollen ankles raised and a stack of unmarked exercise books beside her.

Meanwhile, I attended the preparation camp in Virginia.

It was here that I first met the team I would spend three months sleeping, eating and working with on a tiny icebreaker in the southern part of the Southern Ocean. My first impression was that, in the face of their qualifications, it was a miracle I'd got the job. My second was that it would be another miracle if we made it through the expedition without killing each other.

The first person I met was Kay. She stepped up behind me at the arrival lunch and said, 'Is it part of the training, do you think? To get us used to the disgusting fucking rations?' Later, I would learn she always spoke like this, her Japanese accent thickening as she leaned into the curse words. Later, when she invited me into her bunk and asked if I wanted to fuck, it was that word that made me say, 'Yes, but nothing more.' And later, when she took the photo that made both our names, she said, 'Nobody could have taken that photo if they hadn't fucked their subject.' And I would carry that work ethic with me for decades, long after her death and very public funeral.

Wiry and athletic, Kay would push herself to physical extremes for the best angle, the best shot. 'I would make an excellent sniper,' she used to say, 'if only I didn't give so much of a fuck about life.' Perhaps it was this that made her the unofficial boss, or perhaps because, in her late fifties, she was the oldest member of the team, and we gravitated towards this, the way we never gravitated towards Andy.

Middle-aged and battling it with protein blends, Andy was godson to some famous mountaineer, who funded his activism in two-year chunks. But he was calm in a crisis, and meticulous about regulations. Which, given his role as the official expedition leader, was a good thing – though still not enough to save him ten years later, when the team he was leading found themselves lost in a blizzard.

Next there was Dick, the general assistant who hated his name and insisted we pronounce it 'Deek', and who clearly saw himself as a future Andy – but switched careers and became an accountant after he lost a leg to exposure on a later trip. The other general assistant was Poorna, who hummed to herself and tacked up pictures of her husband and three young children on the wall beside her bunk, who died of infection the following year after being bitten by the leopard seal her colleague was trying to film.

Our expedition had its own videographer – though I soon wished it didn't. Kim doubled up as a marine biologist (which, he was fond of saying, made him doubly indispensable), and his big passion was anti-hunting campaigns. His life's ambition was to make a stand, quite literally, from the back of a whale – which he kept telling Kay she'd have to photograph, till she said she'd take a picture of his corpse instead, 'after the whale's pulled you under into icy fucking waters, you dickhead'. ('It's pronounced Deek-head,' said Poorna.) After that, Kim mellowed a little – or at least until Kay's photo of me went viral and he stopped talking to any of us, and Andy had to report him to the Foundation as being unsuitable for future expeditions.

Also unsuitable, as far as I was concerned, was Noah. A highly skilled physician, he also loved to say the ship was his ark, and made creepy jokes about bunking two-by-two for survival, till Kay told him to fuck off. When I heard he'd fallen into a crevasse and died a few years later, I was surprised at how sorry I was.

Which only left Tap. Tap's real name was Maria, nicknamed as a child because she could barely go half an hour without needing to pee – 'But still a Pulitzer Prize-winning journalist,' as she told us on multiple occasions, 'so don't go thinking the two are mutually exclusive.' Which I didn't, very conscious that Tap was the *real writer* on the trip, and wondering why on earth the Foundation had also wanted me, with no idea my own Pulitzer was only a couple of years away.

This was our team. While Bree fought cramps and sleepless nights and cravings for expensive fruits, I sat in a lecture hall, taking notes alongside my expedition family. Outside, a tropical storm battered the coast, as lightning hurled itself into Chesapeake Bay. Inside, we braved the sub-zero temperatures of the simulation centre, where we practised walking in crampons, where we were taught to test the stability of ice before committing our whole weight.

Here, we learned that the coldest temperature ever recorded in Antarctica was almost ninety below zero, and that the wind chill can make it feel significantly colder than the reading on the screens. We learned that storms can blow up in an instant, and if we saw cloud formations building, we were to return immediately to ship and batten down the hatches. We learned that severe frostbite must be treated within twenty-four hours to prevent loss of limb. We learned to recognise the signs of hypothermia – and that if we ever started to feel euphoric about the cold, it was a sign we were in deep trouble. We learned that, although there are no land predators such as bears in the Antarctic, the leopard seal is a ferocious apex predator and has been known to attack humans, sometimes fatally. We learned that these were only some of the countless ways Antarctica might try to kill us, and that against all of them, teamwork was our best defence.

'The human body is surprisingly resilient.' The trainer told us this while surrounded by the emergency rations and cold-weather gear she had just finished demonstrating. 'But the best way to support that resilience,' she said, 'is to work together.'

*

The billionaire pours another drink and the decanter clinks against the crystal lip. 'Tell me about the expedition.'

The whisky is smooth, expensive. It slips too easily down the throat. 'There were multiple expeditions,' I told him. 'All over the world.' As if I don't know. As if people have ever wanted me to talk about any of the others.

'But the one,' he says. 'To Antarctica – the one with the photo. Here.'

He opens the final box from the packing crate. He watches me closely. From inside, he pulls a padded windproof jacket, warning-red, the Foundation logo printed on the breast. Next, an old-style digital camera, black and clunky. Then a commemorative expedition pin, and a framed edition of Time magazine, the familiar photo on the cover.

When he takes out the final object – a chunk of wood, hand-carved into a Weddell seal – I have to stop myself reaching for it. I hold my shuddering whisky with both hands and force myself to drink.

'This is my most recent acquisition,' he says, and places the seal on top of the framed magazine. It watches me with the inked-on spots of its baleful eyes.

*

You want to know about the expedition? It was boring.

Every day we spent aboard that ship was the same. We hunkered in the cabins and bickered, or wrote exaggerated reports to send back to the Foundation, when the sat-tech and the storms would let us. We took watches in four-hour shifts, staring across ice fields for illegal activity, or for wildlife Kay could photograph.

Yes, we had our little run-ins with the trawlers, and with the mining corporations – the Lidenbrock drill was just taking off in a big way, and all of them were down here, trying their luck – but most days, nothing happened, so even watching for trawlers grew dull. No wonder the old sailors took to carving scrimshaws.

*

Of course, I don't say any of this. I put down the glass and it clinks like a bolted lock. Time to tell the rich man what he wants to hear. 'What do you want to know?'

He tops up my glass. I don't remember finishing it, but I must have because it's empty. His warm enthusiasm is gone now, his eyes calculating and metallic. Almost impossible to look at, impossible to tear away from. He hands me the wooden seal like an interrogation. 'Tell me everything.'

*

So. Let's start with the photo, shall we?

In the end, I suppose, we were always circling back to that. When people ask about the expedition, they never want to know about Kim's research into the summer growth rates of algae, or how Tap wrote the first draft of her memoir on board. It always starts – and ends – with the photo.

*

A wide expanse of sea ice stretches towards the distant peaks.

In the foreground, an icebreaker bears down on it, all bolted metal, smeared and ocean-stained. The line of the camera follows the colossal drill bit at its prow, and just beyond it, as though ready to be speared on its point, is the focus of the image, and the only colour in this monochrome world: a woman in a warning-red parka, kneeling on the ice. With her outstretched arms, she forms a sacrificial barrier between the drill ship and what lies behind her: two mottled grey Weddell seals, a mother and pup.

As the woman blinks the glare from her uncovered eyes, her face dips to her shoulder. The gesture makes her look Christlike:

90

a stained-glass crucifixion against the white, her eyes lowered in grief for all creation. God, she seems to say, *forgive them*.

*

I remember the photo being taken. I remember my knees numb against the ice, the lactic acid building in my outstretched arms. I remember the sheer adrenaline of it, seeing our smaller icebreaker draw up alongside the big one, Kay on the wrong side of the railings, Tap and Noah clinging to her coat as she leaned out over open water to get the right angle. I remember afterwards, the seals adrift and safe and me wrapped in a foil blanket, watching over Kay's shoulder as she flicked through the camera, breathless, her whispered, 'Fuck.'

Of all the photographs Kay took of that incident in the Ross Sea, there were two she published. The first, with my head bowed, was the one that went viral, and the one that became the gesture of the movement that followed. The second was taken a split second later. Blinking away the ice-dazzle, I had raised my head to glare at the oncoming ship, full of rage as the colossal drill bit bore down on me. The world saw both these images, but it was the sorrow and sacrifice that caught people's imaginations, and the anger which had driven it all was lost.

And all the while, Bree was in a hospital in Boston, having an emergency C-section seven weeks before her due date.

As the shutter clicked, the first pains shot through her belly and down into her toes.

Or, as the shutter clicked, she curled and cried out from the dog-haired back seat of the neighbour's car, to save the cost of the ambulance.

Or, as the shutter clicked, the surgeon methodically cut her open and the midwife lifted our son into the harsh light of the theatre, to drag his first wild squalling breath into his lungs.

Who knows? I was in and out of contact, and then there was the complication of time zones and the long daylight, and Bree half out of it with pain and, later, medication. So I've never managed to pin down the moment exactly. It was two days before I even heard I was a mum.

By then, Bree had seen the photo. Everyone had. Later, I learned it was a nurse, turning the communal flatscreen to the news, asking Bree, 'Isn't that your partner?' And Bree saying, 'Wife.'

I remember ice cracking on the other side of the porthole, the scrape of growlers along the hull as I huddled in my cabin. I remember Bree's breath through the tinny speaker of the sat-phone, like canned hope, as she said, 'I've called him Ross. After your stance in the Ross Sea.' I remember being slow with tears. In broken syllables, Bree said, 'I'm so so proud.'

I told her, 'I'm coming home.'

Later, days later, I realised I should have told Bree I was proud of her, too. Recently, I've wondered if this is where it started – the separation, the continental drift – if this was the exact moment we pushed off from one another's shores.

*

I wake in bed in my cabin. Or rather, on the bed, still dressed and with the lights all on, no memory of getting here, but only an intense need to throw myself towards the bathroom – just in time – to vomit a projectile hurl, to thank god I hadn't shut the toilet lid, to hang my head over the bowl. My body tips out of itself, green and vegetal, brown and alcoholic, a smell of cleaning fluids – over and over, till my stomach muscles pull and my ribs ache. I cough. Cough again.

A long time since I've drunk myself into this state. Better to blame it on the sea, though at this precise moment I can't tell whether the rocking is the waves or my own body.

My jaw feels stretched and a watery badness coats the inside of my mouth, gathers in the corners of my lips. When I wipe it with the back of my hand, I discover I'm holding something.

More accurately: discover I'm gripping something so tightly it's pressed grooves, blue-red, across my palm.

The carved wooden seal.

Ross's seal.

I remember seeing it in the box. I remember the billionaire lifting it out, placing it on top of the magazine, holding it out to me like a gauntlet thrown down, like a challenge to be taken up. I remember, vaguely, reaching for it across the table, across almost fifty years. I don't remember what I said to the billionaire. I don't remember if I ranted, if I cried. I don't remember how I'm still holding it now.

I shut the toilet lid and the flush roars like the military plane I took to the South Pole. Still rocking, I sit under the bright bathroom lights as the cold tiles return me slowly to myself. I clutch the seal to my chest, thumb the smoothed wood under its chin, dark and shining from all the times Ross did this as a child. Whenever I went away, he would hold this seal, belly-up, like it was dead and awaiting the skinning knife, and worry his thumb or finger at its throat.

'I have to work,' I used to tell him. 'But this seal is a reminder that I'm doing it all for you.'

And I would tell him about the cramped cabin on the day I found out he was born, Kay sitting on the edge of the bunk, carving the seal with a penknife, saying, 'For your little boy, for his future,' as our icebreaker turned her prow towards north, and me so keen to reach him I barely noticed us leaving the ice behind. I suppose I always assumed I would return to Antarctica sooner, unaware how easily I would be able to move on to other issues, other fights. How easy it was, in those days, to not look back. And I would tell him about the photo, the seal on the ice with her mewling pup, and the Ross Sea he was named for. And I would tell him about the first time I saw him, over a month later, from the doorway in the Boston flat, how his liquid eyes had searched and landed on mine, how I'd dropped my bags and fallen towards him, and his eyes had held on. How they had kept holding on, on and on, throughout the years. 'That,' I used to tell him, 'is the most important thing. That wherever we go, we hold on.'

I try to send Ross another VidNote, but we're still too far from land. The connecting wheel spins, and I have to stop watching it before I throw up again.

I crawl back to bed, wait for the IntuTech to dim the lights. Then I remember I've turned it off, and I have to get up again to do it manually. The ship rolls under me, carries us determinedly, relentlessly south.

*

Did you hear the one about the woman who turned into an iceberg?

She hid most of herself below the surface.

*

It's late when I wake again, wash, dress, clean my teeth and spit the night before down the sink. My head is a battleground, but when I go to down the final whisky miniature to take the edge off, it's empty. Another casualty of the night before. So much for rationing them. I pick up the bottle and find a tiny amber crescent in the bottom, slim as a nail clipping, which I throw back into my mouth. I can barely taste it through the toothpaste, and for a moment I want to throw up again. But the feeling wears off and anyway, at least now I can function.

The waiter with the bunched-up teeth and empty piercings serves me a late breakfast of coffee, eggs and fresh bread. His listing gait seems more natural, now, something to balance him against the waves. As he bends to clear my plate, I'm brought up close to his piercing scars: a row of dots like needle points around the top; a wider puncture through the lobe; a spot like a chicken pox scar on his lower lip. He may not have the friendly, obliging face of his colleague, but he's here and it would be a shame to waste an opportunity. 'Can I ask your name?'

His hand hovers above the empty plate. 'Kip, ma'am.'

'Nice to meet you, Kip.' Conversation started. Now to create a connection, make it personal. I think back to Sharma yesterday in the lounge, telling me about his upbringing. People love to talk about themselves. I point, then wonder if that looks rude. 'Do you miss them?'

'Ma'am?'

'Your piercings.' I turn so he can see my own studded lobes. Creating camaraderie. Forming a bond.

He straightens, holds my half-cleared place setting in one hand, touches the other to his ear. 'A different life.' His eyes are glassy, haunted, as he runs his fingers across the scars. Then the ship lurches and his face snaps back into its professional mask, and he says, 'We had our first sighting of Antarctica earlier, ma'am, and there's an excellent view from the lounge.'

Meaning: go somewhere else so I can get on with clear-up and lay the table for lunch.

I watch him carry my empty plates through to the kitchen. I wait for him to return, but the ornate doors just swing themselves into smaller and smaller arcs, until they click shut. I try the vid again. Still only a connecting wheel, endlessly turning.

*

In the lounge, the packing crate and artefacts are gone, and there's that seedy feeling, smoky grey, of a nightclub in daylight, which may have something to do with the pummel in my head and in my gut. The boat pitches gently. I sit with my feet up on a coffee table, facing the blue and, at the edge of it, the first jagged white.

The ocean plays games with perspective, so the mountain range looks higher than expected – snowy peaks, gold in the caught sun, rising above a bank of mist as though born from the sky. It reminds me of Bree's old children's bible, which she handed down to Ross, and which he used to like for the gory Old

Testament stories. In it, there was a drawing of Heaven as a vast and beautiful kingdom, floating in the clouds. Visible, but never attainable. Not that Ross ever believed in Heaven. Better, I always told him, to work towards a kind of paradise on earth.

When the first iceberg appears in the distance, I go to put on my thermal layers. I hesitate over the parka, with its brazen Plan B logo, but it's warmer than my own jacket and anyway, Sky's paying for the trip, isn't he? When I put it on, the parka hums into life, as the intuition tech sewn into the lining reads my body temperature and the temperature of the room, as it prepares to adjust the coat's warming capacity accordingly. I fiddle around in an inside compartment till I find the switch, and turn it off.

Ross's wooden seal is sunbathing under the bedside lamp. I zip it into my pocket.

All wrapped up and out on deck, I breathe my first fresh air since the Beagle Channel, thirty-six hours before. It's icy now. It bites as I fumble for my gloves, pulls a metallic taste from the back of my throat. My eyes are already streaming.

Sky leans on the railing at the front of the ship. Calmer now, a little of his fidget fallen away in the open air. I brace myself and go to stand beside him. When I lean against the railing, the wooden seal in my pocket presses between my ribs.

'Good morning,' he says.

I try to read his voice, his expression, to remember what I might have said last night. 'Morning.'

'I never get over it, arriving like this. By sea, like the early explorers, watching it all come closer.' He's too pale out here, too screen-bleached, any traces of colour lost to the endless sky. I want to tell him to take better care of himself. 'Not like flying – it's a journey, travelling like this, a real rite of passage. Literally passing from the end of one continent to the beginning of another.'

The end of the world is the beginning of everything. Like one of those snakes consuming its own tail, devouring itself in an attempt to last forever. I'm trying to work out if I should mention the night before, or leave it buried and hope he does the same.

His excitement and furious coldness have both fallen away overnight, and for the first time, he seems content. Warm, even. At some point, I realise, I've stopped thinking of him as 'the billionaire' and started to think of him as Sky. I don't know exactly how this happened. It happened sometime during the part of the night I can't remember.

We're closer to the iceberg now, blue-white against the ocean, a band of turquoise meltwater around its base. No seals rolling in its protective shadow. No penguins porpoising in its lee.

'It's beautiful.' I hear the words lodge in my throat.

He rests his hand on mine on the railing. 'Yes.'

We watch in silence as the iceberg approaches, passes, drifts astern. It's steadfast and solid, as though it has always existed, as though it always will. No hint of how the ocean will melt the substance out from underneath it, of how changing shape will shift its centre of gravity, of how this will ultimately unbalance it. No hint of how suddenly it will flip.

*

He rests his hand on mine on the railing.

*

He rests

(*rest* with its falling *r*, its soft *s*, its inherent sigh; the word is thought to have referred originally to a measure of distance – as in, you travel so far and then your body requires that you stop – as in, after a certain time, your soul requires care)

his hand

(white, like those creatures that live in caves where the darkness bleaches all pigment from their skin, seen so rarely in the light that each glimpse becomes precious)

on mine

97

(thin under the gloves – my knuckles unforgiving against his palm)

on the railing

(wood so polished it refuses to be held, refuses to submit to the purpose it was put there for; below, the painted metal struts already bristle with frozen spume and beaded hearts of ice. I cannot remember the last time I was touched so tenderly by another person).

THE ART OF THE GUILTING

Did you hear the one about the Antarctic land grab?

Course you didn't. It happened like so many coups, quietly, the world turned away and dazzled by the lights.

*

I introduced the word 'guilting' into popular culture forty-five years ago, in the piece that won me the Pulitzer. I suppose you could say it was the most influential achievement of my career.

When I'd first returned, I'd written a piece about my expedition with the Foundation. This had been Patrice's idea – Patrice who had contacted me out of the blue to offer me representation because, she said, 'people all of a sudden know your face, you're a sure thing.' (I never told her that she had rejected me from the slush pile not two years before.) 'We have to capitalise,' Patrice said in that first conversation, 'on the influence of the photo. We have to strike with the follow-up before people forget.'

'While the iron's hot,' I said.

'Our job is to *keep* the iron hot,' she told me. 'Write your account of the photo's genesis. Tell the world what's going on down there.'

So I wrote, and it came out furious. I sent it to Patrice with the note, 'This is only the beginning. The next one will build on it.'

In the Boston flat, I took shifts with Ross, rolled his pram back and forth across the living-room floor to try to get him to sleep, ignored the woman downstairs when she banged against the ceiling. Through spiralling dust motes and the blue city light, I watched for his eyelids drooping, willed his exhaustion to overcome his determination. Then I would throw myself at the desk to write in heady bursts, to the soft hiffle of his sleep-breath, only to break off again when the flood-siren woke him, his lung-full squall demanding the world of me.

Later, after the Pulitzer, a critic wrote extensively about what he called my signature style. 'With those short sharp sections,' he wrote, 'each sentence becomes an intake of breath, each word the last bodily gasp of a dying world. What Cunningham's style asks – asks us all – is what moments will we choose to snatch from the jaws of Armageddon?'

In my own snatched moments of Ross's sleep, I wrote small scraps of features and interviews, finished my reports and gave talks for the Foundation, enough to keep money trickling in while Bree supported us on her teaching salary. Meanwhile, Patrice found a home for the first piece in *Time* magazine – Kay's photo on the cover, my furious words inside.

As I struggled to calm Ross's teething with gels and plastic rings and, on a couple of desperate occasions, a dab of whisky on his gums, the first people read the first piece. And those who read it shared it. And those who shared it shared it again. And those who hadn't read it saw it quoted, saw holograms of influencers and celebrities reading it, discussing it, acting on it, and felt the fury rising with the oceans.

In DC, protestors marched on the Capitol with extracts scrawled across their shirts, with their heads bowed, their arms like crucifixions – and so my pose in Kay's photograph became the symbol of the movement. Other cities followed, whole hosts advancing to chants of WE ARE YOUR OBSTRUCTION and NOT OVER US. Some of them walked whole blocks with lactic acid building in their arms, till they collapsed, shaking, in the street. Some walked unresisting into the gunfire of the authorities and were killed, or badly wounded, or were allowed to pass. Some did shooting of their own, with bullets or (more effectively) cameras, and the world kept watching. The fury grew.

In Canberra, an Aboriginal woman asked a group of strangers to film her as she stood on Capital Hill, her arms stretched wide through the sides of a sandwich board that read THE HEART OF MY COUNTRY IS BURNING. Then she set herself alight. In Rio, a vacationing CEO was discovered speared on one of his company's mining drills. In Lusaka, a man who smashed a tanker of oil into the Russian embassy was found, upon investigation, to have plastered his shanty town home with images of his grandfather's farm, now only dust and concrete.

Governments began to meet in secret. Or they met with fanfares and photographed handshakes. Or they didn't meet and told the press they had.

An art installation appeared overnight in London's Trafalgar Square: stitched from the rags of fast fashion, the artificial pelts of two thousand Weddell seals – each one smeared inside with fish paste so they attracted the gulls, so they began to reek in the late summer heat. On the darker corners of the internet, the sons and daughters of seven world leaders released a film, condemning their parents' inaction and threatening to expose family scandal if nothing was done. On the same day, an environment minister's private plane vanished mid-flight and was never found, and nobody could tell if this was accident or activism.

One by one, governments capitulated and declared the Ross Sea a protected zone. Under the hungry lenses of the world's media, they signed the Ross Sea Agreement. In an effort to block any loopholes, six of the world's most powerful CEOs were also invited to sign, which they did, in unironic green ink.

And so the Ross Sea was protected, and the trawlers and mining rigs were moved elsewhere, and people celebrated, briefly, before returning to their daily lives, their daily struggles, their daily chores.

And I had been declared an icon.

And the power of the corporations to equal that of the governments had been enshrined in international law.

Through all of this, I wrote. Did I approve of what I had unleashed? Some of it. Was I proud? Hell yes.

Words had become my activism, the fuel for other people's small fires, and all I had to do was stoke enough of them to make a blaze, then strike the match. *Words*, I wrote in the piece that would win me the Pulitzer, *must weigh themselves against the truth, and find themselves equal. Writing has become both my calling and my guilting.*

*

What is a guilting?

A guilting is not a confession. It is not a bargain for forgiveness. Nor should a guilting be a punishment. Yes, you can wear it on the body – as a ring, a pendant, a tattoo – but it isn't there to weigh you down. It shouldn't be a difficult load to bear. In fact, I wrote, that is the whole point of a guilting – to manifest your guilt into a physical object, so you no longer have to carry it in your heart.

It is simply an acknowledgement: this is what I've done; this is how I've hurt people; this is where I made the wrong choice. I am not asking for absolution. I am not allowing myself the luxury of self-flagellation. I am simply making myself aware, and that is all I need to do.

Even at the time, I wasn't sure I believed it. Even then, I wondered if I was taking the easy way out. Bree never commented on the essay, and I never asked her opinion, though I watched her read it the day after I'd sent it to Patrice.

If enough of us acknowledged the problem, I decided, eventually somebody would have to act.

*

This book is probably a guilting.

*

Perhaps I ought to tell you about the humanist burial site, four years ago in Vermont – the outdoor service, the trellis creeping with leaves, so reminiscent of our wedding decades before. The only difference was the HoloPlayer, projecting life-size holograms of Bree into the aisles – as a gangly teenager in Georgia, or middle-aged on the arm of her sister, or at the beach dome with Ross and his boys – so it was as if all of her past selves grieved there with us. The late September sun slanted through them, the colour of melted butter, but already there was a chill in the air, and the mourners huddled perceptibly closer.

Bree had chosen this place herself, back in the early days of the illness, when we were still together. She had been adamant about the outdoor venue, come blazing heat or depths of winter. 'If you're all gonna cry,' she'd said, 'you may as well water the flowers.' She'd made me drive her up here to check the place over. To *normalise it*, she'd said. I'd told her visiting your own grave was morbid, and kept my eyes on the road. The end was years away, the doctors had assured us of that, and there were treatments, now – palliative, but enough to slow the progression, to limit loss of function, to pass off the memory loss as just regular ageing, at least for a while. 'This burial ground might not even exist by then.'

There'd been an argument several nights before, after I answered a vid call during Bree's routine check-up at the clinic. Bree had lashed out that I was callously stepping over my wife's illness to get to my career, and in turn I'd accused her of being too busy glamorising her condition to remember the rest of the world existed. Things had been hurled and broken, doors and hearts slammed shut. So my main memories of that first exploratory visit are of the echoes of that argument, and of nervous crocuses, feeling their way through the grass.

It wasn't till the funeral itself that I realised how small the place was. Perhaps that was why Bree chose it. Perhaps she knew, even then, how people would fall away from her, piece by piece, as she fell away from herself.

I'd arrived late. From the back of the congregation, I mumbled along to the songs and responses, shivering in my satin suit dress. At the front, Ross wept and Hanna wrestled their children into line. Bree's sister stood up and read too quickly from her vid, about how community-minded Bree had been, about all the many children Bree's teaching had inspired, how she had been a wonderful mother to Ross, a doting grandmother. Even in childhood, she said, it was clear Bree had an infinite capacity to love.

At the end of my row, a grey-haired Bree laughed at something off-camera, her holographic eyes not quite meeting mine. Yes, I thought. Yes, that's true. I waited for her sister to say something about Bree's marriage. I waited, strung out and jittering, for my name to appear.

Instead, she read a stanza from some bland generic poem I was sure Bree would have hated, and invited us all to observe a minute's silence, to listen to the rustle and chirps of Bree's beloved nature. We bowed our heads and pretended our eyes were closed. I watched the other mourners trying not to fidget. Nobody looked back at me. Then the celebrant announced the final song, and the holograms went out.

And just like that it was over. A ceremony. A life.

On the edge of it all, I waited. Mourners gathered in the aisles to mingle, briefly, before the cold drove them back towards the IntuTaxis. Hanna ushered the children past me without looking, her face all horizontal lines. Ross followed them. At the end of my bench, he wavered.

'Ross.'

He stopped. I saw Hanna glance back, but he waved her on, his eyes following them all the way to the taxi lot. When he did look at me, it was as if I was another hologram, a ghost. 'I wasn't sure you'd be here.'

'Of course I came.'

'We thought you might not be able to make it.'

I regretted the suit dress. I regretted a lot of things. I touched a thumb to the krill tattoo on my wrist. 'Ross— '

'Rob.'

'What?' Out of the corner of my eye, I saw the celebrant approach, but something about how we were standing changed her mind, and she turned instead to Hanna's parents, to help them along the path.

'I changed it,' he said. 'It's Rob now.'

'Since when?'

He didn't answer.

I said, 'It was Bree – your mum – it was her that chose it.'

'I know the story.'

I wanted to ask if he'd ever told Bree. She had never mentioned it – but then, it was her memory that was the problem. And anyway, I hadn't seen her for over a year. Not since she hadn't known who I was, and neither of us, I had decided, needed that heartache on top of all the others.

He waited, his eyes scanning my face as though there was something he expected me to say. When I asked, 'How've you been?' they cut away and I knew that was the wrong thing. 'I'm not giving up on you,' I told him.

He looked again towards the queue of IntuTaxis, where Hanna stood with one hand on the open door and the children's faces bobbed like lifebuoys through the tinted windows. He said, 'My family's waiting,' and was gone.

I sat on the bench as the remains of the small crowd thinned and disappeared. The surrounding trees were starting to brown, curling up at the edges like damp paper. Fallen leaves gathered in low ridges, where they had been raked away from the ceremony area. I sat till my joints were stiff and the shiver had set into my bones. When the next group of mourners arrived, I had to be asked to leave.

On the journey back to the big empty house outside Boston, I turned on auto-drive and called the only person I had left to call. Patrice comforted me for almost an hour as I sobbed my way down the interstate, till my tears were spent and my throat hoarse. Then she finally broke the news: she had handed over her last few clients to AJ and was retiring – for good, this time. 'I'm sorry,' she said, 'I didn't want to tell you today, of all days, but since you called . . .'

'No, it's fine,' I heard myself telling her. 'Really. It's fine. I'm fine.'

As soon as I reached home, I started to pack. A week later I found the flat in Edinburgh, cheap and exposed to the weather. I viewed and bought it over the vid, then booked myself on an airbus to Scotland. Everything I took with me fit into two suitcases. I was, I told myself, ready to move on.

But it's impossible, isn't it? Leaving the past behind us. It follows us wherever we go, settles like dust over new furniture, sets itself up as a frame around every unseen view. The rusting red bridge through my Edinburgh window became an echo of the bridge in Frisco. I told myself it was a coincidence, choosing this place – that I wasn't punishing myself with that view. I told myself a red bridge was a red bridge and nothing more. As I sat in the smothering damp of my new kitchen, watching the haar roll in up the Forth Estuary, I wondered if anybody had even noticed me leave.

The next person I spoke to was my solicitor, when he called a couple of weeks later, to discuss contesting the will. 'Legally,' he said, 'you're still Bree's wife. It's a pretty strong claim.'

But the money was left to Ross – or Rob – and I wouldn't take a penny of it. I left Ross a VidNote to tell him: footage of the old red rail bridge as it disappeared into the fog.

ANTARCTICA

Ask any two historians about Antarctica's Golden Age, and they will probably disagree on its dates.

One might say it began in 1922, with the end of the Heroic Age of Exploration and the death of Shackleton. The other, in the 1950s, with the move towards international scientific co-operation on the continent. Or perhaps on 23 June 1961, the day the Antarctic Treaty entered into force.

Similarly, they might argue over its end date -- was it with the arrival of the first Lidenbrock drills in 2046, or did it end when governments started to fund mineral scans in the decades before that? It's rare that we notice things disappearing until they're already gone.

*

There's ice in the path of the ship, break-up from the West Antarctic Ice Sheet, bergs and growlers scattered on the oily sea. If I press my face against the cabin window, I can look ahead, to where a current of drift ice curls across the *Lone Star*'s path like a swirl of milk through coffee. The ship cuts through. Beyond it, the dark hulk of land.

There are other ships now, too. Trawlers netting the rich polar waters, cargo ships on their way to or from the continent, some high in the water, others laden and making their slow way north.

I sit on the bed under the painting of the iceberg and open my vid. It's been two days, now, since the Beagle Channel. Two days since I last messaged Ross.

On the vid, the connecting wheel spins, falters, spins, then connects, an umbilical pull to the outside world. Until that point, I hadn't noticed the ship knuckling in around me. I take a deep breath and press call.

The screen frames a shot of the pillow; broad and white as an ice sheet, the wooden seal at its centre, nose raised to the camera. A pleading shot.

'Hi love, it's Ivy. Mum.'

I zoom in on the two inked dots of the seal's eyes. I zoom in too close, till they become blurry, and it's impossible to tell how much is poor image quality, how much is pigment, bleeding into the surrounding wood.

'Just to let you know, we made it. Antarctica. I'm thinking of you.'

Soundscape includes the background rumble of the ship unzipping the waves. After a long moment of listening to this, I zoom back out.

'Miss you.'

*

I feel the ship slowing as the waiters serve us lunch. It's the same two as always: a skeleton crew. The one with the piercing scars – Kip – and the one with gap teeth and floppy hair. I try to catch Kip's eye and smile, but his gaze rests somewhere above my head.

Through the curving picture window, rocky islands drift, sway, then come to a stop. Other ships are everywhere now: nondescript government-owned vessels; slick corporate operations flashing their logos like credentials; the occasional hulking rust-bucket, held together by barnacles and greed – all of them anchored, all of them waiting.

Maretta sees me looking and says, 'For the Polar Regulations Bureau. We have to wait for our permit.'

'How long does it take?'

'A couple of days,' she says, riffling through her couscous with a fork. Today the food is Moroccan, a rich lamb tagine that infuses the dining room with the smell of cloves and paprika. I know without asking that the lamb is farm-reared and organic, from the way it disintegrates when I press it to the roof of my mouth, from the way the flavour seeps between my teeth and down the back of my throat.

'But for us,' Sky says, 'a few hours, tops. I do have *some* pull with these people.'

Meaning: he probably has a corporate stake in the Polar Regulations Bureau. Meaning: he is almost certainly profiting from the permit fees.

Which means, I suppose, that at least some of that money is going back into Antarctic conservation, which has got to be better than some politician's pocket.

Sky excuses himself. As long as we're anchored here, he tells me, there's signal – and as long as there's signal, there's work. He says this pointedly, and I don't mention I already know.

*

In the slim window after lunch, I change into my outdoor layers. While I tug off my trousers, I try the pass-chip again.

The connecting wheel spins. I pull my socks the right way round and set them aside. As I dig in the drawers for my thermals, the vid screen flashes, and the chip connects. It unlocks a series of online folders, but when I open the first one, it spills into a string of meaningless symbols. A code. Data which requires digital decoding on top of the physical pass-chip. Whatever this information is, it's well protected.

I set a standard translation program running, then project the vid onto the cabin wall so I don't have to keep checking the screen. On the bed, I lay out my clothing. Woollen thermals, leggings and shirt, trousers, thin woollen jumper, thick woollen jumper, high-tech fleece. Waterproof coat and overtrousers. Hat, scarf, woollen inner gloves, waterproof outer ones. Sun shades for the glare. Thin socks for comfort, thick socks for warmth, waterproof boots with a thick moulded tread.

Above it all, the vid projection flickers as the symbols rearrange themselves. Slowly, they become a string of numbers and words.

No, not a string. I pull my thin socks back on and reconfigure the display settings into three columns: names of companies; percentage of ownership; and net worth.

The numbers are static so this can't be a live stream. I scan the list.

At the top sits Cirrus Holdings, listing a hundred per cent ownership and a value just over three trillion dollars. Sky's. Further down, shares in all his competitors – Taiga, PacifiCorp and, yes, the Polar Regulations Bureau. Shares, even, in the GDPs of several countries. The complete list of Sky's holdings I've been unable to find anywhere else. Running down the columns, I try to do quick calculations in my head, but the numbers are too large and there are too many of them.

Besides, what the data is telling me isn't just what shares Sky owns and in what corporations. It's that he owns the whole market.

I try to work out who might have access to this information, who might need to hide it behind the painting in a guest cabin. I remember Maretta at dinner, trying to give me the specifics about Plan B, her boss cutting her off; I remember the photo of her parents – the inner bruise behind her professional façade. Sharma would certainly have access, but also presumably much better hiding places. A disgruntled crew member, gathering intel on his boss – though on this technological marvel of a ship, crew members are few and far between. I shudder. I think about Kip, perhaps forced to remove his piercings because they don't match his livery. Or the floppy-haired, gap-toothed waiter with the friendly face.

I go back to the main screen and try the second folder. A different code, with a different set of symbols. I check the third and fourth. All scrambled. All distinct. Each one, it seems, will need decoding individually – hours of work and processing. I check how much time I have left and realise I'm out of it.

I take the pass-chip out of the vid port and place it on the pillow, where it sits dull and heavy as a false tooth.

*

The loading bay is a deck below – an array of pulleys and lashings and metal gangways, one side open to the water. Sharma works alongside a man I haven't yet come across, with a shaven head and darting movements like a hungry bird. When I introduce myself, he nods in time to the water lapping against the hull. 'Aisi,' he says.

'Aisi's my second-in-command,' Sharma tells me, as he motions for me to stand back.

Together, the two men winch an expedition boat into the sea to bob alongside, then load in bulging waterproof sacks, sealed buckets and plastic drums, till the prow nudges up out of the water.

'Food and shelter,' Maretta says. Even dressed in full water-proofs, she manages to look flawless. 'Just a precaution. The weather can change suddenly out here.'

'Yes,' I say, meaning: I was doing this before you were born. I nod towards the rifle slung across Sharma's back. 'And that?'

He sees me looking and frowns, 'Security. It's my job to be armed.' Which is of course true, but I'd expected something more discreet. It must show in my face, because he lightens and says, 'Distances are big down here. The rifle lets me deal with danger before it can get too close.'

I want to ask what kind of danger he expects. After all, this isn't the Arctic, where the threat of polar bears makes firearms a necessity. But he waits with one foot on the rim of the boat,

117

the other on the metal runner at the edge of the loading bay, holding the railing against the uneven bob of the water. With his other hand, he takes my arm in a sailor's grip. I'd like to refuse him – to show Maretta I can make it into the boat without help – but I'd forgotten how cumbersome I am in so many protective layers, and I let him guide me into the expedition dinghy. X-Ped, he calls it. Nowadays, everything gets shortened to its function. From beside the engine, the other man – Aisi – nods, a dipping beak.

Sharma helps Maretta in to sit opposite me. 'Sky not joining us?'

Maretta shakes her head without looking at him. I expect him to put his foot down, refuse to leave his boss unguarded, but he only glances at me, then at Aisi, then back at Maretta. Clearly his issue is not with leaving Sky alone, but with me. When he unmoors the boat, it feels like a shrug, and I get the feeling a line has been crossed, though I can't work out where, or who's crossed it. Probably me. After all, this little venture is my idea.

I have persuaded Maretta to take me ashore. She protested – how it wasn't on the itinerary, how there was too much ecological damage at a site like this, and wouldn't it be better to wait for a pristine landing once we reached Plan B – but it felt halfhearted, and I suspect she might also have been suffering from cabin fever. Maretta strikes me as someone who needs to be *busy*.

Besides, I told her, it would be good for me to see Antarctica at its worst, so I have something to pit against Plan B when we finally arrive. This was a wheedling argument, the kind Ross might have used as a boy, trying to con his way into a second ice cream. Transparent, but too much effort to keep resisting. In the end, it didn't take much for Maretta to agree.

*

From out on the water, the *Lone Star* gleams, sleek and whitemasted, her hull dusk-blue against the grey waves. Around the bay,

118

drill ships and mineral carriers hunker in shades of brown and grey. Dirty green trawlers wait with logos blazoned across their flanks. Among them, a smattering of off-white cruise vessels cater to those unable to afford the longer trip to Eastern Antarctica, where the icescape is less industrialised and the wildlife more pristine. Fluorescent orange X-Peds zip between the waiting ships and an imposing building on the shore, processing and issuing the permits.

We speed towards a rocky beach at the edge of the bay. Beyond it, craggy hills, half-smudged with snow, push unsuccessfully towards the clouds. I feel Maretta's eyes on me and look away. Overhead, skuas circle and dive for scraps from the ships, bony wings like elbows as they squabble for spoils.

I've always hated skuas – their jackal opportunism, how they taunt the penguin colonies, steal untended chicks. But these are something more. As two of them circle the X-Ped, talons stretched, we have to keep our heads low so Sharma can bat them away with the emergency paddle. When they keep coming, he unslings the rifle and fires a warning shot into the air. The birds scatter. My heartbeat scatters with them.

'I've never seen skuas attack like that before.'

Maretta shrugs. 'It's learned behaviour. Humans mean food. Scraps. The more people come down here, the more aggressive they learn to be.'

I watch the skuas circle the ships, belligerent and hostile. Perched on decks and railings, they throw back their heads and laugh.

With so much human activity, it's easy to believe the lie that we might actually belong down here, that this landscape might be safe. I look to Aisi, impassive behind the engine. When I breathe in, it smells of fumes and fuel from the ships, the release of human waste into the water.

They always used to say, the winter-overs and long-term expeditioners, that away from the stink of the penguin colonies, Antarctica had no smell – just rock and ice, not even the sweet rot of decomposition. 'It's the first thing you'll notice when you get back home,' Andy told me, as we set out on the expedition all those years ago. 'How rich it all smells.'

Not true. To me, Antarctica always smelled of iron, a cutting red smell that stuck at the back of my throat and pierced the top of my nasal cavity. 'Can't you smell it?' I'd asked the team, but they'd only shake their heads. It was two days before I realised the smell was my own cold body, and by then there were other smells – damp wool, ripening sweat, sharp underwear when the cold made me chicken out of changing it. The smells of my body became the smells of the landscape, and when I went back home, back north, they abandoned me.

I pull my hair across my nostrils. The only smell is the floral-scented shampoo from the cabin, and even that is thin and unreliable.

Aisi leans his weight against the tiller to turn the boat, then draws it back into himself. He moves as though he feels the X-Ped's passage through the water with his whole body, as if the cold currents are in his blood. Completely in control, and the most natural thing in the world.

'Can I try?' The words are out of my mouth before I even know I've thought them.

Aisi looks at me, then at Sharma, who shrugs and takes over the tiller. The boat rocks as the two men rearrange themselves, Sharma's rifle slung back across his shoulders, and I find myself gripping the edge of the boat as water slaps at the sides.

'Here.' Sharma tilts his head to beckon me over. 'You're right-handed?'

'Yes.'

'Sit there.' He sits to the right of the engine and indicates the space opposite. I shuffle my way along the bench towards him. When I get up to cross the boat – crouching, trying to keep my centre of gravity as low as possible – the floor tilts under my feet and I tumble, crash into position beside the engine.

'Sorry,' I almost say, and stop myself.

Maretta turns to look at me with her cool professional disinterest and I have an urge to push her in. During our training all those decades ago, we learned that hypothermia is not the only way icy water can kill you; it can take up to half an hour for hypothermia to set in, even in the coldest of seas. The immediate danger comes instead from cardiac arrest, a sudden spike in blood pressure, or more commonly, sheer undiluted panic: the unexpected immersion sends the body into shock, so you forget to breathe, or swim, or even hold your head above the water. In many cases, the mind tricks the body into letting itself drown.

I turn away from Maretta and back towards Sharma and the thrumming dark engine in between us. 'What do I do?'

'Step one,' he says, and he unhooks a springy cord from around his wrist and slips it over mine, to cut the engine in case I fall overboard. The kill cord. The term drifts back to me from across the years, chilling and inhuman, as Sharma guides my hand to the tiller. 'At the moment it's idle,' he says, and shows me how to put it into gear. 'The more power you want, the further you twist the handle. Got it?'

I turn the handle towards me, just the slightest touch, and feel the X-Ped respond. I ease up and she stills again.

'Good. Now pull the tiller towards you to turn right, and push it away from you to go left.'

'So it's back to front?'

'If that's the way you see it.'

The space between the moored ships feels wider, now. I suppose it takes navigating through a landscape to truly understand the scale of it. I practise steering a few times, carving S-shapes across the water – small at first, then wider as my confidence grows. As a passenger, the X-Ped had felt puffed up and unwieldy, her flat base smacking the waves as she strove across the bay – but there's a surprising amount of power in the small boat. I can feel it thrumming up through my hand, into my arms and shoulder, till

I imagine the throb of the engine vibrating my bones to dust. I find I don't care. If I crumble, so what? It's heady, almost hedonistic, being at the tiller, feeling my every impulse played out in the boat's travel across the water. Like bringing a wild animal under my control. I open the throttle and race towards the rocky spit of land we'd been making for.

'Slow down when we get close,' Sharma yells over the roar of the engine. 'Try not to go sideways-on to the waves.'

I mean to nod, but my body is too tense, too tightly caught in the grip of steering the boat. The rocky beach races towards us, and there's that same destructive impulse, the one that wanted to push Maretta overboard. I picture us speeding faster and faster towards the land, till we crash right into it in a shower of pebbles and seafoam – or till the momentum skids us across the water, up the rocky beach and on forever into the Antarctic sky. The spray is cold stars on my face, and the air lashes against them. I smile. I close my eyes, imagine the sudden agony of impact, and open them again. I twist the tiller to slow us down. Across the boat, I feel Sharma relax as well, while Maretta straightens her white-knuckled fingers.

I try to work out what I need to do to land. I can feel the wavelets below us, gesturing us into land, so I hesitate, switch the boat into neutral. My hand sits idle on the tiller, caught between the urge to drive on and a deep resistance to the dead stones ahead, not even a seal carcass to break the barren shore. The X-Ped is like a horse that can sense its rider's uncertainty. When she starts to drift, it's as if she shares my reluctance, turning her prow away from the endless grey. Opposite me, Maretta also turns her face away, out towards the slew of ships – as though the lifeless rocky beach is beneath her attention. Then a skua shrieks and she startles; the cool façade slips for the thinnest of moments, and her face is the face of a child, terrified of the world, gripping a photo of her parents, smearing the frame with her grief.

'Ms Cunningham.'

I remember what Sharma said, about not going sideways-on to the waves. I push the tiller away from my body, try to pull the X-Ped back around towards the shore, but the engine is idling and she doesn't turn, just carries on drifting. Somewhere inside my body, my own tide is dragging me away. Maretta, clutching the photo. Ross, rubbing the smooth dark belly of his wooden seal, his arms stretched towards me. Begging me to stay. Later, the Helsinki hotel room – too-soft carpet, plush pink walls. *You're coming home?*

The X-Ped is side-on to the beach, now. I push again, can't connect my brain to why she won't turn. Wavelets slap her side, rock her unsteady in the water. I push and feel my seat on the side of the X-Ped shift, give way, then resettle.

You're coming home?

I have a flight . . .

'Ms Cunningham!'

Sharma reaches over to put the boat into gear. His face is close to mine and I feel as though I've been reprimanded – but at the same moment I remember how the engine works and I open the throttle so the roar fills my head and the noise is like slamming into a brick wall. And as I open the throttle, a wave smacks side-on into the X-Ped, lifts her side out of water and tips me back – my hand off the tiller now, and too late I make a grab for it but I'm floundering, my feet no longer connected to the floor, my body sliding back out of the boat and the water slams against my back, and no wonder people go into shock, no wonder I've forgotten to breathe because there's no air in my body any more, only cold, only solid unstoppable cold, and I'm gasping and gulping and it's sharp water and I can't drag the air in past it – and then I see Sharma, one hand gripping the side of the boat, which is somehow above him, now, the other gripping the front of my life jacket, holding me to the boat, and his face is still close to mine, and in it I see that same destructive will, that same desire to let go. And I want to gasp at him to hold on, but my throat is all fire and salt and ice and I can't speak, I just beg him in my mind, *hold on*, and I watch his eyes fill with hatred, feel his grip loosen, before he blinks, tightens it again and says, 'Hold on.' And then Aisi is leaning his whole weight against the far side of the X-Ped, Maretta beside him, as if they could fight the ocean and win.

And the boat flops back down onto the water and rocks there, gentle and unconcerned, a grazing mammal.

When Sharma lets go, I slip from the bench onto the floor and huddle there, force myself to count my breaths. In for four, out for four, over and over. My back is drenched and frozen and I hug my arms around me, still shivering. Still gasping shallow icy breaths.

Aisi digs in the emergency supplies and hands me a foil blanket, which hums with IntuTech as I wrap it around my shoulders. Without speaking, Sharma takes the tiller and guides the X-Ped away from the rocky grey shore, back towards the *Lone Star*. In the bottom of the boat, I huddle in the warmth of my IntuTech blanket, staring at nothing, feeling the eyes of the others skimming over me and away.

*

In the lounge, I sit with my back to the ships and the divebombing skuas, a hand to the side of my face like a blinker, so I can't see them reflected in the fractured mirror. I try to pretend I'm scratching my temple. I say. 'I thought it would be like riding a bike.'

Maretta hands me a coffee and pours one for herself. I fiddle with the handle of the cup so it rattles on its saucer, as she lays out a scone, jam and butter from a silver platter. I half expect her to cut it for me and remind me to take small bites. 'Things can change a lot in fifty years.'

I want to say, 'How would you know?' Though of course she

124

knows, and I have to push the image of that small frightened child from my mind. And anyway, what I really want is a drop of whisky in my coffee. She ought to have offered me one, for the shock, but I'm damned if I'm going to ask her for it. I eye the bottles, all lit and amber, strapped against the wall. 'Is there a map?'

Maretta thinks for a moment, then says, 'I should be able to call one up.'

'What about a paper one?'

'Paper?'

'With actual edges and creases and print.' I mean the sort of map she'd have to leave the room to find.

There's a pause in which I watch Maretta decide I'm being too demanding, and then decide to be professional despite this. She agrees she could check with the captain. 'Maybe we have something for emergencies or tech failures.'

'Could you?'

Another pause. 'Now?'

I say, 'Only if it's not too much trouble.'

'No, no,' she says. 'Not too much trouble at all.' And then she's gone.

I carry my coffee across the lounge – I'm still shivering, a few drops on the saucer – but then I'm behind the bar, choosing my whisky, the nearest, lift its golden glow to ease off the cap, pour in just a smidgen, enough not to smell it through the coffee, then OK, just a smidgen more, a slug, then back on the shelf. I take a gulp of coffee and it blisters my mouth, but the heat pours through my stomach and into my arms and legs, and I feel my body settle.

I carry the cup back over, avoid looking out of the window on the way. I arrange myself in my armchair, legs crossed at the ankle, one hand in my lap, the other supporting my chin as I gaze into the middle-distance. Nonchalance is harder than it looks.

After minutes of nothing, I take out my vid, check for messages, then put it away. I take it out again, to worry at the shallow notch of the vid port, think about the pass-chip waiting on my pillow in the cabin. In the absence of any other ideas, I set the vid to record, then pocket it again.

When I take another sip of coffee, the whisky is a bright fire at the back of my throat. The shiver has almost gone, now. In its place, my body tingles from the subterfuge. It isn't that I think anyone would mind me taking without asking – but I'd forgotten how good it feels to keep secrets, to have somebody to keep them from.

Still no sign of Maretta. I have the urge to do something else rebellious and unpredictable. Some unnoticeable act of vandalism – a small tear in the underside of a cushion, maybe, or a scratch along the wooden board below the window. Something trodden into the carpet by the table leg. Which is petty, obviously, but beneath it is that old restless energy, rekindled first through the power of manoeuvring the X-Ped, then again just now: the power of knowing something nobody else does, and choosing not to tell.

With one last check towards the door, I knife half a pat of butter from the porcelain dish. The butter is hard with cold. Condensation beads its pale yellow surface, so when I try to spread it down the narrow gap between the arm and cushion of Maretta's chair, I have to push it off the rounded blade with my finger. It slips between the leather into the body of the seat.

I sit, skin zinging, and sip my coffee. If there are sensors in the lounge, feeding my behaviour into the IntuTech's predictive algorithms, I hope I've just thoroughly confused them.

When Maretta returns, it's with a satisfied smile and a battered map bulging at the folds. I suspect she's never failed to fulfil a professional request, and I suspect this is a point of pride for her. She makes to lay out the map on the table, but the table isn't big enough, so she spreads it extravagantly across the floor.

126

I put down my cup – try to distance her from the smell of stolen whisky – and lower myself to kneel opposite.

'Is this what you were looking for?'

I smooth the creases with my palms. It smells of old books kept in the damp, the continent spread against the blue like a huge white comma. 'Where are we now?'

Maretta points to a red dot and the italicised words *Polar Regulations Bureau* at the northern end of the Antarctic Peninsula: the curling finger of land that reaches out into the Southern Ocean, the continent's thin strip of vulnerability. Thinner still, since the break-up of the Larsen Ice Shelf. There's a chip in the silver of Maretta's highly polished fingernail. I notice this and feel victorious, and then ashamed.

'And the Plan B site?'

She hesitates, then indicates an area further south – unmarked – on the western edge of the Peninsula. I spread a hand over the narrowing sea ice around the western half of the continent, over the wide white expanse of the much bigger East Antarctic Ice Sheet. Thank god this, at least, is still intact.

I used to do this with Ross – sit on the floor, with him perched in the diamond of my crossed legs, my old expedition maps spread out before us, as I traced the routes for him with my finger. 'This,' I would always tell him, 'is where I was when you were born.' And I would point to the Ross Sea with its white barrier of sea ice, spell out his name for him from the blue letters.

I find it now, a large triangular inlet in the lower half of the map, now titled Ross Sea Protected Region, the text in self-satisfied environmental green. I cover Ross's name with my thumb. Somewhere along the edge of it is Cunningham Peak, ritually named for my efforts fifty years ago. I look, but the map's scale must be too small to show it.

'That's the area you campaigned for?' Since declaring herself a fan on the first evening, this is the first genuine interest Maretta has shown in me. She says, 'We learned about it in history.'

History, for god's sake. I try to imagine a teenage version of Maretta, somewhere between the lost child and the woman she's become, but it's impossible. She's too much of an adult, with her severe haircut, her sombre fitted suit. Probably she wore it on the X-Ped under her waterproofs.

'I had that photo as my vid screen for years.'

I don't need to ask which photo. 'Why?'

'The usual. A single woman making a stand, the underdog fighting authority. What child wouldn't be taken in by it?'

I notice the phrase *taken in*. 'This area,' I point to the green border on the map, 'the Ross Sea and all around the bottom here – it was already meant to be protected. The Antarctic Treaty made the whole continent a non-industrialised zone – and it worked, at least till the Lidenbrock drill came along in the '40s. You're too young to remember.'

Outside, an orange X-Ped loops the bay, churning white water in its wake. When it pulls up alongside the *Lone Star*, I can see two figures in branded black waterproofs, calling to someone on the ship. I lose sight of them as the X-Ped steers in closer to the side.

'Your expedition.' Maretta says. 'The Ross Sea Expedition of '48.'

'That's what they call it in history class?' Her face falls, but I watch her sweep her disappointment out of sight, drop her professional smile into place like a heavy carpet. I try not to revel in it. I think of the much-held photo of her parents, the inked heart below it. 'We safeguarded this whole area, the *Ross Sea Protected Region*. But all that industry didn't disappear, it just moved along a bit.' I point at the blue just outside the Protected Region boundary, at the Amundsen Sea in one direction, the swell of Victoria Land in the other. 'There are still trawler nets and longline fishing all out here, summer drilling right along the Peninsula.'

'Why didn't you fight it?' She does her best to sound curious, but I can hear the accusation in her voice. As though I owe her decades of thankless fight, just to live up to her childhood hero worship. As though I owe her anything at all.

'It was a losing battle. The corporations would never have gone for it, not back then.' I resist the urge to tell her she'd understand if she were older. 'I focused on other things – the rainforest, ocean clean-up – fights I could actually win.' *Like rebuilding the barrio where you grew up*, I think, but am not quite petty enough to say.

'And did you?'

I shrug. 'Some of them.'

She says, 'It's why we brought you here. When Sky asked me to solve the Cunningham problem— ' She checks herself.

'The articles.'

Her face is a drawn-down blind. Through the window, the orange X-Ped pulls out of the shadow of the *Lone Star*, steers away into the scatter of waiting ships. 'To bring you back down here, remind you what we're supposed to be fighting for.'

'To get me on-side?' I can hear the whisky rising in my voice and try not to laugh. 'Glad he thinks I'm worth the effort.'

She sits back on her heels, eyes me over the top of her coffee cup. 'Sky gave me my second chance, Ms Cunningham. It's a principle I've lived by ever since: that everyone deserves one, no matter what.'

'Still, it'd have been easier for him to just file an injunction.'

On a breath, like a small bubble rising unstoppably to the surface of a lake, Maretta says, 'Exactly.'

*

Later in my cabin, with the duvet pulled tight around me, I play back the recording. I try to shut out the sounds of the ship, slipping further from the bay and the Polar Regulations Bureau, further into the night. I turn the vid up to full volume. Even then, Maretta's voice is only a hiss of static.

I turn the word through my head, long into the night. *Exactly.* So soft it almost never happened.

And only when I wake the next morning will I think about how someone had been in and folded my thermals away into the drawer, had turned down the covers and laid my sleepsuit on top. How I had put it on and got straight into bed, my mind already churning.

How I hadn't had to move the pass-chip from the pillow.

WHAT THE SEA GIVES BACK

Whenever I think about the ocean, I think about the Spilhaus Map.

Imagine a map of the world, but instead of prioritising land masses – brightly coloured blocks arrayed against a vague blue background – it focuses on the oceans. Or, more accurately, *ocean*, singular, since there is only one. Imagine a united mass of blue, with the continents stretched and fractured to fit at its fringes. In the centre, the small white comma of Antarctica gleams like a set jewel.

Several times during my career, I've used versions of this map to demonstrate interconnection, to encourage people to see the world afresh. My favourite version is one illustrated with the whirling arrows that show the major ocean currents: clockwise around Antarctica, the cold blue arrows of the circumpolar current bleeding red as they swirl out into the broad plains of the Pacific and the Atlantic, into the smaller corner of the Indian Ocean. The currents carry their nutrients north, then return warmer waters to the south.

There's a balance to it, and I like how this mirrors my own migrations: Edinburgh, to Boston, to Antarctica, to Boston, and finally back to Edinburgh. The reaching out, the looping return. Compared to this, Ross is an unfinished sweep – Boston to Frisco to Abu Dhabi to who knows where – an arrow shot into the void.

I think again about the ocean as a single entity, one blue heart beating against all the continents' ribs, with me aboard the *Lone Star* at its centre, and the meandering global current still connecting me, distantly, to Ross. It may take a thousand years, but the water always comes back to where it started.

*

I remember how Bree shook me awake that day with a smile full of soft morning breath and the words, 'Hey there, superstar.'

I dragged myself out of sleep – the kind that only comes after a heady night. My dress was still strewn across the chair, and I could see the Pulitzer certificate on the desk, innocuous beside the room service menu and list of spa treatments.

'Time to get up.'

When I checked my phone, it was 4.15 a.m. I'd been asleep for two hours.

'Come on – I have to show you something.'

I buried myself in the pillows. 'Remind me again why I love you.'

While Bree stuffed things into bags, I showered off the night before. I stuck my upturned face under the water. I brushed my teeth twice.

By the time we were checked out and driving through the outer fringes of New York, the sky was a pale blue wash, readying itself for the sun. I tried to persuade Bree to turn on the auto-drive while she let herself wake up, but we hadn't yet had the new car long enough for her to trust it. Besides, Bree was like me, always needing to feel in control of where she was headed. Through the sleek glass-sided buildings, navigating the construction works for what would later become the Manhattan Sea Wall, then over the East River into the suburbs, we passed old electric cars and sleek new auto-drives all headed for the city. Going our way, there was only an ancient diesel-driven banger, coughing out fumes, which we overtook. After that, we saw no one. We passed extravagant stone-faced houses behind ornate electric gates. Gardens burst their colours over high walls, and turbines and solar panels gleamed from tiled roofs. The further we drove, the more palatial and gated the mansions became, until they finally gave way to low timbered homes in pastel colours, porches with flynets and easy chairs, a motif of anchors, buoys and driftwood. The paintwork grew salt-scoured, and as we turned at an intersection, the sun burst through a gap in the buildings and everything was suddenly lit gold. In the new light, the road and the houses and the birch trees lining the street looked artificial, as though everything might be hollow at the back.

'Where are we going?' I felt dreamy and light-headed.

'You'll see.' Bree tapped out an irregular rhythm on the steering wheel. 'D'you need to stop for coffee?'

I shook my head, basking in the feeling of being not-quite-there. 'You know we should've stayed an extra couple of days in New York.'

'What about Ross?'

'Your sister likes having him, doesn't she?'

Bree stared straight ahead at the almost empty road. I watched her cheek moving where she chewed it, and I counted her slow blinks.

I said, 'I mean for the press. Professionally speaking. If there's extra coverage about the prize – I ought to be there for that, make myself available.'

We were driving over bridges by now, some old and low to the rising water, their channels and inlets passing bold and blue below us – some Bailey bridges where the unstable ground had flooded and collapsed. An oystercatcher took off from the mudflats. It veered towards the windscreen, then suddenly away.

Bree said, 'Patrice knows how to reach you.'

I dug out my phone to check for messages, but it was too early for anyone to be in touch. By rights, I should still have been sleeping it off. The morning-after taste was starting to cut through my toothpaste. I reached for the water bottle and took two deep swigs, but it was lukewarm, staling. In these specific words, I thought: this early start had better be worth it. I decided not to annoy Bree by saying them out loud. Then I said them anyway.

Bree said, 'I hope so too.'

I kicked off my shoes and leaned back to rest my bare feet on the dashboard. Bree always hated when I did this, but I loved seeing my feet with the wide flat road unspooling ahead of them. I smiled at Bree and wiggled my toes. Bree turned up the air-conditioning.

*

We parked in a tarmacked lot beside an old brick lighthouse, empty apart from a handful of weather-battered electric trucks hooked up to the charging points. The salt smell hit us as soon as we stepped out of the car, and with it came the unseen crash of waves, the raucous call of gulls. There was a promise of heat in the day, but buried, for now, by the North Atlantic breeze. When I tugged a jumper over my head, my stiff joints creaked. I yawned and clicked my jaw. I needed to click my hip, too. I leaned on Bree's shoulder and tried to roll it out, but I couldn't make it go.

'D'you recognise it?' she asked.

We'd come here three years earlier, on our anniversary – had driven down from Boston through the snow and bad weather warnings, on a day I'd said was too cold for the beach. (Bree had said, 'You've been to the South Pole, for god's sake, woman up.') The sea air had whipped at our skin and I'd been convinced the trip was a mistake. I'd braced myself as we climbed the wooden steps up the sandy ridge – until suddenly, there was the beach, spread out for miles in either direction, the kind of wide and pristine sand you hardly ever saw, even back then. The sea was foamy with cold where it crashed against the shore then dragged back, and the low sun lit everything soft and soporific. When a flock of sanderlings darted from the water, pecking for worms and molluscs in the surf, they cast long shadows of themselves up the windswept sands.

We had huddled in blankets by the long grass, watched the sky purple and the sun sink into the water, leaving a trail of fire across the waves. Afterwards, in the car, shivering and with the heating blasted on, we had kissed the salt from each other's skin, made awkward and difficult love. Then we'd driven to the only unshuttered café we could find, where we ordered beer and chowder with blissed-out grins.

'OK, you're right,' I'd told Bree on the drive home. 'That was special. Thank you.'

Now, I said, 'We missed the sunrise.'

'I wasn't aiming for the sunrise.' Bree led me up the wooden steps to the top of the ridge. There was the beach. There was the surf. There were the darting sanderlings, even – but the beach wasn't empty.

Stooped figures roamed with slow concentration, their shadows stretched along the sand like barcodes as they picked up food packets, plastic bottles, scraps of netting with their long-handled litter grabbers, as they dumped them into multi-purpose sacks.

'What happened?'

'Nothing happened.' Bree tried to take my hand, but I pulled it away.

'Last time, it was clean.' I kicked at the rusted remnants of a beer can. 'Spotless.'

Last time, Bree told me, she'd got talking to the woman at the café: a bunch of volunteers came down here every morning, to clear whatever had been washed up overnight. 'That's why it was so spotless. They make it that way, every day.'

'So it was never real.'

'Morning!' A stubbly man in a hooded anorak waved us over.

Bree said, 'Just because someone's had to work for something, doesn't mean it isn't real.' And I followed her across the sand.

'Don't suppose you two girls are here to help with the trash?' The man rustled the rubbish bag as he spoke and his teeth clicked together like castanets.

I waited to see if he would recognise me. A lot of people did, especially environmental types. The man reached with the grabber to pick up the frayed toothbrush at my feet.

'Sure,' I heard Bree say. 'Why not?'

'Hell, I wasn't serious. It's this damn landfill. Businesses ship it all off, and I swear half of it goes overboard, ends up right back on these shores just the same. Damn pain in the ass.' He wipes the constellation of sweat from his brow. 'Still, we'll be done in about an hour. You girls have a nice day.'

'No really,' Bree said, 'Put us to work. It'll do us good.'

'Well, if you're sure . . .' He handed Bree his bag and grabber, and she passed them to me. 'I'll fetch you another set from my truck.'

When he'd gone, I asked, 'How come I'm the only one with these?'

'You heard – he's fetching another from his truck.' Bree nodded towards a scattering of bleached plastic fronds, caught in the sand. 'Why don't you start on that patch, and I'll take the section further down?'

'I'm not one of your students,' I wanted to tell her. Instead I turned away and said, 'Sure.'

It was boring work, moving from litter to litter – toys with snapped-off limbs, shards of glass, packets that fell apart when I touched them, so I had to grab each one multiple times over. Soon, the sun had cut through the early morning cold to redden the back of my neck, and my lips were dry with salt. I took off my jumper to tie around my waist and brushed the salt-frizzed hair from my eyes. So much for glamour and photo shoots. 'Why did you bring me here?'

Bree leaned on her litter-picker and shaded her face against the sun.

'This is some sort of moral lesson, isn't it?'

'I wanted to come here together, to a place we both love.'

'And the litter picking?' I dumped my rubbish bag, waved my litter-picker at the beach like a gesticulating man in a Victorian painting. 'What, I win a Pulitzer – a fucking Pulitzer, by the way – and you just can't wait to bring me back down to earth?'

I saw her face harden. Let it, I thought. If I was behaving like a spoiled child, then she had started it by punishing me like one.

'Screw this,' I said. 'I need to check my phone.'

'Well then. When they ask you how you celebrated your win, make sure to tell them: you had the opportunity to help a local community reverse the environmental impact of a corrupt federal government – only you chose to fight with your wife instead.'

'If this is a fight,' I told her, 'I sure as hell didn't fire the first shot.'

She went back to her litter picking. 'I'm sure you'll manage to fire the last.'

*

The whole drive home, neither of us spoke. I rubbed my feet against the grits and grains of sand in my shoes. The car was full of the smell of the sea, and I wound the window down to let it out. When Bree stopped to use the bathroom, I called Patrice. There had been enquiries, Patrice said, after a brief congratulations, and requests for interviews. 'Do you want the numbers?'

'Yes,' I told her. 'Yes of course.'

Back in the Boston flat, as Ross burbled happily on the rug and Bree danced his teddies across the floor, I made the calls. I did interview after interview, the same answers rehearsed and trotted out each time. Yes, I was thrilled and honoured by the Pulitzer. Of course I would continue to lobby governments and corporations. I was working on another feature, yes, and a book, as it happened, but I couldn't give too much away just now. Well, I had spent the day battling the effects of unregulated big business at the level of local community. No, the fight was far from over.

Somersaulting a fluffy pink rabbit off the edge of the sofa, Bree snorted. Ross kicked his legs and giggled.

*

Just a few months earlier, we'd taken Ross to the beach dome outside Boston – the first of its kind in North America: a promise of tropical sunshine in the middle of an east coast winter, part of an entertainment chain which would soon have outlets across the country.

Bree had discovered it in the early weeks of pregnancy while I was away, not yet on the expedition but preparing for it. It had soothed her, she said, lying back in the artificial sea under the too-blue sky, letting herself float on the gentle nudges of the wave machine. It made her rounding body feel weightless. So, when Ross was born and I was home, she had insisted we take him.

We carried him in from the bitter Boston cold, swiping our cards at the turnstile: past the enquiry desk with its bored assistant, via the changing lockers with their smells of body odour and shampoo, to squeeze into our swimsuits, then down the concrete ramp onto the beach. It was early morning, the middle of the week, and the beach dome was empty but for a couple of hardcore sunbathers withering in their winter tans, and a pre-work swimmer breasting serious lengths of the shore-line.

Ross's eyes were bleary at the artificial sunlight. I remember his look of adoration as Bree carried him out into the ocean, as she held him gently on the surface. His surprised hiffle as I touched his forehead with the chlorinated water.

I've never believed in god, but Bree had insisted on some kind of baptism – a hangover from her faith-centred upbringing. There was something purifying, she said, about being touched by water. As Ross's eyes widened in shock and then in infant joy at being back in his element, Bree whispered, 'You, Ross, were named for the sea. So we baptise you with the ocean, and promise to love you even from across it.'

'Amen,' I wanted to say, but didn't. Ross smiled up at us, as the waves rolled in from the painted horizon.

*

And I remember five years later, maybe six – a weekend, this time, and the golden sand a cacophony of coloured towels, of beach balls and inflatable floats. Nostalgic, in the face of disappearing coastlines. The dome echoed with the shouts and splashes of children, the jingle of food stands from the prom.

The one thing the beach dome never quite got right was the sound. It was almost there, in the hush of breaking waves and the gull calls played from hidden speakers – but echoed back, like the sounds in a warehouse or a school hall. It was just one thing Ross loved about the place.

His face lit up as he ran down the sand, skinny in his neon yellow trunks, weaving between sunbathers and a fractious sandcastle competition, as he raced for the sea.

Bree and I had brought books for the afternoon – and alcohol smuggled through in our water bottles as though we were teenagers. We grinned at each other as we swigged, already drunk on sunshine and the piped scent of saltwater. Bree's smile was slow and lazy – rare that she did anything slowly since Ross was born. I remember watching him splash in the shallows, how he turned to wave, kicked up diamonds. We waved back and, satisfied, he returned to his paddling.

I remember the tingle as Bree rubbed tanning oil into my back, already gritty with sand. I wanted to turn and kiss her, to lead her into the shallows and make love under the water. We couldn't, of course. So much of parenthood was wanting to and not being able. I closed my eyes and felt Bree lie on the towel beside me, the back of her hand a narrow slip from mine, the hairs on her arm close enough to make mine tingle as our bodies entered each other's electrical fields. I knew, from this, that she wanted me too – that she was also allowing herself to fantasise, desire jumping the synaptic gap between us.

I don't remember when I first became aware that Ross was drowning.

I don't remember who noticed first, or whether either of us spoke. I don't remember anything except that suddenly we were both on our feet, that the dome was silent (except of course it wasn't), and the only thing happening anywhere in the world was Ross – his small body too far out and under, then up, hands grabbing at the waves, a not-quite cry, a struggle, a frantic splash, then under.

I remember sand flying. I remember running feet. I remember the water's hold as it pulled him deeper in, his angular thrashing, how he emerged from the waves, how he was raised into the light to breathe.

I remember how I stood on the shore, frozen, and watched Bree charge towards him, watched her seize him, pull him back to the safety of the land. I remember how my body kicked me into action only after he was already safe – how I wrapped him in a towel, rubbed him dry till his skin reddened and he squirmed, till he said, 'Mum, stop.' I didn't once look at Bree. I held Ross close, told him over and over, 'I love you, I love you so much.'

As we were leaving, a man in a Hawaiian shirt recognised me and called his two teenage daughters over for a photo, which Bree took. In the picture, I'm not quite looking at the camera. My smile is as wide and blank as the artificial sky.

ART/ARTIFICE

In the morning before breakfast, I walk agitated laps of the deck.

I woke early, searched for the pass-chip: swept my hand under the bed, hauled the pillows onto the floor, shook the covers over the rug till my arms ached. I'd known all along I wouldn't find it, a discovery I was never supposed to have made. I try not to think about it, but it niggles like a missing tooth.

I walk laps of the deck.

I begin starboard, where the stairs let out through the fat PlastiGlass door, its thick rubber seals and high lip marking the end of safety. The deck is painted with a running track, which loops the bounds of the ship. I picture Sky running circuits, rising early to worship at the temple of his own body, before getting down to the daily business of wealth – but I remember his bruise-ringed eyes and spinning fingers, and the image vanishes. A crew member in full IntuTech gear scrapes the thin layer of ice from the deck, salts the track. As I pass, he nods, says, 'Good morning' with his voice constricted from the cold. I smile in response, then set off clockwise around the ship.

The sky is cloudless, pink at its edges. Night still clings to the ship: a cold sweat of frost and rime coats the metal, and the ropes and stays above me shiver in the frozen air. My breath leaves me in billowing clouds of white. Away from the shipyard of the Polar

Regulations Bureau, the channels are grey and eerie: ice-crack and lap of water, the occasional cry of a skua. Once, through a dip in the topography, I glimpse a distant ship. Fifty years ago, even when I was here on the expedition and actively looking, we could go days without seeing another vessel.

I tried to explain this once, almost a decade ago, in Helsinki. Campaigning for the ratification of an Antarctic Industry Cap. In front of the world's most influential executives and conglomerates and entrepreneurs, I argued for the real-terms removal of industrial activity in Antarctica. The loss of income caused by the Industry Cap, I told them, would pale in comparison to what we would lose as a planet. I should have known they would never let it pass. That I would never be allowed to walk away unscathed.

The channel is edged with glaciers, their slow push down the valleys, invisible grind of soil and rock far below their glittering surface. Relentlessly undoing the landscape. In turn, the glaciers themselves are being gradually undone.

A warning, that's what I was. To all those after me who thought of sticking their heads above the parapet, of fighting a passionate but imperfect fight. *Remember Ivy Cunningham. Remember the Helsinki affair – and stand down.*

As I watch fractured growlers of ice driven under the prow of the ship, the crew member approaches, his body tilting with the roll of the ship. Breakfast, he says, will be being served below deck. If I'd like to warm up.

When I thank him, he hovers, as though he's forgotten what comes next. Then he says, 'Ma'am,' and returns to scraping the deck.

In the absence of the IntuTech which might prevent it, my underarms sweat into the downy prison of the parka. I let them. I enjoy the dampness clinging to my skin out of sight. In our pre-expedition training on the edge of Chesapeake Bay, it was drilled into us, again and again: never let yourself overheat; never let your base layers get damp; sweating can easily lead to hypothermia.

I unzip my coat to let the chill rush in. It digs like knives into my colding skin, cuts at the damp patches under my arms. Maybe that's the definition of luxury, to ignore training in favour of the whims of the body, a heated cabin with unlimited high-pressure hot water only a minute away. From the prow, I walk the quarter-lap back to the starboard side door, back down into the ship, and the pattern of the day.

*

I sit opposite Maretta as the waiters deliver eggs and fresh bread to the table. I watch her meticulous chewing and think about her hushed *exactly* – but after yesterday's stilted conversation with Kip, I'm loath to lay any cards on the table while he's here, so we eat in silence.

The pass-chip still worries at me like an open sore, and when Sharma arrives to say Sky would like to speak to me in his office, I feel my breath catch. His expression is as inscrutable as ever.

'Of course,' I tell him. Then, like a prisoner trying to go to the gallows with dignity, I add, 'Thank you, Sharma.'

Maretta's spoon slips against the saucer. Three dots of coffee soak into the pristine tablecloth.

*

Not so long ago, Maretta would have been my type. Not in the way Bree was my type, to love and let myself be vulnerable with, or in the way Kay was my type, to share experiences and desires. There are so many ways to be attracted to a person.

I tried to explain this to Bree once, one unseasonably hot October at a rooftop bar in Manhattan, both of us sprawled and talking slightly too loud. The sky turned purple and the city's mirrored glass unlocked itself into a mosaic of lit windows. I told her, 'I'm attracted to you because you're beautiful, obviously.' I had perfected, by this point, the art of the compliment. 'But also because I can be myself around you. You look at me and see right

147

through the bullshit, and that's sexy and terrifying and the most incredible feeling in the world.'

'But?'

'But. Sometimes it's possible to be attracted to someone because they're out of reach, you know? Like a celebrity or a one-night stand.' Although at this point, I knew, Bree had never had a one-night stand. 'Someone who's attractive precisely *because* you don't know them, and they don't know you. Because they could be anyone.'

Bree downed her fourth mojito and said, 'So what you're saying is, you have desires I can never fulfil?'

Which was typical of Bree, misreading a moment of honesty as criticism, and I wanted to tell her not to be so fucking needy. Instead, we went back to the hotel – ambient lighting, crisp cotton sheets, a nineteenth-floor view of the park all paid for by some magazine I don't remember – and I undressed her, kissed each patch of skin as I brought it into the light, told her, 'You're everything.'

But yes, I thought afterwards, as I stood naked at the full-length window, daring passers-by to look up. There were things Bree couldn't give me.

When I was younger, the girls I met in the student union bar were always poised and put-together. I'd walk them back to their rooms, wait outside for them to invite me in, and each time one of them did it became a kind of victory. I always left before they woke next morning.

It was meeting Bree, ironically, with her lessons on appearance-as-armour, which helped me understand – that what I'd felt was attraction-as-inferiority-complex. At summits and conferences, meeting women whose every surface seemed slick and polished, I felt the same attraction, the same desire to witness the ugly sweating chaos of their climax – and to feel myself in control the entire time.

When I think about Maretta, I think about those three dots

of coffee on the clean white tablecloth, and it's that same urge to tip her over the edge.

*

At the back of the *Lone Star* is a polished spiral staircase. I follow it from the main deck, down to a single unstaffed desk, a transparent PlastiGlass partition, and Sky's office beyond. It's the sort of office that pretends to have everything on display: ergonomic chair, vast mahogany desk facing the panoramic window, screens all set to blank. Against a wall, a cabinet with an old metal key in its lock.

No sign of Sky. I check the staircase, then try the PlastiGlass partition door. It opens. I hold my breath for an alarm, or for the tell-tale relaxation music to betray my presence, but Sky must have turned off the IntuTech in here, because the only sound is the slim rumble of the ship. I slip inside.

The office smells of polished oak flooring and someone else's elbow grease. Something unexpected, too – some acerbic chemical I can't identify. The sea today is grey and choppy, small mouths biting at the rocks.

Now I'm inside the office, I'm not sure what I want from it. Only that the pass-chip was my only other source of information, and without it I feel powerless.

Checking again for feet at the top of the stairs, I try the screens – but they're biolocked, and even if there were time to hack a bypass, I'd never have the skill for tech like this. I try the desk drawers – perhaps whoever found and confiscated the pass-chip delivered it directly to Sky – but only two of them open, and they reveal nothing but a copy of Maretta's Plan B information sheet, and the usual assortment of sleek office stationery, all in shades of silver.

I turn the key in the cabinet lock and it clicks, loud through the empty office. I glance at the staircase again. I open the doors.

At first, I'm not sure what I'm seeing. Everything is colour and texture, the chemical smell overpowering, till it shifts and settles into a painting. Oils, maybe. Acrylics. A wide canvas stored on its end, paintwork of blues and whites and greys. It's all fat and deliberate brushstrokes, or the swept curves of a palette knife, three-dimensional, so I want to reach out and touch it. When I tilt my head, the swept colours transform into icebergs littering a dark blue bay, a grey-hearted mountain looming above. I pull the canvas forward. There's another stacked behind it, and another, and another, all the same artist – the same as the painting in my cabin – all icescapes, all opulent with texture and paint.

'What do you think?'

I turn so fast I almost let the paintings fall. As I steady them, I can feel the hard shine of brushwork under my fingers.

Sky stands in the doorway, hands in his pockets so his shoulders hunch forward. He nods at the paintings. 'Well?'

I think the paintings are beautiful. I think they perfectly capture the movement in an Antarctic icescape, the way ice can grab the light and break it. I think the paint mutters like the scrape of sea ice or a hidden glacial creak.

I think the man who owns them is moments from condemning me.

'Are you a collector?'

'Yes, as it happens. But these are just for fun.' His leg judders in time with the engine, wilder, until he springs off from it and crosses to stand beside me, one hand on the open cabinet door, finger tapping against its edge. He says, 'They're mine.'

It's a moment before I understand what he's telling me. It's difficult to marry them: these bold brushstrokes, with the fidgeting man beside me. I look back at the canvas. 'How long have you painted?'

'Since I was a child. Nothing technical – they wouldn't make a gallery. But it helps me get to the truth of things, figure out what's buried under all the everyday stuff – I'm sure you can understand that.' I nod. He makes to close the cabinet, then stops, one hand on the key. 'What's that word you used again? In your Pulitzer article?'

'Guilting?'

'Yes,' he says. 'Guilting.'

He closes the cabinet and directs me to the chair. He stands by the window, silhouetted, and I wonder if it's deliberate, to stop me seeing his face. I have to remind myself that he's an expert at this game, too, that he's played it all the way to the top.

He says, 'Sharma told me about yesterday.'

I can't tell if I'm being reprimanded. After the confusion of the pass-chip disappearing, yesterday's brush with Antarctic waters feels like days ago. I wonder if he knows about Maretta's hushed 'exactly', or about the butter pat melting into the belly of the leather chair.

'Are you alright?'

'Fine,' I tell him. Then, because his silhouette is a thumbscrew and it feels as though more is expected, I add, 'Sharma saved me. He stopped me falling out of the boat.'

'Did he now?' A smile curbs the studied cut of his accent, though I don't understand what's amused him. When I smile back, his voice turns serious. 'Look, I wanted to apologise – if you'll let me.'

'It wasn't your fault – I was a bit of a reckless driver.'

'Not about yesterday. For how I was when you first came aboard. It wasn't my idea to bring you here, not originally, and I know I didn't do much to make you feel welcome.'

I chew over his words while I work out how to respond. It would be rude to agree with him – after all, I'm still his guest – but to deny it would feel like letting him off the hook. 'What I wrote about you,' I say carefully, then stop. I try to shrug as though it's no big deal, as though I haven't spent the past eight years chasing him like a rabbit into the dark. 'It wasn't kind.'

'No.'

'Put it behind us?'

His silhouette is tense against the backlight, silent. When he does speak, it's on an in-breath, as though he's caught himself in the middle of a thought. 'I remember my dad, once – I don't know why, some lost possession, maybe – he took me to the top of our building one night. The lift was broken – he made me walk all fifty-eight floors.'

In all the interviews I've watched, all the articles I consumed at my kitchen table, I've never heard him mention his father. I hear my breath catch again.

Sky must hear it too, because his outline stiffens. After a long moment, he continues, 'I remember looking out of the tiny corridor window. From there, you could see the harbour floods, the abandoned park, the main freeway running out of Sydney. The lights of the cars, red and white, stuck travelling in their separate directions. All of them, my dad told me, had chosen their lane, and they had to keep going forward. He said it was the only way any of us would ever get anywhere.'

'As in, *you can't go back*.'

Sky nods. 'Of course, he meant places like home or the office or the simulators. Ordinary, unambitious places. Places with a clear route.'

I listen to the scrape of a growler along the hull: small hunk of ice, kissing the side of the ship. His silhouette in the window is still pulled taut, and I can't help feeling he's holding something back. 'Why Antarctica?'

'Scott. Amundsen.' He shrugs. 'Mainly the Boss.'

Shackleton again. Explorers from a supposedly heroic past. I watch the grey snouts of glaciers through the window, nosing down to the sea between the rocks. 'What about *you can't go back*?'

'Plan B isn't an unambitious place.' He makes a small clicking noise in the back of his throat, which at first I read as anger. Later I will understand it as dismissal of his father's views. Then

152

he moves away from the window to lean over the table, and his face is lit by that familiar enthusiasm, anglepoised like a photographer's staged shoot. 'Did you ever learn about the gold rush?'

'California?'

'Australia. Victoria, in the middle of the nineteenth century. Word gets out that somebody has found gold, so next thing you know, the fever's set in, and people come flocking. Pickaxes, sieves. Tented slums. Sluicing and digging and blasting – all clinging to their little scraps of hope.'

'A boom town.'

'Exactly,' he says. 'And this was, what, fifteen, maybe twenty years after Melbourne was first colonised?' Out of the shadows, now, his face a white flag. I appreciate this – playing the game, but kindly. From somewhere out of sight comes the long low blast of a horn. Another ship. 'Less than twenty years to go from an indigenous population to a horde of colonisers digging up the land. Not even a lifetime. My dad might've been all for never looking back, but it was one of those stories I couldn't tear myself away from.'

'So when people started to squabble over Antarctica . . .?'

'I had to have a piece of it for myself.'

*

From the lounge, I hear it sound again: that long low horn, closer now, as a ship noses into view along the channel, led towards the *Lone Star* by the bright white figurehead of a naked woman. Her breasts stick out like scoops of ice cream, and her sculpted hair is unfashionably long, belonging to a bygone age of seafaring. She's the only part of the ship that looks cared-for. Brown stains leak like tear tracks from the hawse holes in its sides. The rest of the hull might once have been red, or orange, or dark green, but is now so rusted I'm surprised it isn't shedding an oxidised trail in its wake. The deck is a forest of communications receivers, and crane arms for cranking bulging nets from the deep. A krill trawler.

The *Lone Star* has also slowed. Perhaps an impasse. The channel looks wide enough, but there are always hidden rocks below the surface.

I sit with the vid perched on the table, projection off so only I can see what's on the screen. I want to check the armchair where I deposited the butter – to see if my subterfuge has been discovered – but two men are cleaning the atrium just outside the lounge door. The brawny man from the deck this morning; a slender, smooth-faced man I haven't seen before. They wear old-school sailors' outfits, caps pulled low over their eyes as though they, like the liveried waiters, are a kind of masked performance. Something about the way they ignore me makes me feel I'm not supposed to be here, but I can't see any reason why I shouldn't be. I've tried to speak to them, but they only nodded, then went back to their cleaning. They remind me of the waiter, Kip, after I asked about his piercings – that same fixed gaze, the same professional disinterest.

Perhaps I'm being paranoid. After all, it was the same fifty years ago with the Foundation: a clear divide between those of us there for that one expedition, and those who belonged with the ship. Not for Kay, perhaps, who was more outgoing. But for some of us. For me. 'Just how it always is,' Noah said as he cata-logued his medical supplies. 'We all have our own jobs to do. It's the separation of Church and State.'

'OK,' I said, 'but which of us is which?'

And he looked at me as though it was obvious his calling was spiritual, and surely mine was too.

I try to ignore the cleaning crew, and tap my fingers against the keys, but nothing comes. No information. No pass-chip. No words surfacing from that pit in my gut. Not for the first time, I wonder what I'm doing here.

The trawler in the channel is a hive of giant petrels, wheeling and bombing to scavenge spilled krill from the deck. Clearly, the ship has already raised its catch from the depths. In the golden window before they begin to toxify, the millions of krill will be processed on board: a continuous procedure of pulverising, freeze-drying, packaging in airtight wraps.

Meanwhile, the ship will head north. Her white-breasted figure-head already looks towards port, thousands of miles away – in Singapore, perhaps, or Rotterdam, in LA, Manila, Santos, a concrete city of containers and cranes, drones and trucks and rails. The krill product will be craned to the dockside, to begin its various journeys, to medical warehouses and packaging plants, to hospitals and food marts, into the jigsaw puzzle of people's apartments, into a million bodies who will never meet.

The thought of all this is like the edge of a towering cliff, and I have to close my eyes against the spin. When I open them again, the trawler is sideways-on to us, its flaking logo visible: a fat cleat knotted with rope. Moor & Co.

The name rises from the pelagic dark to tug at some flung line – a worry, a snag.

Moor & Co. I've seen it somewhere recently. A list of names among other names.

I close my eyes and it's there. The file I accessed with the pass-chip. A company somewhere near the top of the list. A high percentage.

Sky. The billionaire – although even that moniker is an under-statement. He has a controlling interest in so many companies, why shouldn't this company be one of them? Moor & Co, trawling Antarctic waters, profiting from unsustainable fishing only a day's journey from his own conservation site.

I sit. I watch the ship. I wait to feel surprised.

When I check the vid for signal, the connecting wheel just turns.

*

I find myself in the cabin. Again.

Lounge, cabin, elliptical rounds of the deck. Vary the order. Repeat.

155

I can't stop remembering what Sky said about the Victorian gold rush, wanting to colonise a piece of Antarctica for himself. Moor & Co, the trawler, his list of companies. In my cabin, I grip Ross's seal in my fist, worry at the smooth patch under its chin. I try not to think about Sky's collection of artefacts, try not to let myself feel like one of them.

I wish we could go ashore – properly, this time, however horrid the spit of land. At the very least, I wish I could let in some air. Without the IntuTech to regulate airflow, the cabin has started to smell fusty. But the picture window doesn't open. I run my fingers all around the black seal at its edges, just to make sure.

Lounge, cabin, deck.

Repeat.

*

Remember: this book is a guilting. A record of guilt.

*

I walk laps of the deck.

I walk till my calves burn and my face bites from the cold.

I walk in a pattern. I'm aware there must be sensors on deck, feeding into the IntuTech analysis, aware of the ship learning my behaviours, predicting my moves. I do it anyway. In my outdoor shoes and branded Plan B jacket, in my hat and two pairs of gloves, with my scarf pulled up over the lower half of my face, and my bladder pressing from the cold, I walk the track that loops around the deck. Two laps, striding at pace – Bree always said I walk too quickly, as if there's a crisis I'm always on my way to attend.

So I walk fast enough to work up a sweat. After the second lap, I pause to lean against the railing at the prow, watch the water as the ship cuts through. Sometimes, I see penguins porpoising across the waves – sometimes close enough to distinguish the flash between light and dark, sometimes only a distant ripple. Sometimes I see the spume and rolling back of a whale, or else a dim shape where a seal turns in the shelter of a berg. Sometimes I just listen to the glaciers and the calls of skuas and giant petrels, the rhythm of my own ragged breath.

*

Late in the morning, we pass a fuel plant. Ambitious pipes and barrels and buildings nestle like a grey forest on the bare rock, all needle and steam and frost-dulled chrome. Workers scurry below – clouds of breath on the air, boots stamped hard against the dirt – and below them, deep below the surface, the machinery vibrates the rock, draws up the slick ancient bodies of oil. I wonder if Sky has shares in this place, too. Offshore, two huge cargo ships are infernos-in-waiting. Impossible, down here, to retain any sense of perspective.

Kay used to talk about this with photography. In Antarctica, she said from the deck of our little expedition icebreaker, the normal rules of composition aren't enough – it's too sweeping, too *fucking unbelievable*.

And so the metal prow of our icebreaker found its way into many of her photos. Whenever we landed, she would trek to the tops of snowy outcrops to look back the way she'd come, so her shots nearly always contained the ship, small bright focus in some expansive bay. Or else they contained one of us, gazing out across the ice, or as a tiny red dot on the horizon. It introduces the human element, she said, pulls the viewer in. I think about this often: how a person can be drawn in against their will.

Each time I rest at the prow of the ship, I allow myself five minutes, until my eyes glaze over from watching the waves, or till the sweat-chill becomes too much and I have to start walking again.

Round the deck, clockwise. From the prow, where the bridge looms above with its tinted panoramic windows. Along the

157

starboard side, past the door to the stairwell, the bright lifeboats suspended just below the railings, and around where the painted track cuts corners off the stern. Here, I give one eye to the churning wake. Then back up the port side, more lifeboats, a view of the complex citadel of masts and instrumentation overhead. Back, finally, to the front of the ship.

Round one more time. Then wait. Watch. Remember.

I find myself running the same memories on repeat.

THE SAME
MEMORIES ON
REPEAT

When Ross was a child I took him to a nature reserve. It was a two-hour drive from the new house north of Boston, which we'd bought after the flood-risk zone had crept too close to the old flat. Normally, visits had to be booked weeks in advance, but at the last minute I'd used my connections to wheedle a rare full day of just the two of us, where I would turn off my vid, and teach Ross to enjoy the world outside of a screen. For years, this was one of my favourite memories.

We arrived late in the morning, Ross sticky and grumbling from a journey without any digital distractions. After hooking the car up to a solar charging point and loading the food from the ice box into my backpack, I chivvied him from the empty parking lot, through the gate that marked the boundary of the reserve, and down the winding track through the woods.

The light fell slant and dappled, and we both strained to see where creatures snapped and rustled between the trees. Was that a bear, or the broken stump of an old beech? A stray leaf, or a squirrel perched on a high branch? A trick of the light, or the white scuts of retreating deer? We walked till Ross forgot his grumbles from the journey, and he ran ahead along the track.

I followed more slowly, careful of the stones and roots sticking up under my feet, the weight of the backpack pulling at my shoulders and across my hips. Twice, Ross ran out of sight around a corner, and I had to call him back, my voice swallowed by the dark between the trees. I started to wonder if there really were bears in there, and what I would do if we came across one. The fingerpost at the car park had said the trail was only a mile, but I felt as though we'd been walking for longer.

Then, without warning, we were through. The track ended and the woodland opened out onto a grassy meadow, with roe deer grazing the edge of it, ready to dart away between the trees. At the bottom, grass gave way to reeds, and the reeds thinned out into the breeze-rippled waters of a lake.

Ross ran into the meadow with his arms out and the deer bolted. From somewhere to my left, a flock of birds took flight with a sound like canned applause.

I laid out the picnic blanket and we sat in the shade of the trees. Hungry from adventure, we stuffed ourselves till our eating slowed to grazing, and our slow smiles spread. We played catch in the long grass, and afterwards I checked Ross's ankles for ticks. We'd brought books, and we lay side by side, dozing and reading as the meadow flowers rustled, as seed pods dried and popped around us. Against the smells of earth and greenness and fresh water was the smell of sun block heating on Ross's skin, a fat white smear of it across the back of his neck. At the edge of the lake, we scouted for mayflies and water boatmen. We lay half-hidden as the thin white flash of an egret stalked the shallows. I taught Ross about conservation – which was, after all, why I'd brought him here. I remember telling him, this was what I did for a job: helping people understand why places like this were important.

When the sun dipped behind the trees, we packed everything into the bag and headed back along the track towards the car. In the moth-light, bats darted between branches, snapping up a feast as the world turned dusky and blue. I could feel the heat still radiating from Ross's body, our heads light and limbs heavy from a day in the sun, and he smelled of gentle sweat and grass and the dusty earth. A sickle moon rose to wink through the branches.

Years later, one Thanksgiving, when Ross was an adult and Keira still in her highchair, we sat at the table with our waistbands straining and the fat solidifying around the remnants of the turkey, and I told Hanna about this day. 'It was such a special place,' I told her. 'Ross was only young, he probably won't remember.'

'Sure I do,' he said. 'The place with the bugs.'

And Bree said how Ross had been bitten half to death by the time we got back, and could barely sleep for days with all the itching and the cream she'd had to slather him with.

I said, 'I don't remember that part.'

Hanna laughed. Bree topped up my glass and said, 'Of course you don't, honey.'

*

But I do remember another day out – a few years after that Thanksgiving, a few more before Helsinki – with Keira, this time. From their PacifiCorp house on the side of the hill, we took the whining trolley car into Frisco. The trolley was crowded, and kept having to stop to let the circuitry cool down, or so maintenance workers could press cold-packs against metal rails that had warped in the heat. By the time we reached the aquarium, we itched and grumbled with sweat, so I pulled Keira past the smaller tanks to the brief respite of the ocean zone, to bathe in the cool blue light. 'Places like this,' I told her, 'help to remind us that all life came from the ocean.' Places like this made me yearn to go back to it.

Keira stared into the artificial deep, her small sweaty hands starfished against the PlastiGlass. Later I would learn PlastiGlass was one of Sky's many patents, that the aquarium was owned and managed by one of his myriad companies. Back then, I merely watched with the same admiration as everyone else: groupers, angelfish, a reef shark on its quick-turning prowl. A flurry of golden trevallies flashed like skittered coins, as a humphead wrasse lumbered towards them.

Two manta rays soared overhead, and a chorus of oohs and vid cameras tracked their progress. Keira touched a small finger to the tattoo at the base of my thumb. 'Granny, what's this?'

'It's a krill.'

She traced its curling shape. 'Like the cooker?'

'Not grill,' I told her. 'Krill. The most important part of the Antarctic food chain – so maybe they're the most important animal in the entire world. Almost everything in Antarctica eats krill, or eats something that does.'

A whale shark, flecked and enormous, drifted above us as though it had somewhere to go.

'Granny, look!'

Time was, I was against keeping animals in tanks. Now, I wondered if it might be the last safe place for them. I let Keira lead me across the tunnel, to follow the whale shark's progress till it receded into the blue.

Why, Keira wanted to know, did the whale shark grow so big, when all the other fish were so small?

I tried to explain about feeding patterns and thermoregulation, about pelagic zones and heat loss, the link between whale shark body and body of water – but her eyes went glassy as the aquarium walls, so I ended up saying, 'Because the ocean's even bigger.' She looked at me like she couldn't understand what the ocean had to do with any of it.

*

And I remember the park down on the bay, regenerated after one of the floods, overlooking the wreckage of the old prison and the imposing red bridge. Me and Keira and Bree. A ladies' day out, Ross had called it, which might have annoyed me if it had come from anyone else.

It was a typically grey Frisco day, with a fog threatening to roll in off the Pacific, and so half the city had brought their kids to kill time on the sims and the IntuTech apparatus. All Sky's, I realise now. All that intuition tech, gathering information right from childhood, collecting enough data to predict and so control all human behaviour. No wonder he got so rich so quickly.

Sometimes, Bree worried all these new gadgets would kill children's imaginations, that IntuTech was destroying the spirit of adventure. But as I watched Keira strike out across the reactive surface of the splash pad, as it wobbled and caught her in response to the anticipated placement of her feet, as she squealed and dodged the carefully timed sprays of cold water, I thought I had never seen her more alive.

I still have the photo of her from that day. I don't remember who took it, me or Bree. In it, Keira's face is a thrown-back laugh, her shoulders up in shocked delight as the water shoots for the back of her neck. The old red bridge in the background. It's another of those images I keep returning to.

Keira reached the edge of the splashpad and waved. From high up in the bleachers, we waved back. The dog grunted and snuffled our ankles.

As a slip of sun pushed through the cloud, delighted shrieks rose and sharpened and blended with the scavenging calls of the gulls. Around the edges of the park, children hooked into simulators jumped and yelled at the adventures playing out through their headsets. Music blared over the external speakers.

The park would never have been my choice – I was always pushing for forest hikes or picnics up the coast – but it was easier, here, to keep Keira entertained. And besides, Bree said, the noise and barely ordered chaos reminded her of school. Ever since the diagnosis, that had seemed important to her.

We watched as Keira left the splashpad and wandered over to the IntuTech animals. They stood almost life-size at the far end of the park – model tigers and snow leopards and orangutans and cuddly red pandas and impatient wolves – advertised by the park's publicity material as 'educational'. The animals were static, all waiting for a child's touch to bring them to life, so they could croon and purr and lean in for cuddles as though they were well-trained pets. In my head, I was already writing the thinkpiece: the damage these so-called educational initiatives were doing; how they gave children a false understanding of their relationship with the natural world; how they perpetuated the myth of a tame wilderness. At least in zoos, I would argue, animals remember how to savage an unwanted hand. I watched Keira run her finger over the forehead of an IntuTech lion, down the soft slope of its nose. The lion yawned and shook out its mane.

Later, while Bree went to buy ice creams from the kiosk and the dog ignored us in his hunt for dropped scraps, Keira asked, 'Do animals love us back?'

'You mean the lions and elephants in the park?' This, I remember thinking, was the perfect outrage fodder for my opinion piece.

She shook her head. 'Real animals. Ones that live in the wild.'

'Most people aren't very nice to animals that live in the wild.'

'You are.' She kicked a stone and it clattered against a drain. The dog skittered after it, skidded to a splay-legged stop, then looked around at her for more. 'Daddy says you have to put animals first because of your job.'

'I suppose I do.'

'What about him?' She bent down to scratch the dog between his ears, and he flopped onto the pavement, his fat tongue lolling and a sliver of drool at the corner of his mouth. 'What if he doesn't know to love me back?'

The dog rolled over, his legs bent in the air and his belly bared for attention, and Keira giggled.

'It's OK,' I told her. 'I definitely think he loves you back.'

*

Mid-afternoons in the Edinburgh flat, I would pour myself the first drink of the day. It's a rule I made for myself: I would vid-call Ross, the camera pointed at the remnants of the spidery red bridge across the Firth, and if he answered, I would tip the gin down the sink. I made this rule for myself around the same time every afternoon. Every time he didn't pick up, I would knock back the drink and pour myself another.

The second drink of the day is always the most beautiful. The first is fiery, a rush towards oblivion. The second is a slow tumble through it, like a dance. I liked to tell myself I could take it steady, then swill the gin around my mouth till my teeth ached. More and more, I couldn't remember how I got to this point in the day: what I might have done all morning; how quickly the afternoons drained away. It's why I chose this place, so time could become insignificant – the flat cheap and storm-battered, the streets prone to flooding from the Firth, so that whole weeks could pass with no way in or out of the neighbourhood. I would catch myself, more and more, perched on the arm of a chair or standing at a threshold, staring at nothing.

If the press could see me – if they still cared – they would run headlines about how I was drowning my sorrows. Scavengers, the lot of them, like the skuas, squalling for the scraps thrown over-board. And besides, they would have been wrong, because sorrow isn't something you can drown. Sorrow is amphibious. It consumes whatever it touches. Feed it whisky and it sucks in the peaty fumes. Give it wine and it plays drunken ballads on the xylophone of your ribs. Try to exorcise it with diet plans and wellness regimes, and it learns to eat sweat, to suck the fat from your cells. Sorrow is a smell stuck in the nostrils, a repeating taste at the back of the throat, a plate of fried eggs, a serving of kippers. The only way out of it is through.

So the drink is not a destination but a journey.

A commute, if you will. Even before – at parties and summits and conferences and book launches and award ceremonies and networking events with free glasses of something cheap, or in the old Boston flat with Bree's wine-cold hand on my hip – it was always a journey, towards the life I wanted to live, the person I wanted to be. 'Here, Ms Cunningham,' somebody would always say, 'have another.' Or else they wouldn't say anything, but a uniformed waiter would take my empty glass and wordlessly replace it with a full one.

That's the journey the drink was making: to the sort of person who people noticed if I went without.

KATABATIC – MEANING, A STEPPING DOWN

By midday, hunger kneads my stomach and fills my head with air. They warned us about this, fifty years ago, during our training for the expedition: how quickly the body burns through calories at these temperatures, how we would start to crave sugar and cheese and fatty meats and butter cut straight from the block. Funny how I'd forgotten.

I rest against the railing at the prow. Through the ringing cold comes the light rhythm of shoes on deck, and Maretta jogs into view. Even in her thick sport suit, she looks unruffled. She's already so focused on her run that at first she doesn't see me, and when she does, she falters. She half raises a hand, and I nod back.

I wait for her to pass before I set off again on my own laps, striding faster to compensate for her presence. Maretta runs anti-clockwise to my clockwise walk, so each time we meet, I have to steel myself to smile or ignore her. We meet three times in the time it takes me to walk one lap, seven in the time it takes to walk two. While I stand back at the prow, scanning the glinting water where absolutely no wildlife stirs for me, Maretta passes behind me twice. The third time, she slows, wavers, stops. 'See anything?'

'Not yet.'

'How was your morning?'

I shrug. I know I'm supposed to ask the same question back.

Maretta peers into the water from her spot on the track, as though stepping outside the painted lines even for a moment would be unthinkable. I want to ask her about her hushed *exactly*, about what I'm doing here, about whatever Sky is holding back – but who knows if she'd tell the truth and anyway, I'm damned if I'm going to feel indebted for anything. I try to work out if I could phrase it so as not to give her the satisfaction of my ignorance.

For a second, she also looks as though she might speak, and both sets of words teeter in the crackling air. Then she glances away from the water, back towards the centre of the ship, where Sharma is emerging from the stairwell, a smart black vid-cam hung around his neck. She says, 'Well, see you for lunch,' and starts up running again.

The cold is inside my head now, and the tips of my fingers are numb. I need to stand under a warm shower before lunch.

At the door, Sharma looks past me, to where Maretta approaches on her next lap. We will arrive at Plan B that evening, he tells me in his flat professional tone. I'll want to be on deck when we reach the border.

'Will we go ashore?'

'Sky will show you.' He teeters for a moment on the threshold, as though unsure if he's coming or going. I'd like to ask him what, exactly, the billionaire will show me – but warm tendrils reach out from the stairwell and hook me in.

*

At lunch, I have to force myself not to eat too quickly. Kip and the floppy-haired waiter have brought out creamy shellfish tagliatelle, all curled pink prawns and coins of monkfish, a scattering of iridescent mussels with their mouths open like badly kept secrets. Another country's cuisine; another culinary conquest. I

172

should have kept a tally. As I wind the pasta around my fork, I try to remember how Bree used to do this against the bowl of a spoon, to control the tangle and keep the sauce from splattering. I have an urge to cut it up, the way I did for Ross when he was little, but I don't want to seem uncouth and anyway, I haven't been given a knife. Across the table, Maretta eats the way she always does, the intake of food a precise and diminishing mechanism.

To distract from any clumsiness, I ask, 'What time will we arrive?'

Sky wipes a runnel of cream from his chin. Eyes bright, he says, 'We'll reach the border just before sunset – it's the most spectacular light – the whole place coloured like a painting.'

He takes deep gulps of water and the ice clinks against the glass. He reminds me of the children in Bree's class – the sort of barely contained excitement Bree always used to say would end in tears. I want to put my arm around him and tell him it'll all be OK. Instead, I say, 'I can't wait.'

*

As soon as lunch is over, I change back into my outdoor layers and head up on deck. At the door, the IntuTech scans me in my branded parka, then winks green to let me out. I take a deep breath of fresh, unprocessed air.

The day is bright – too bright, I'll think later – and I stand at the prow of the ship and lean as much into the railing as I dare. When I squint ahead, as if I might already be able to catch a glimpse of the famous Plan B, there are only rocky shores and the dirty spilled mouths of glaciers – but there are clusters of penguins on the stony beaches, and a giant petrel screams and wheels overhead, its bulbous beak like something prehistoric. Up to my left, a high icy ridge glitters in the sun like magnesium flares. As I begin my customary laps, I can almost feel the IntuTech calling out my patterns, watching me click predictably into them.

Two laps, then a pause to watch from the prow. Another two laps. Another pause.

I'm resting against the railing when the sky darkens like someone switching off a light.

First the darkness, then, a half-moment later, the chill. It drops onto the deck and lies there, and I stuff my hands under my armpits to hug myself warm. The ship has slowed – or stopped. I can't tell. On land, the ridge gathers a shadow of cloud along its lip, close to the ice like congregating ghosts. There's a silence like the world has been turned off. Into it, a low seductive whistle.

I try to lean into the sound, the way I leaned out over the railing to stare into the oil-blue water. The whistle rises till it becomes a rush, then a rumble, then a waterfall roar – but on deck, not a breath against my skin.

Up on the ridge, the soft grey ghosts begin to roil, then to fall. They fling themselves over the edge, hurtle down the slope towards the bay, towards the ship.

Katabatic . . .

The word is in my head before I've even remembered what it means, but already I'm running for the door, for the safety of its ship-tight seal. Running, and my feet slam the deck, the painted track. I can't hear them over the roar, but I can feel them, slam, slam, up through my bones, a shatter, but I have to reach the door – I reach it and I shove – shove harder, shoulder my whole weight against it, but it won't open. The IntuTech light winks red. Danger. Difficult conditions – what? – not compatible with opening the door. 'Fuck.' The wind is at my back, at my heels, it claws at my elbows. I rip the cover off the keypad but I've been out of the game for too long, the tech is too complex. 'Fuck.' Slam at the buttons, and the wind is in my hair, in my hood, it bites at my fingers on the metal keys as the display flashes orange – a question mark – and I take a chance and jab the button to accept, and it sticks but then, yes, the light flashes green, thank god, and the latch unclicks as I'm tugged back by the loose flaps of my jacket, as the door is wrenched from my hand. I screw up my eyes and hurl myself over the lip, inside. I'm inside. I throw my whole weight back against the door, slam it shut.

Safe. Inside. Breathe.

I lean against the wall. The wind screams and kicks at the door beside me. All my joints tingle and my body is an army of wasps, a swarm rising up to defend itself. My breath comes heavy, fast. I'd forgotten how it feels to fight.

In for four. Out for eight.

Katabatic wind. It comes back to me, now, here, on the safe side of the door. Literally, a *stepping down*: when the higher, colder air from the ice sheet at the centre of the continent is pulled out towards the coast, where it clashes against the warmer air, the warmer waters, to create sudden and violent storms. They taught us this fifty years ago, training for the expedition. In Antarctica, they said, a katabatic wind can reach almost ninety metres per second. If you see one coming, head for safety, don't look back.

In for four. Out for eight. I try to shut out the storm rampaging just the other side of the door. I wait for my bones to stop singing. I count my breath, the way Bree used to do with Ross, whenever he woke in the night.

In for four. Out for eight.

It was always Bree he called for, after a nightmare. I would lie awake and listen through the thin walls to Bree's murmured counting, till her calming rhythm rocked into a tune, low music as she lulled him back to sleep.

The wind is a furious screech against the side of the ship. It scrabbles to claw me out.

In for four.

There was always a creak of floorboards as Bree reappeared in the bedroom, as she tucked her cold limbs back into the duvet, back into the curl of my body. Some nights, I would pull her in,

175

kiss the tilted stretch of her neck, make hushed love to the slow rhythm of her breath.

Out for eight.

Sometimes, I would pretend to be asleep.

In.

And out.

Gradually, I become aware of the suffering closeness of the landing, the stairs winding down and away, the warm air rising up them from the cabins. In the dark crooks of my body, I feel shivery and damp. I force myself to move. Away from the wall and the headrush of noise at the door. I sway, grab the banister.

In for four.

Out for eight.

Step by step, I climb down and away from the storm.

In the cabin, the storm presses its dark fur against the picture window. I draw down the blind. I turn up the heating as high as it will go, till the vent blasts Saharan air, loud enough for me to hear it over the wind.

I take off my coat and gloves and scarf. I strip off my jumpers and thermals. I take it all off right down to my underwear. I want to put on my sleepsuit, to tuck myself into bed and cover my head with the blanket. But it's the middle of the day, and I need to find out what's going on.

I try to vid-call Ross, but any signal there might have been is butchered by the storm. I dig my inside clothes back out from the drawer. Slowly, heavily, I put them on. I make my way towards the lounge.

*

Snow hurls itself against the panoramic windows and smothers them in darkness. In the onslaught, the warm-lit lounge has become a sanctuary, the howling rage drawing us all together.

176

Sky. Sharma. Maretta. And now me. Kip stands behind the bar, his livery at odds with the forces of Antarctica unleashed.

'Thank god,' Sky says when I arrive. He holds a glass of something that could be whisky.

Somehow, I manage to catch Kip's eye, and he nods and pours one for me. 'Everything OK?' I take the offered drink and sip, and the heat slips down towards my diaphragm. I hadn't realised how cold I still felt, or how shaky. In the mosaic fragments of the mirror, the sky cuts itself into dark ribbons.

'Sky was worried about you.' Maretta purses her lips as though she can't understand why he would be.

Sky says, 'We all were. These Antarctic storms are enough to terrify anyone.'

'I'm fine.' Now I've calmed down, I notice the absence of the juddering engines. The ship tosses and rolls entirely at the mercy of the storm. 'We've stopped moving.'

'Too dangerous, apparently. We'll wait here till it blows itself out.'

'Any idea how long?'

He looks to Maretta, who looks to Sharma, who says, 'A few hours, maybe – these storms are unpredictable, even with the best technology in the world. We may as well make ourselves comfortable.'

'Have a drink,' Sky says unnecessarily. When I take a pointed sip of my whisky, he smirks, then looks away. Maretta watches me drink with her lips still pursed, her gaze dark as the battering storm. Outside, I can't even see the mountains anymore. The lights flicker.

Maretta is the first to excuse herself. 'Work to do,' she says, with another frown at my whisky, and she breaks our small circle.

Sharma watches her leave. Only when she's gone does he say, 'I'd better check on the crew.'

Sky knocks back the rest of his whisky, hands the glass back to Kip. I want to ask them to stay, to counteract the wild cruelty of the storm through force of company, but before I can think of a good enough reason, Sharma is gone, then Sky – 'I'll be in my office, if anyone needs me' – clinging to his regular pattern in the face of the pummelling wind.

Just me and Kip, now, and the dark and roiling storm for company. He pours me another whisky, but when I invite him to join me, he only shakes his head.

'Tell me about yourself, Kip.' It worked with Sharma – no reason for it not to work again – and I need a voice to shut out the roar of the wind.

But Kip just scratches the piercing scar at his bottom lip and says, 'Thank you, ma'am. I'd rather not.'

I turn a slow circle, arms wide, to indicate that we're alone, that he doesn't need to be so professional and aloof – but the floor lurches under my feet, the ship a bottle on a roiling wave. I sit, hold my whisky in both hands. Pretending to scratch my chin, I peer up at the ceiling for cameras. Nothing visible. I wonder if Sky knows about the butter down the side of the chair. I wonder if it's still there. I glance back over at Kip, who looks furtively away, checks each of the spirits is fixed correctly into place.

The wind slams against the windows, and the ship jolts. It rips into my body, rattles my organs, flings hands across my ribs like grappling hooks. Behind the bar, Kip leans on his elbows and watches, unspeaking, his expression passive, his body tilting with the pitch and roll of the storm.

STORM

There was a storm, too, the night Keira was born, a squall blown in from the Atlantic. There were no flights out of Boston, so we drove through the pounding rain, Bree having to struggle on in manual just to keep the car on the road till we reached an airport that could fly us west. The plane shuddered as the wind took hold, and Bree gripped my hand. 'We don't tell them,' she said. 'Not today.'

'No,' I said. 'Not today.' Besides, neither of us had processed it yet ourselves, this illness, this *dying*, though it had hulked in every room ever since the diagnosis, demanding to be both looked at and ignored: the monstrosity of knowing that, from that day on, I was always one moment closer to being alone.

We arrived in Frisco bedraggled and exhausted, to a confusion of noises and smells: the lemon-scented ward; a tang of disinfectant; the bustle against chrome fittings and polished floor. Hanna was in her own room – I remember the nurse mouthing, 'Comp-li-cations', as though the body were something to be ashamed of. Then Ross – 'Come in, come in!' – bouncing to show us his new daughter.

Although of course, she wasn't technically his daughter, was

181

she? Not technically our granddaughter, either. I remember the thought, and I remember hating myself for thinking it.

*

When Ross first told me he was seeing someone, I'd hugged him on the steps of the big house outside Boston, so tight I could have squeezed him out of existence. He'd met Hanna, he said, through a dating scheme. He was working for PacifiCorp by then, and rarely had time for anything else; Hanna had recently come out of a relationship and was looking to move on. The algorithms, he said, had worked perfectly.

That afternoon, I took myself to bed with a migraine. I often got migraines in those days, when I was stressed or worried or angry, before I knew how to drink them into oblivion. Sometimes I could spot the warning signs in time to keep them contained. This one had come up out of nowhere.

Blinds drawn, I lay in the artificial dark, surrounded by the rustles and clanks of the house, the indecipherable murmur of Ross and Bree talking downstairs. My head needled from inside my skull. The pain beat along to my pulse and I tried to lie as still as possible.

For a long time, Ross had been drifting. I'd thought the PacifiCorp job might give him a sense of purpose, but instead he'd become ragged, frayed at the edges. Nothing held his attention. If we watched a vid-sim together, he would wander out into the kitchen halfway through. If we went for walks, he would drag his feet the way he did as a teenager. Now, I wondered why I hadn't suggested dating before.

A nauseous stab. In for four. Out for eight. I shifted my head onto the cool part of the pillow.

*

It was only a few days after this that Ross told us Hanna was pregnant.

182

'Already?' I looked up from where the coffee percolated on the countertop – real coffee one of the luxuries we still allowed ourselves, though even then it was becoming difficult to get hold of. 'You've barely been together five minutes.'

'It isn't mine.'

The percolator gurgled. I could hear my heart loud inside my head.

Bree said, 'I'm so, so sorry, honey.'

Ross looked between us, then laughed. 'No – no, she didn't *cheat*. She was pregnant already, before we even got together. We just didn't realise.'

'But the other man . . .?'

'Off the scene.'

'So . . .'

'Look,' he said, and his face shone in a way I hadn't seen for years. 'I know it's all soon and new and complicated, but this is a good thing. I'm going to be a dad.'

I didn't know how to respond. I looked at Bree, who pulled him into a bear hug and said, 'Well then, I'm happy for you.'

*

In the private room in the hospital in Frisco, I leaned in to look at the snuffling red-wrinkled face of my new granddaughter.

I expected to love her instantly, the way I had loved Ross, to flounder in this new and unlooked-for miracle. I looked at her and felt nothing.

I watched Bree gush and sob. I watched as she hugged Hanna, carefully, around the baby, as she dragged Ross into a tight proud squeeze. I watched her brush aside all thoughts of her illness, ready to replace her vanishing memories with these bright new joys. I had become a dead fish, too long out of the water.

I made the right noises, obviously. I've made a whole career out of that. I cooed and coddled, put my hand on my chest and let my eyes well up. I told them the baby was beautiful – which she was, but only in the way all new life is beautiful. When Ross said, 'We're calling her Keira,' I said it was a lovely name. Even when they asked me to hold her, I smiled down into her sleeping face, hummed that lullaby I used to sing for Ross. Visiting was limited, so they only had to believe it for an hour.

Then we left the ward. I walked with Bree down the too-clean corridor, out into the dense Frisco smog. We took an IntuTaxi to Ross and Hanna's new corporate-owned house on the hill, overlooking the city, perched between wildfire and flood. Then we showered and dozed as the sounds of other families echoed through the cheaply built complex. And all the time, I wondered, when and how did I get like that? And how could I come back from it?

Over the years that followed, I tried to make up for it with gifts, till Ross started saying, 'You spoil Keira rotten, Mum,' though I could tell he never really objected. 'That's a granny's job,' I told him.

Or I would mention her in speeches and campaigns, as an example of what I was fighting for. In my youth, I told the vids and mics and cameras, I had been passionate and idealistic. Now, for Keira, I would be fierce.

Perhaps the problem was that there was too much of Hanna in her. Hanna was always cold with me, though she could vid-chat with Bree for hours. But sometimes, I would catch something of Ross in her, too, an expression picked up despite there being no genetic link – his stubborn frown, his serious sense of play, that same old-man laugh like a busted valve. Once, when their dog barked at a passing bird, she jump-started exactly the way Ross used to, and I had to remind myself it wasn't him, that the child Ross was gone and a gangly man loped through the world in his place.

I got a tattoo. Just a small one at the base of my thumb. A single Antarctic krill.

Bree rubbed her thumb over it and asked what I was apologising for. 'Nothing,' I told her. 'It's just a tattoo.' Even though the guilt must have been written on my face. Even though guilting was her word to begin with, so surely she knew one when she saw it. She asked, 'When have you ever made a mark without purpose, Ivy Cunningham?' I didn't answer, and she didn't ask again. While she busied herself with her own mortality, I busied myself with anything but. Support for an Antarctic Industry Cap was building. At symposiums and conferences, as I gesticulated to emphasise my point, the tattoo caught my eye: a single krill, separate from the swarm, scratchy and angular as my heart.

*

The storm around the *Lone Star* continues to rage. All afternoon, I imagine I can hear all my organs screaming.

Over dinner, nobody speaks. Once, I try to say something about the raw power of nature, the timely reminder of how little we can control. I see Sky's face and I stop.

*

After, we gather once more in the lounge: me, Sky, Sharma and Maretta. With the glow of the old-fashioned lamps, it feels as though we're gathered around a campfire. I catch myself wondering what would happen if the light went out, what monsters might emerge from the dark.

'What should we talk about?' Against the noise of the storm, my voice is a pilot light, flickering.

Sharma says nothing. Maretta purses her lips as though she doesn't trust what might come out if she opens them. Eventually, Sky asks, 'Any idea how much longer?'

Sharma shakes his head, but still doesn't speak. He pours a round of whisky and sits back in his chair, out of the circle of lamplight. Sky picks up his glass and drains it. His leg jitters against the batter of noise. As he holds out his glass for Sharma to refill, he says, 'A different Antarctic storm, then. Captain Scott.'

Maretta nods studiously. When Sky looks at her, she flushes. 'Tell us.'

Maretta brushes something non-existent from her lapel to hide the false modesty in her voice. 'I'm not sure I'm the best person . . .'

'Of course you are.' Sky's voice booms, then fades against the ceaseless roar of the storm. 'Of course you are, Maretta. Your memory for details . . . Tell us the story of Captain Robert Falcon Scott.'

She sips her whisky through pursed lips. She glances at me, teacher-like, as though to check I'm paying attention, as if I haven't heard the story countless times before, as if I couldn't already tell it a million times better than she could. Then she presses her palms to her knees, takes a breath, and begins to recount the history as though reading from a textbook: 'Captain Robert Falcon Scott was a polar explorer at the beginning of the twentieth century. His ambition was to be the first man to reach the South Pole. He led the Terra Nova expedition to Antarctica, where the men set up a base and spent two years conducting scientific experiments. In 1912, Scott took a party of men to make their attempt on the Pole. When they arrived there, however— '

'When they *struggled* there,' I can't help saying. 'They didn't just arrive. The men were weak. Exhausted. Bitterly cold and desperate for success.'

'Yes.'

Sky drinks another slug of whisky. 'Go on.'

'They struggled there,' she says, 'only to discover the Norwegian flag. Amundsen had beaten them to it.'

'Thirty-five days,' Sky interjects. In the low lamplight, his eyes catch mine. 'That's how late they were. Think about it – nobody has ever been there in the history of humankind, and then two teams make it barely a month apart. Can you imagine how defeated Scott and his men must have felt? All that struggle, all

186

that suffering, lugging their gear over the peaks and crevasses of the Beardmore Glacier – they took ponies, for god's sake – only to find another flag waving in the wind. Mocking them thousands of miles from home.'

The lights flicker. I hold my glass with both hands, say, 'No wonder they never made it back.'

'You think?'

'That kind of failure . . . it's enough to make anyone lose hope.'

Sky sits back in his chair. He looks at me with those ice-blue eyes, as though he's a priest awaiting my confession. Only when I look away does he gesture for Maretta to continue. She takes a delicate sip of whisky. 'Like Ms Cunningham said, they never made it back. They got caught in a blizzard and died.' She says this with a shrug.

'Exposure,' Sharma says, as though he remembers it personally.

Sky says, 'Just a couple of days from base camp.'

'They knew they weren't going to make it,' I add, telling the story together, now, each adding in what we think matters most. 'One of the men walked out into the snow and disappeared, because he thought it would give the others a better chance of survival.'

'"I am just going outside and may be some time."'

I nod. 'Titus Oates's last words.'

'Supposedly.'

'They never found his body.'

Sky says, 'You know Scott wrote a letter to his wife? *To my widow* . . . A few of the men did – wrote letters to friends and family, sending their messages out into the void.'

'He kept a diary.'

'Yes.'

'Right up to the end.'

'"For God's sake look after our people."'

I say, 'It's a hell of an edict. A hell of a last proclamation.'

Sky nods. His fingers continue their nervous pattern around his glass. Outside, the katabatic winds howl their warnings, rock our tiny metal ship.

Eventually, Maretta says, 'If only more people had listened.' Her lips are pursed again. She looks at me and says, 'Well, I think I'll call it a night,' as though there is any possibility of sleep, as though the storm isn't baying at the sky, as though the ship isn't locked between its punishing jaws. 'Good night, Ms Cunningham.' When she stands, there's a smear at the back of her crisp suit trousers: the butter down the side of the chair has finally melted and leaked out, and I feel a cruel sense of victory that Maretta's the one to be caught by it. I glance at the others to check if they've noticed, but Sky is frowning into his glass. After a few minutes, he drains it, then, as though our communal story was the only thing keeping him tethered, he follows Maretta from the lounge. Then there is only me and Sharma.

The lounge feels darker with just the two of us. Less of a sanctuary. I wait for him to speak, but he just sits, ankle resting on his knee, and sips his whisky.

'You must've seen some storms, Sharma.' I refill my own glass, take another long-drawn sip. 'On the boat.'

'Must I?' His smile is sardonic, but then it clears, and he stands and clicks each of his knuckles in turn. When I wince, he half shrugs and says, 'Sorry. It's been a long day.'

He says it with an air of dismissal, and I can't help asking if I'm being sent to bed as well.

'Wouldn't dream of it.' He gestures to the decanter of whisky on the table. 'We both know that even if I told you to, you'd revel in doing the opposite. Don't we, Ms Cunningham?' He says it lightly, the sardonic smile back at the corners of his mouth, but still I shiver. He must notice, because he nods once more to the whisky and says, 'Stay – enjoy the night.'

Then he's gone, too, and I'm left alone, the decanter the only warm glow at the centre of the blizzarding storm.

By the time I leave the lounge, I can't tell if I'm stumbling from the drink or the pitch of the storm. My feet feel unsteady on the thick pile carpet as I count off cabin numbers in my head.

It's the open door that stops me – in the yellow corridor, the blue sliver of artificial daylight. Through it, a narrow stairwell descends into the bowels of the ship. Where the rest of the *Lone Star* gleams chrome or polished wood, this is scuffed metal, tired grip paper on the treads.

An unknown stair is as good as a Keep Out sign for setting the journalist's instinct tingling. A chime of clarity through the whisky fug. On that first day, I tried all the doors on this corridor, and only Maretta's cabin yielded results. Now, another unlocked door – impossible to tell whether it's been left open by accident or on purpose. I check the corridor behind me. No one. I hold my breath. No sound but the creaking and banging of a storm-thrown ship, an intensely humanless sound. I take a step and stumble, and my heel rings out against the metal stair. I wait for someone to come running. No one does.

I take another step, and another, more careful now, bracing myself against the narrow walls. Every few steps I lose my footing, clang, hollow and sad, reverberations mourning up through the heart of the ship.

Halfway down, I must trigger a sensor, because another light flickers on. I pause again. Below, a heavy metal door is fixed open, its small glass pane reflecting the toes of my shoes. From beyond it comes a sound like wind across the mouths of bottles, so faint against the storm I have to hold my breath to hear it.

The stair is still empty – no footsteps along the carpeted corridor above. I keep going, quietly as I possibly can, till I reach the doorway at the bottom. Through it is a half-lit room. A cubby, really, a bank of consoles covering one wall: orange lights pulsing in a complex pattern I don't know how to read. Like a dance, intricate individual flickers come together to create this single soporific rhythm. Without meaning to, I find myself breathing in time with it, my heartbeat calming as my eyelids start to droop. The whisky, probably. Exhaustion from the storm.

I blink myself awake. The consoles are labelled: *lounge*; *dining room*; *bridge*; *deck – fore*; *deck – aft* . . . All alight, all flickering. Under *cabin 3*, the lights are out.

The control centre for the ship's IntuTech, channelling all its data through here. Apparently, it hasn't gone unnoticed that I've disabled the system in my cabin – but by whom? And why have I not been challenged about it?

Against the opposite wall is a desk, a pulled-out chair, a HoloPlayer beside a trio of biolocked monitors. Above them, framed on the wall like an icon of a minor saint, is the photo from the expedition. The photo of me, kneeling on the ice, arms outstretched to block the path of the ship.

I start towards it; my movement must trigger another sensor, because the HoloPlayer winks awake, flickers scrambled light against the walls, then resolves itself into hundreds of images. Photos. Articles. Vid-spots playing on a silent loop. They cover the walls, bleed through one another as they jostle for space. My entire career – every article I've written, every speech I've ever made, all gathered here. In tribute? Or as an accusation? Above the desk, the expedition photo drowns in the Holo-light; the glittering photo from Helsinki is superimposed on its icy backdrop, its cruciform arms.

My spine crawls as if I'm being watched. I hold my breath, hold myself so still the room forgets I'm there. When the HoloPlayer flickers off, I'm plunged back into darkness and the pitch and swell of the storm. The orange lights of the IntuTech keep pulsing in their soporific dance.

*

In my own cabin, I try Ross again. Nothing.

I can't purge those images from my head – cacophonous, my entire life hurled against the walls as flickering light. But why? And by whom? Not by Sky – he has his own much grander office, no need for hiding down grubby stairs. One of the crew, then. The IntuTech controls would suggest Sharma, or perhaps his right-hand man, the birdlike man from the X-Ped – but why would either of them bother? And hasn't Maretta always been a fan of mine? Didn't she hero-worship that exact same photograph of me when I was younger? Nothing quite fits, and I itch with it.

I pace the small route from bed to sofa to desk to bathroom door. Each time the ship lurches, I plant my feet and throw out my arms to the furniture. After two laps, I collapse onto the bed. The images didn't feel like hero worship, or fandom. They felt like evidence, gathered before a trial. Collated, ready for sentencing.

The storm nags at the sealant around the window. The howls of long-dead explorers circle the edges of my dreams.

*

When I wake, the storm still rages, and I feel as though I've only slept a couple of hours – but when I check the time, it's already morning. I force myself out of bed.

Out of habit, I climb the stairs to where the heavy door leads out on deck. The wind darkens the PlastiGlass, and in my little vestibule I feel like a caught fish, with a petulant child hammering against the tank. The display on the door's IntuTech says the temperature outside is −24°C, the wind speed 110km per hour. I'm not wearing my thermals, or my parka, or my outdoor boots; even here, I can feel the cold.

I rest my hand on the door handle. Again, out of habit – or maybe something else.

The images from last night flash before me: decades of my career, compressed into a single room barely bigger than a cupboard, campaign bleeding into campaign till they all collapse in on themselves and I no longer remember what any of them were really for. I remember what Sharma said, how I could be counted on to do the opposite of whatever I was told. Contrary.

From here, from the inside, from the relative warmth, I could work out how to override the IntuTech. If I wanted to, I could force the door to let me out.

If I did open it, if I stepped out into the swirling dark, what would kill me first? Hypothermia? Frostbite? Would the wind carry me away overboard? Would I drown in the Antarctic waters? I could go through this door and nobody would stop me. Nobody would even know.

I can't stop thinking about the photo above the desk: me on the ice in front of the seals, head bowed, my cruciform arms blocking the path of the ship. The photo from Helsinki super-imposed over the top – the beginning and end of my career.

My hand against the handle twitches.

The draw is there. The draw is always there, like standing on a precipice, deciding whether or not to jump.

*

In the lounge, I try to write. Here, surrounded by windows, the wind is a magistrate hurling down judgement. Once or twice, the storm lifts just enough that the mountains swim through, before it drops again and everything is obliterated. Everything but the small lit ship, its handful of occupants.

The vid screen flickers, an arrhythmic heartbeat. My fingers hover over the keys. In the atrium, the two cleaners are back. Perhaps they clean at this time every day. Perhaps they have been sent to keep an eye on me, or to gather more evidence against me. They look pitiable in their comical sailor costumes: one large and brawny, the other slender-faced, with chapped lips and a mole at the corner of his nose. This time, I don't try to speak, and the cleaners, in turn, ignore me. I sit with my back to them and wait for the words to come.

All I need is one sentence. A way in, to exorcise the night before onto the page. I've done this enough times – I know how to let the words draw themselves up from the deep. Or maybe all I need is to vid-call Ross, to reach out through the blockade of the storm. It would make a nice story.

But no. All I really need is a drink – an interim between not writing and writing, between sleep and work. Drink as a way of stepping outside the self. Drink as a threshold. Drink, yes, as commute.

My hands are dead birds hanging from a barbed wire fence. I want to do something tactile. To cook a meal, I decide – a small banquet for two or three people.

I hate cooking. I hate having to source specific ingredients, the precision timing, how easy it is to screw up at the eleventh hour. I don't remember the last time I cooked something that wasn't reconstituted. Now, though, I want to cook like we did in the old days. Me and Bree, hands brushing, hips flirting up against each other in the tiny Boston kitchen. I want to peel and chop fat cloves of garlic, to crush them with the flat of an old knife, knowing their bitterness will cling to my fingers for days. I want onions fresh enough for catastrophic weeping. I want a knob of butter in the pan, the slow melt, the auditory pleasure of its sizzle. I want the spit of peppers as they hit hot metal. I want to pour two white wines from an over-priced bottle I picked up at the convenience store on the corner, with condensation that gathers around the bowl of the glass, that runnels under my fingers. And I want to be able to drink just one glass, slowly, with Bree sipping the other one beside me.

Behind the bar, the bottles clink and rattle in their racks. Too early. I can still hear the two men moving about, just out of sight now towards the stairwell – or perhaps the storm is too loud and I'm only imagining it. I tap my fingers against the keys, raise a string of nonsense letters on the screen the way I used to as a child, playing at creativity.

How often did Bree and I cook like that together? Once a week, maybe? Once a fortnight? We were both so busy, and, later,

193

I was always away. I close my eyes and try to remember the specifics of a single meal we cooked together. Something with aubergine, perhaps. *Eggplant*. I remember the flick of Bree's wrist as she peeled potatoes into the sink, the heat in the kitchen, steam from the pans sent spiralling by the sliver of air through the window that barely opened.

Mostly, what I remember is that window, the glass furred and blackened at the edges – how Bree would squeeze her hands through the narrow gap to plant riotous flower boxes, which were always dying in the fumes from the street below.

The air in the lounge feels close and muggy, wet as it slides into my lungs. God, what I'd give to be able to open a window. To let some of the outside in. I close my eyes again.

Through that kitchen window was everything I loved about Boston: broad-leafed maples that rustled up against our second-floor apartment, their branches catching the 3 a.m. holler of drunks, or bearing pigeons like scratty iridescent fruit. When the storm-warnings came, twigs scratched at the window frames and the leaves plastered themselves flat against the glass. One autumn, a whole murmuration of starlings stitched in and out of view, raucous at such close quarters, before they settled as one between the golding leaves. All that week, the pavements and bins and chained bicycles below were richly splattered with shit, and the bewildered rats scurried through it with scraps of chicken skin from the food cart on the corner.

It was common knowledge that the man who owned the food cart kept a yard stick with a paddle nailed to the end of it, for swatting rats that came too close. Also that, when he thought nobody was looking, he would feed them on scraps and gristle. 'For your babies,' he would murmur, as they legged it with their plunder towards the shelter of the communal bins.

Sometimes, the council emptied these bins, in roaring automated trucks that woke us in the early hours before dawn and sent the urban foxes slinking back into the shadows. Sometimes not – and they would bulge with fat eco-plastic sacks (it was that kind of neighbourhood), which leaked mould-smelling juices into the gutter, and commuters would walk the narrow gap between this and the deluge from the freshly watered window boxes.

I try to type with my eyes closed, and without thinking. This was something I was taught at university: how to set a timer and keep on writing, till you've reached down through the noise of the day and into whatever words lie buried in your gut. Like Sky, painting to get to the truth of things, to dig it out from beneath the tedious quotidian.

I write for four minutes without stopping. When I look back at what I've got, it's just an unrelenting block of expletives.

*

We eat lunch with the blinds down to try to shut out the storm. Roasted vegetables in flaking pastry. I fork it listlessly around my plate. I want to bring back the camaraderie and shared stories of last night, but every time I try to begin, the wind hurls itself against the hull of the ship, and my thoughts scatter like the images from the HoloPlayer.

Into the stifling roar, Sky says, 'I want to paint you.'

My first thought is that old movie my parents used to watch, the line about French girls. I say, 'I don't know if it's appropriate.'

He colours, and my heart goes out to him. 'Not like that,' he says. 'No, I mean – I haven't done many portraits, but with landscapes, you learn them as you paint. I want to take this opportunity to get to know you better.'

Which, perhaps, is another reason it might not be appropriate, though I don't realise this till later. I notice Maretta has stopped eating. As much to ruffle her as anything else, I say, 'Sure. Why not?'

*

Sharma pulls out a protective sheet to cover the floorboards and hefts a sturdy easel into the centre of the office. The cabinet unfolds to release a trolley, which he clamps into place to serve as a stand for the paints and palettes and cleaning water. He unpacks the brushes and jars. He places a fresh canvas to the easel, then clips it in against the pitch and roll of the storm.

Sky watches, giving small direction. 'Normally I'd work with natural light. But in the circumstances . . .' He nods towards the darkening howl at the window. The light in here is yellow, like melted butter. When Sharma leaves, the buffer of a third person vanishes with a click. Sky indicates the chair across the room. He asks, 'Do you mind if I . . .?' Then he manipulates me without waiting for a response.

I hold my breath. To go so long without human touch, and then to be moved so mechanically – a tilt of the head, a pushing back of the shoulders – is a new kind of emptiness. When he's finished, I say, 'Thank you,' and it comes out jarred.

Sky positions himself on the other side of the easel. I watch his eyes flick from me to the canvas and back again, a clean brush balanced between finger and thumb. I try not to wriggle, not to break the position he needs me to keep. There's already a line of sweat at the nape of my neck. My ankle twitches. I want to cough, just to break the silence, but his focus is so intense, and I don't know how small a thing it might take to shatter it.

At last, he dips his brush into a pot on the trolley – the palest wash, for the least possible mark on the canvas – and begins.

I watch the concentration as it travels from his eyes up to his furrowed brow, then drops to his mouth. He doesn't bite his lip or set his jaw the way Ross used to – but at the height of his focus, he looks as though he is about to speak, until the words become swallowed, transmuted into paint. He stands poised, brush tilted to avoid drips.

'Do you ever lose control?'

'I wouldn't be a very good artist if I couldn't control a brush.'

I shake my head, then remember I'm supposed to be keeping it still. 'In writing,' I say, 'there's a technique where you write

196

without thinking. Losing control is the whole point – it helps you get at whatever you're keeping buried underneath.'

He dips his brush into the spirit jar: a single dip to clear the bulk of the paint, then a deliberate press against the side of the glass, till he can twist the brush-head clean. He blots it on a white cloth to check for paint residue, then dips it again, before setting it aside to dry. When he's finished, he picks up a new brush and says, 'I paint to learn about my subject, as much as about myself.'

'And what are you learning about me?'

He smiles. 'That you're more of a journalist than you think you are.'

I catch his eye and smile back. If he didn't want me to pry, he shouldn't have positioned me as an interrogator: face-on to the easel, square-shouldered, all nose and chin and eyes. It's the position I've adopted on podiums the world over, not flattering, but strong. It says, my words are a battering ram, and they are coming to break down your doors. I'm pleased Sky can see this determination is still inside me. I try to decide how to frame my next question.

He lifts his brush from the canvas. After a long moment, he says, 'My dad was always one for control.' In all the interviews I've watched, I've never heard him talk about his family – and yet here he is, talking about his father for the second time. 'We lived halfway up a high-rise in Sydney, and he worked in the city. Middle management in a middling firm. Aim for the middle, he always taught me, where it's safe.'

He's quiet for a while, only the sweep of bristles across canvas. My legs threaten to cramp. My shoulders stiffen. When he pauses to swap brushes, I whisper, 'Go on.'

He examines the bristles. 'He was obsessive about money. Rent, bills, food, always in that order, and whatever was left at the end of the month, he'd split into equal thirds: one for savings, one for charity, the rest on women.' He speaks in a rush, floodwater tearing through a levee. Outside, the storm roars in agreement. 'That's how he ended up with me – I was dumped outside his door one morning with a stack of spare nappies and a note saying I was his.'

'And were you?'

'Probably. There's no signal, by the way, in case you were thinking of cashing in on that little scoop.' His voice is acerbic as the spirits stripping the oil from the brushes.

I say, 'I wouldn't do that.' What I mean is: *I wouldn't do that any more* – and this takes me by surprise. Since when were certain stories off limits? I think back to the night he showed me Ross's seal, try to remember what might have shifted within me.

'Wouldn't you?' He pauses again. When he looks up from the canvas, his eyes are the cold brass of a weighing scale, and I hold my breath so as not to tip the balance. Then they soften and he says, 'You know, my dad was terrified of catastrophe.' Outside, the dark has dropped right to the surface of the water. No sign of the icy peaks, not even the palest smudge of a glacier. We could be the only people left in the entire world. 'Crime, illness, natural disaster. The company he worked for managed loans, and whenever catastrophe struck, he was the one who wrote the company's clients into poverty. I saw what that did to him. When he thought I was in bed, he would sit up for hours, calculating and recalculating, staring at his savings balance on the screen.'

'He must have been so proud of you.'

He half-laughs. Sarcastic. 'The only thing that obsessed him more than poverty was wealth. *Injustice.* He had it on his bedroom ceiling, painted in fat red letters: EAT THE RICH. It was the first thing he saw every morning, the last thought he had before he went to sleep. He disowned me after I made my first billion.'

I picture Sky, huddled under the blanket, listening to his father counting savings in the next room. Clutching his secret aspiration to his chest like a wounded animal. Picture Ross, crying for his mother in the night. I say, 'That must've been so hard.'

'Being abandoned?' He squares his shoulders like something settling into place. 'Yes. Yes, it was.'

HOW TO PAINT ICE

Start with blue: a soft sad wash across the canvas.

All ice is blue at heart. The bluer the ice, the deeper, and so the further back in time it lets you look. This, Sky tells me, is what his paintings attempt to capture: a past world, a climate long-since disappeared.

Once you understand the blue, he says, you need to soften it. Nobody can stare directly at the past without a filter – so apply the paint with a sponge or palette knife: a surface thick or bold or dazzling enough to hide the imperfections underneath. Think of this as nostalgia.

Learn not to be afraid of white paint, which is a moon riding high above an ice field, the sun glinting from a cornice, the portable glow inside a drift. Still, apply this with thin brushes. Too much light can overwhelm the viewer.

Remember to take your time. After all, this is what ice is: time, frozen solid. If possible, carry the ice in your head for days before picking up a brush. Carry it for weeks. Months. Years. You cannot tell the story of the ice without telling your own story in its place.

So do not begin until the story you are painting has melted, and there is no one left but you who remembers it. Until the only record is a deep blue glow on your inner eye. If you're lucky, you will not have to begin at all.

YOU ARE NO
LONGER LUCKY

Late into the afternoon, I become aware of a cavernous ringing, and for a moment I can't place it. Outside, the ridge and glacier and rocky shores are reflected in the still waters of the bay. It's only in seeing them that I realise the light has lifted and the wind has blown itself out, the air so loud in its stillness I don't know whether to shout or whisper. My chest is still hollow and aching from Sky's story, and for a moment it's as if the stillness is ringing inside me. I want to call Ross.

Sky stands with his brush raised, staring out of the window. A bead of paint drops onto the protective mat, and without thinking, I stand as though I can reach out and catch it before it hits. Sky turns to look as I hover, half in, half out of the chair. 'Sorry.'

'Are you OK?'

I nod. I sit back down, but my face is burning and I've forgotten my pose, so Sky has to come over and arrange me again. Close to, in the mix of daylight and warm nostalgic bulbs, he's paler and more drawn than ever, the circles under his eyes an oil spill, casting his eyes deeper into his head. I can't stop picturing all those nights as a child, lying awake as his dad counted out his mediocrity, those sleepless nights as an adult since his dad disowned him – and before I know what I'm doing, I've drawn him into a hug: stooped, the way Ross always was once he became an adult;

and I can feel the awkward angle of his shoulder blade under my arm. He pats me on the back in return, and I pull away without looking at him. Again, he asks if I'm OK, and again, I nod. The blue-white light through the window feels false, as though I'm drifting into a hologram. 'Onward?' We've been talking most of the afternoon, but now my voice comes out choked.

'Onward.' Sky still stands in front of me, his own tone whispered, reverent. 'First thing tomorrow.'

'Tomorrow?'

'I want you to see it in daylight.' The schoolboy excitement steals, soft, across his face, and he makes a visible effort to rein it in. 'Besides,' he adds, 'I want the crew to check the ship at first light for damage.'

I try to pull up the sagging corners of my face. Now we can move, I want to be gone, to put this howling bay behind us forever.

Sky notices and smiles. 'At least now the storm is over, you can get some air.'

Into the new quiet, Sharma knocks to tell us dinner is ready. I look to Sky for permission, as though I'm the child and he's the parent.

'Go,' he says. 'I never eat when I'm painting.' The way he says it, it sounds like he's a great master. Perhaps he is, what do I know? When I stand, my legs are stiff and all my muscles ache from trying to hold the same pose for too long. I wait till I'm out of sight before I stretch out my joints, let my hips and wrists and all my knuckles click.

*

Sky, I know from my kitchen-table research, is not his real name. Or at least, not the name he was given at birth.

With my body square-on to the canvas, I learned how he chose it because it reminded him of all those retro corporate phrases people use to fling about – *blue sky thinking, reach for the sky, the sky's the limit* – phrases which his father always hated. Why, his father would grumble, can't anyone be comfortable with the middle?

And so Sky hoarded these phrases like forbidden toys, whispered them to himself under the covers in that high-rise Sydney apartment. *Teamwork makes the dream work. Live the dream. Back in the saddle. We're riding the gravy train now, biting the bullet, squaring the circle. Let's nail this jelly to the wall! Uptick, upsell, upmarket.* And *onwards and upwards* – always *onwards and upwards*.

The sayings became a prayer, and his god was always ambition, his rosary the flickering decimals of currency. In the cocoon of his childhood bed, he breathed in the cotton-burn smell of the Quik-Dry, and when he breathed out, it was with determination for *more*.

*

Around the same age, at around the same time, on the opposite side of the world, Ross was stowing magazines at the back of his wardrobe. It was the '50s, during the brief resurgence of print publication, when everything was retro and Ross complained in the language of our grandparents that Bree and I were *so uncool*.

When I discovered the magazines, tucked neatly under a pair of worn-out school shoes that should have been donated years before, I expected nudity: men and women in compromising but wholly unoriginal positions – the sort of mild rebellion I'd squirrelled away myself at that age. Instead, I saw flat earth, faked disasters, secret corporate takeovers planting electrolytes in people's brains.

And climate denial. Headline after headline of climate denial – in block capitals splayed across glossy covers. I showed them to Bree, who was trying to build an engine out of household waste ahead of a first-grade lesson on sustainability. 'I know, he's had them ages.'

'How long is ages?'

'Couple of months? Pass me that egg box.'

She had a length of cut-up knicker elastic wound around the fingers of her left hand, and her skin was puffy with loss of circulation. I handed her the egg box. 'Did you talk to him about them? What did he say?'

'I ain't the reason he has them, Ivy.' She let go and the construction spun across the coffee table and clattered to the floor. 'Shit.'

'You think this is about me?'

'No,' she said, 'I think this is about Ross.'

While Bree fidgeted with the engine, I tucked the magazines out of sight under the sofa. That evening, I listened through Ross's bedroom door to the thuds and rumples of a teenage boy occupying space. I heard the wardrobe door open and close. Heard it open again. Heard the muffled tumble of things being dragged out. I stood on the landing and waited for him to emerge and confront me. The floorboards creaked. The bedroom door stayed shut.

Later, after Bree was asleep and the sliver of light under Ross's door had been turned out, I sat up, leafing through the pages. You forget what it's like, to hold a paper magazine: cheap print that leaks ink onto your fingertips, the limited boundary of its form – something that has been killed by the infinite possibilities of clicking through on a screen or vid-sim. In the lamplit lounge, with only the low hum of appliances as witness, I held my breath to hear my fingertips squeak on the glossy paper, to hear the crinkle as I turned each page.

It was impossible to tell whether the writers believed their own stories, or whether they were just out to make money from others who might. I read about government facilities at the edge of the world, and the ice wall that stopped most people reaching them. I read about hostile takeovers, conducted through hacking and data manipulation, sometimes by corporations looking to boost stocks, sometimes by governments (which were either Chinese, or American, or Russian, or Atlantean, or alien). I read till the light outside the window began to lift, and I heard the first bird sing the dawn into being. Then I stashed the magazines back under the sofa, and tucked myself into bed next to Bree as though I had been there all night.

That morning, after Ross had left for school, I returned the magazines to the mess at the back of his wardrobe. I never mentioned them to him, and when I looked for them again six months later, they had gone.

*

When I step out on deck after dinner, I breathe so deeply it makes my eyes smart, and I have to wipe them with my glove. The sea is flat and purple now, a royal depth. Scatterings of ice, broken up by the storm, look mauve in the dimming light, and the peaks reach pale and amethyst into a dusky sky. I wonder if Sky is seeing it, from down in his office, if the dusk-light tints his painting purple. If I close my eyes, I can still feel the hug of his awkward arms, his bony shoulders so like Ross's.

It hits me, then, that the storm has ended and I still haven't tried to call Ross. For a moment, I'm frozen, halfway between my spot at the prow and darting back inside. Then I see Maretta, leaning her arms over the railing, watching the night draw in. She raises a hand, and I don't feel I can leave.

She beckons me over. 'Is Sky still painting?'

'I think so.' She's positioned herself in my usual spot, right at the prow of the ship, and I wonder if this is deliberate. 'You weren't at dinner.'

'I ate early,' she says. 'Look.'

A chink of gold lights the jagged edge of the mountain, a warning beacon, setting the snow aflame. The last glimmer of sun, I think, caught by the peak from below the horizon, and I wait for it to cool and vanish. Instead, it grows, burns more riotously gold, till it burgeons into the fat yellow coin of a full moon. It lets itself be cradled, briefly, in the lee of the slope, then lifts into the deepening blue like a boat loosed from its moorings.

Maretta waits till the moon has floated clear of the mountain, its edges distorted by haze and its gold face pocked and shadowed, then says, 'About the other day.'

I say nothing, wait for her to incriminate herself.

'What you said, in the lounge. About the articles you wrote – the ones about Sky.'

'I remember.'

'"It would've been easier for him to file an injunction."'

There's something about moonlight that sets its own rules, that unlocks guilt from the body. Golden/guilting/glint. The cold seeps through my thermals, I want to stamp feeling back into my feet, to tuck my hands into my armpits for warmth. Instead, I lay the question before her like a sword: 'Why am I here?'

We're alone on deck, but still Maretta scans the ice-riddled waters, glances up at the drifting moon and along towards the starboard door. Nothing moves except the slowly yawing ship, the occasional wash against a floe. 'I believe everyone deserves a second chance, don't you?'

I don't know if that's what I believe, but I nod anyway. I need her to believe I'm on her side.

'I want your opinion on something. Your advice.' She glances again towards the starboard door. 'He wouldn't want me doing this.'

'Sky?'

She gives a faint shake of her head as though to clear it of water, then takes a deep breath and starts to speak. Again, the lines sound scripted, rehearsed. 'The tech that Plan B runs on – it's intuition tech of course, like everything Sky does – but the main development which has allowed us to create such an expansive conservation site is the Chillers.'

'Yes.'

'Ground-breaking technology, designed to keep an environment in stasis without producing counteractive waste energy. Everything is recycled back into the Chillers themselves, which means nothing leaves the Plan B site – not even residue heat. It's the perfect system.'

Her voice is low; I strain to hear her over the sound of my own breath. When she pauses, I say, 'Go on.'

'Plan B is a pilot project, as much about Sky's passion for the place as anything else – the tech isn't quite perfect, there are the usual wrinkles to iron out in development – but if we can roll it out across the rest of Antarctica – to other key sites right across the world – it could halt climate collapse. It could help restore the balance we need across the globe.'

'A miracle cure?' It comes out cynical and I want to take it back.

Maretta looks again towards the starboard door. She lowers her voice further, so her whisper mingles with the shifting sea. 'What if I told you the technology was stolen?'

The water darkens as the blinds are drawn in the lounge below. I wait, remember what she told me about being head-hunted from one of Sky's rivals. Taiga, that was it. When she doesn't speak, I say, 'Corporate espionage isn't really my area of expertise.'

She traces a pattern of waves in the condensation forming on the railing, small drops that meld together then part. 'If any accusations were made . . .'

'If accusations were made, there would be investigations, and the development of the Chillers would be tied up in legal knots for years.'

'Decades,' she says.

The moon has drifted further from the peak. It dances in the gap between the mountain and a snow-thickened ridge. Around it, stars peer hesitantly into the bay, as though checking for certain that the violent storm has passed. 'Why are you telling me this?'

'I told you, I used to worship you. Balancing on that ice – I thought you were my hero.' She doesn't look at me. Again I think of those three spots of coffee on the pristine tablecloth, and stand taller. How long has she nurtured this secret, how long has it been rooting in her brain? I think of Sky as a small boy,

EAT THE RICH weighing thick and heavy above his head. I think of him painting in his office below, struggling towards some hidden truth.

Into the dark, I ask, 'But what do you want me to do about it?'

A small cough answers me, polite and affirmative. Beside me, Maretta stiffens, and I watch her face arrange itself into its usual polished mask.

Half-lit through the open door, Sharma's expression is impossible to read. Impossible to know how much he might have heard, how much he might know already. He says, 'It's an early start tomorrow. Sky asked me to check if either of you wanted a nightcap.'

Sky, I think, should still be painting.

Maretta declines. She wishes us both good night, and is gone – as if she could have advertised any more clearly that she has something to run from. But I've been playing the game for a long time. I make some comment about the cold and allow Sharma to escort me back inside. After the deepening blues and purples, the light in the stairwell is spongy, and my eyes prickle in the heat.

I request the drink in my cabin. 'I'm getting old,' I tell him. 'I feel the chill in my bones.'

*

I take a moment to appreciate that the whisky he delivered is a large one, then drag a long, heady sip through my front teeth to swill around my mouth. When I swallow, heat pushes through me and begins to thaw my bones where, yes, alright, maybe I do feel it more than I used to. From the wall, Sky's painted iceberg glows, pale and vulnerable against the tumult of the sea. I sit on the sofa with my back to it, my feet up and the vid open on my lap.

The Question of the Stolen Chillers.

No.

The Problem of the Stolen Chillers.

No.

I imagine AJ assessing the title's potential for viral reach, which is of course zero. 'It isn't *dynamic*,' I can almost hear him saying. 'It doesn't *deploy*.'

Chilling Truth at the Heart of Antarctic Conservation.

I sip my drink to stop myself cringing. The cursor flashes. It flashes again. My fingers hover over the keys, an avalanche waiting to fall.

I could do it so easily – write about cover-ups at the whims of the super-rich, and who is forced to keep their secrets for them. The words are all there, like muscle memory. The old habit itching to return. The old reputation. *Ivy Cunningham: taking on those in power, bringing the truth to light.* Not a big enough scandal to secure my name, perhaps, but enough to make the nationals. Enough to get me out of those grubby IntuNet conspiracy sites.

And if it prevents the roll-out of a technology that could quite literally save the world, then so what? The world has been saved before. People only find new ways to condemn it.

I check the signal. In the aftermath of the storm, the connection is weak and slow, like it's struggling to push past something. But it works. I send a quick VidNote to Ross – the moon through the window, over the deepening purple water – then I search the IntuNet for information on the Chillers.

I go for public information first – search for press releases from the early days of their development, interviews with Sky about testing. The loading wheel turns. Again and again, I have to re-enter the same search parameters as the connection lags. Like a ship dragging something else in its wake. Like there's someone else piggybacking on the connection.

I shake myself; we're miles from anywhere. From anyone. And besides, I'd forgotten how good it could feel, digging into a subject. Like picking the layers from a scab. I use my old media login to access restricted databases, and am surprised it still works. When I check the patents archive, I find the Chillers registered to a subsidiary of Cirrus Holdings. I search their public database for results of the Chillers' scientific trials, for testing records, for anything I might be able to use as evidence. The loading wheel turns. I trawl university lab records and corporate engineering programmes. The connection cuts out, begins again. I search for 'Chillers' and 'Cirrus Holdings'. I feel like I'm climbing a steep hill with someone riding, parasitic, on my back. When I hunt for any mention of breakthrough heat exchange technology, there's nothing, as though somebody has gone to a lot of effort to expunge the data from the network.

I throw my vid down on the bed in frustration. I pace the room, try to work out what Bree would've done in this situation. Would she have confronted Sky head-on, or gone behind his back? Would she have published Maretta's revelation in secret? No, not without proof. Bree was often combative, but she was always sensible about the consequences. 'Rock the boat,' she used to say, 'as damn hard as you can. You just gotta be prepared to swim.'

I keep pacing. I pick up the wooden seal, then put it back down. I tap my thumb against the screen, resisting, resisting . . . Then I give up and call AJ. Instead, I get his Executive Administrative Coordinator. His 'assistant', though apparently both needing and providing assistance are now things to be ashamed of. I try not to think of Bree.

The assistant crackles into frame, slight and eager, his shaved head tattooed with geometric patterns. When I start to talk, he cuts me off, saying, 'I'm so sorry, I'm having trouble receiving you, possibly due to extreme weather or third-party interference, could you try switching to audio only please, thank you.' He speaks as though it's all one long scripted sentence.

His image goes white, so I turn off my own video as well. 'How's this?'

'Hello, yes, that's much better, thank you so much for co-operating, can I ask who's calling please.'

'It's Ivy. Ivy Cunningham. I wanted to speak to AJ.'

His voice crackles from the speakers, rehearsed and distant. 'I'm sorry, could you repeat that for me please.'

'Ivy Cunningham.' I feel myself growing hot as I spell it out. 'I'm a client.'

'Cunningham . . . Cunningham . . . Certainly, one moment, let me see if he's free.'

I realise I haven't checked the time difference between here and Manhattan. Perhaps it's still office hours. Perhaps he's working late.

The assistant's voice crackles back through the speakers. 'Yes, he is available, Ms Cunningham, just putting you through.'

The screen flashes twice and I catch half an audio trailer for a new vid-sim, distorted by the bad signal, before AJ's curly hair and overbearing smile pixelate onto the screen. In the background is a glitzy gathering of people, the clinks and chatter of a party. 'Cunningham! How goes it in the land of the rich?' I hate how he uses my surname like that, as a wager on familiarity. I watch his grainy image frown. 'Wait, why can't I see you?'

'Bad reception, sorry.' I try not to sound too gleeful at not having to show my face. 'We've been off-grid the past couple of days.'

He drops his jaw in exaggerated horror. 'God, how remote is this place?'

I don't answer. I wait as he switches to audio. The tinny music and chatter grow fainter as he heads to a more private room to take the call.

'So, seriously Cunningham. How's the trip?'

'Good. Interesting.' Now I have his attention, I'm reluctant to share too much too soon. Better to keep him baited. 'It's just an article they want from me. Or a feature, or something – some way of lending my voice to the project, a way of showing I'm on-side. I don't have all the research yet. I'll send something over when I do.'

'Any sense of a timeline?'

'Not yet.' After a calculated hesitation, I say, 'I think there might be a scoop.'

Silence. Then, a released breath that comes through the speakers as a rush of static. 'What kind of scoop?' His voice is hushed, a reverent whisper.

I can't help whispering too. 'A conspiracy.'

'Personal? Or political?'

'Corporate,' I say. 'Environmental.' I consider mentioning the cost, the damage Maretta's story could do – but now I have his attention, I'm reluctant to put him off. 'Like I said, I'm still digging.'

He says, 'It sounds perfect for you.'

This throws me. It is perfect for me – the perfect intersection of every aspect of my career. The perfect bait. 'What if I'm being played?'

'Ms Cunningham, listen.' I note the more formal address, his voice low and cautious. 'You have a choice here. You can write their feature, the one they want you to write, and what happens to it will be up to them – I can't guarantee you any kind of exposure.'

Exposure, we used to say, is something you die of. 'Or?'

'Or you can follow this other story, make it a radical exposé of whatever the billionaire is hiding, and we can bring the world's most powerful man to his knees.' *We* . . . As if he's risking anything. As though anyone other than me would take the fall if it went wrong. I can hear his excitement filtering through. 'But we'll need evidence, Cunningham. Rock solid, you understand? We have to do this by the book.'

'You want me to do it.'

'I can't make that decision for you,' he says, though the speed at which he says it suggests he wants to. 'But that's your brand, isn't it?'

'My brand?'

'A doubling down after Helsinki – sticking to your guns. Following that ruthless agenda no matter what.'

'I'm not sure that's the best idea . . .'

'It has to be,' he says. 'After Helsinki.'

THE OTHER PHOTO

I've told you about the first – in the Ross Sea, with my arms raised like a messiah – but there was a much later photo, which also shaped my career. A second image on which everything turned, taken nine years ago in Helsinki, me gripping a wine glass in the low strategic lighting of a hotel bar.

In this second photo, my hair is silver. Needle-sharp crows' feet corner my eyes, and I'm wearing an asymmetrical red suit that contours with my body. A power suit, Bree called it, although by that point, everything I wore was about power.

Earlier in the day, the Ivy in the photo has given a speech: well-rehearsed and emphatic, received with a standing ovation. Now, in the photograph, in the low-lit room, in Helsinki, she celebrates.

Ivy stands in front of the bar. Behind her, a server with his back to the camera reaches into the array of glittering bottles. Light dances across the bar's polished surface, and in the brimming shots of clear liquor lined up along it, and along the stem of her glass. In front of her is a woman in a low-cut dress, who also dances with light.

Ivy stands in front of the bar. Ivy stands on a table in front of the bar. The woman's head is between Ivy's legs, her face turned up, mouth open. But the Ivy in the photo doesn't look at her,

219

and the glass at the end of her outstretched arm is a crystal flash, tipped to a precarious angle. The lighting is soft, sophisticated. In it, wine sloshes across her wrist and glitters. Glints.

Ivy looks straight at the camera, and opens her mouth to speak.

*

'He doesn't want to speak to you, Ivy.'

Two years after that second photo was taken, Bree shrugged and leaned back into the armchair. Around her, the other residents of the home worked through brain exercises on their vids, or watched the birds that flocked and squabbled around the garden feeders. 'It's important,' one of the carers told me once, 'that our residents feel able to connect with the outside world.'

I hated seeing Bree there, hated that she thought I was the one who'd made it necessary. Sometimes I wondered if that was why she'd chosen this place – close enough to visit, far enough to make me have to work for it – to punish me for making our own home *unsustainable*. That was the word she'd used, scientific and environmental. I don't know whether that was deliberate.

'Can you talk to him for me? Apologise?'

Bree shook her head as though it weighed too much for her.

'Then at least tell me how he's doing.'

And so Bree would fill me in on Ross's news: his promotion; that Hanna was pregnant again; the move to Abu Dhabi. ('Why?' I asked, and Bree said, 'Why d'you think?')

Sometimes, Bree would forget what she was saying part way through. Sometimes she told the same story twice, or with different outcomes. Later, she would forget she'd spoken to Ross at all, and I would have to glean what snippets I could from the carers.

The first day that Bree didn't know me was the last day I visited. I remember walking into that care home with its non-slip paths and high-backed armchairs, and Bree's eyes searching, searching for something familiar in my face, her terror when she couldn't find it – when she pulled her hand from mine and screamed, 'Don't touch me! You have no right to touch me!' The carers scurried to calm her, kept saying, 'It's OK, it's OK,' over and over, when of course it wasn't, how the hell could it be? Afterwards, I sat in the car park and wept, till I became aware of the carers, watching me through the break room window. Then I let the car drive me back to the big empty house outside Boston, where I tried to remember which items had been Bree's and which had been mine. Bree had taken some things with her when she left, but there was still furniture she had chosen, unwanted gifts (given and received in both directions), photographs and artwork we had picked out together – impossible to untangle.

I spent two days boxing things up, driving them out to the donations centre. By the time I was done, the house looked desolate, sun-shadows and picture hooks showing what used to be. I called Ross, left him a message, saying, 'It's over. I've lost you both.'

*

I wake early, an itch under my skin. From the bed, the parka hanging on the back of the door is a shapeless dark, the silver iceberg winking from the sleeve, its bulk below the surface. A secret hidden in plain sight.

What if I told you the technology was stolen?

A story – and all mine for the breaking. If I want it. If I can get the proof from Maretta, if I can get her to trust me enough to hand it over.

Balance – isn't that what icebergs are really about? Don't they float according to their centre of gravity? As the warmer water melts away what's underneath, doesn't that centre of gravity shift, and won't the iceberg suddenly flip?

From somewhere below, there's a low rumble. It shivers through me as the ship starts to move.

*

When I arrive on deck, the railings are still rimed and glittering, and the sky has the pale uncertainty of dawn. The atmosphere is like the shattered mirror on the back wall of the lounge. Each of us throws back something different. Maretta's eyes flick towards me, the smallest of betrayals. After that, she doesn't look at anyone. Sharma stands wary and observant beside Sky, whose excitement trembles through his whole body. His gaze is triangular, from me to Maretta to the bay narrowing ahead of us, where the water sparkles so brightly it's impossible to look at it directly. Behind us, the crew are out on deck to witness our arrival: the waiters – Kip and the man with floppy hair – shivering in their livery; a man in an exaggerated chef's outfit; the two cleaners in their sailor costumes; and two actual sailors in full IntuTech waterproof gear – the birdlike man from the X-Ped, and a small, shrewd-looking man with epaulettes and an insignia at his breast. The captain, presumably. All men, all standing as though weighted to the deck. Is that why Maretta decided to confide in me – some bizarre ideal of sisterhood? Again I get that prickling feeling, of being surrounded by such vast wilderness, and so little to hold fast to. Eleven, including myself. I'm glad I didn't know before the storm hit that we were so few. Nobody is speaking. It has the feeling of a poorly attended school fete, everyone there out of social obligation.

'For the original explorers,' Sky says, his voice a serrated blade against the quiet, 'moments of arrival must have been marked by naming a place or staking a flag.'

He says this as though he's seeking my approval. His fingers are back to their repeating patterns, finger to thumb to finger to thumb, spinning shapes from his knuckles. I nod. The crew stand silent sentry behind me.

Ahead, the bay continues to narrow, till it becomes a rocky channel. After the darkness of the past two days, the ice on either side seems whiter, and ahead, it intensifies into a glare so bright that even with my snow-glasses, I have to shield my eyes. I wonder whether someone will announce when we've crossed into the conservation area. Then I understand what I'm looking at, and realise no one will need to.

It starts as a trick of the light. A shimmer in the air, like vapour. The sky made solid. I find myself rubbing my eyes.

Then the sun clashes against the surface, and the light transforms into a wall – transparent, half a kilometre high and stretching away from the channel in both directions. PlastiGlass. Military grade and almost indestructible. To seal off the test site, to mark the border of Plan B. Not just a line on a map, but a line along the ground, and up into the air. On this side, chaos. On the other, a perfectly orchestrated world. Whatever its origins, it's impossible to deny that Plan B is a victory of technology and engineering.

'See the Chillers?' He can't keep from bragging about them. He points to the insulated engines around the base of the wall, white to blend in with the ice, each boasting its gleaming solar panel. 'We have nearly four and a half thousand, each adjustable to a fraction of a degree. They work on IntuTech – reading temperature, atmospheric pressure, light levels – a thousand different data points.'

'Impressive.' My voice feels small against this enormous angular structure.

'It's the same tech we used to preserve the underwater wreck of the *Endurance*, but next level. More finely tuned. Not only do these Chillers adjust in the moment,' he says, 'but the intuition tech means they can predict approaching atmospheric changes and alter their own settings ahead of time. Nothing is left to chance.'

I say, 'It's a giant cage.'

Maretta gazes resolutely forward.

Sky frowns. 'This is a perfect environment. Why would anything want to leave?'

Closer now, and the wall towers above the ship, claustrophobic, despite the sun clattering off every surface. I can't help thinking of Roman walls, of the Great Wall of China – other emperors desperate to declare the bounds of their domain. A searing flash as the PlastiGlass channels the light. I blink as the ship moves forward, and then we're through the narrow break in its defences. Inside the conservation area. Inside Plan B. Around us, the ice glitters and winks at its reflections. We've arrived.

PLAN B

From the ground, it would be easy to think Plan B was a perfect circle – that the Chillers and PlastiGlass walls curve round to meet themselves as though drawn with a compass. In reality, it's full of irregularities, and its shape is a hulking cloud, cumbersome and on the verge of snow.

Along the southern edge is the ridge of mountains that back-bones the Antarctic Peninsula: bare rock pulled free of the surrounding snow and ice, as between them, glaciers push their creaking fingers towards the sea. Here, rock and ice and snow give way to a pattern of stony inlets and beaches, where ice floes scrape up against each other, and where smudged lumps of Weddell seals and crabeaters loll and grunt. The beaches are littered with rusting metal contraptions, used by whalers and trappers centuries before – imported, I will learn later, as a kind of exhibition, a nod towards the earlier days of Antarctic exploitation. Around them, colonies of gentoo and Adélie penguins laugh puff-chested in their sleek black jackets, and pink the stones with the sharp tang of scat.

At the centre of the site, a splendid sparkling ice shelf, a hundred metres thick, hurls back the sun like an allegation. From beneath, the sea whispers its slow disintegration of the ice, and swarms of krill gorge on the phytoplankton, plump themselves for the penguins and the seals and the colossal gulps of whales. Below them, sea snails and brittle stars push into the soft mud. Against the protection of underwater cliffs, giant sea spiders crawl through forests of sponges, brachiopods cluster in their shells and wavering corals sift scraps from the chill water. This is an ancient ecosystem. Its creatures grow slowly, over multiple human life-times, waiting out millennia in the underwater dark. And everywhere, the Chillers work to keep this frozen world in its state of equilibrium.

The *Lone Star* slips along a channel, slow in the presence of abundant wildlife. Stitching a path ahead of the ship, a minke whale puffs clouds of spume. On deck, I'm not sure whether to applaud or say a solemn prayer. Sky is right – it demands some kind of ritual to mark our passage from one place to another. Beside me, he's all grin and bounce, and for a moment, I forget this whole place is fake, held in stasis using stolen technology. He reminds me of Ross as a toddler, clapping his hands to see his demands presented to him, his every wish made manifest.

Sky takes out his vid and opens up a program I don't recog-nise. When he points the camera towards where the edge of the ice shelf sticks out from behind a spit of rock, the ice shelf on the screen lights up an artificial blue. He taps to select it, and the screen gives back a list of measurements. 'What do you think?' he asks.

'What am I looking at?'

'Diagnostics. Here.' He tells the program to analyse, and the readings are replaced by a series of words: STABLE; PERFORMING ACCORDING TO PREDICTION; MINIMUM RISK.

'It's all interconnected,' he says. 'This program, the data readings from the IntuTech on the ship, the Chillers around the site, the millions of other sensors we have here – they're all constantly sharing information with the central Plan B system. A colossal IntuTech database, and all of it accessible right here.' He taps the vid. 'Over the seven years we've been building, we've input millions of data points, created thousands of individual algorithms, studied the behavioural patterns of all the wildlife within the site, the tracks of the glaciers, the melt rate, right down to the smallest currents drifting against the beaches.' I try not to look at Maretta, as Sky says, 'It's the ultimate in IntuTech engineering. If it's successful, we could use these systems all around the globe.'

'For environmental purposes, of course.' Maretta's face is so still, it's as if she hasn't spoken.

'So on your vid . . .'

He says, 'I can point this at anything or anyone inside the Plan B boundary, and the IntuTech will give me its readings, an analysis, and predictions of its future behaviour.'

'Anyone?' I glance at Maretta, her narrow lips.

'In theory,' he says. 'Yes. In practice, there are . . . complications.'

Maretta says, 'The intuition technology has weak points where Sky himself is concerned.' It isn't hard to see through her clipped professionalism to the smirk hovering just below the surface.

Sky frowns. 'Not *weak points*. Disruptions.'

'Yes, of course.'

'Deliberate disruptions,' he says. 'Everyone – every*thing* – is governed by desires and fears. The things that drive us. At its most basic level, that's how the IntuTech works: the algorithms determine the weightings of various driving forces, and use these to calculate a person's most likely course of action. The more things and people we can calculate this for in any given environment, the more accurate our overall results.'

'But the disruptions?'

He shrugs. 'I like to erase certain readings, alter my own data points, just enough to keep myself unpredictable to the IntuTech.'

'I see.' I try not to think of my own attempts to do the same, the bank of lights in the cubby, the ones marking out my cabin all in darkness.

'Predictability is bad for business. My own predictability, anyway.' He points the vid at the minke whale, blowing up spume ahead of the ship. MINKE WHALE: PERFORMING ACCORDING TO PREDICTION. MINIMUM RISK. 'Got to stay ahead of the game somehow.'

Not a cage, then, but somewhere to submit these things to his intense and scrutinous gaze, like a museum cabinet, or the tanks in the aquarium in Frisco.

The crew have begun to disperse. I didn't notice when they started to leave, but when I turn around there are only the two waiters left, still shivering in their livery. Then the waiters leave as well, and it's just me and Maretta and Sky.

'Where's Sharma?' I didn't notice him leave, either. This shakes me, the way it did on that first night when I didn't remember his name.

'Readying the X-Ped.'

'To land?'

'He needs to run through the safety checks.'

I nod. It was another thing the expedition training drilled into us all those years ago: if you're going to land, make sure you scout the area first.

'We'll go downstairs for breakfast,' he says, 'Then you can take a look at your painting before we go ashore.'

'It's finished?' The change of subject catches me by surprise.

'It might still be damp in places, but it's ready for a second pair of eyes.'

*

All the way down the stairs to his office after breakfast, I feel I ought to say something. I'm aware this place is a technological marvel. 'A miracle of engineering,' I could say. Or, 'You must be so proud.' Or, 'I hear this entire project is built on stolen tech-

230

nology and lies.' But I keep thinking of his shoulders when I hugged him, angular and awkward and so like Ross's. And of how he positioned me, face-on to the canvas, how he looked through the reputation to see me as I used to be. How he chose to paint me the way he must believe I can become again.

The office is bright this morning, in the sun off the bay. In my outdoor gear, I'm already itching from the heat of the sun through the glass. The easel has been moved for the natural light, so it faces the window. Through it, I can just see the corner of the ice shelf, half-hidden by a rocky outcrop.

'Ready?' he asks.

From the door, all I can see is the rough wood at the back of the canvas. It makes me think of execution scaffolds. 'Does it look like me?'

'I think so.'

'Show me.'

Sky guides me around the desk, around the easel, and the sun through the window hits me like plunging into a too-hot bath. The picture comes into view.

It's definitely my face – I can recognise the angle of my nose and square jaw – but stylised through heavy paint, like his icebergs and rocky shores. It stares out of the canvas. Unflinching, I'd thought. Strong. Only now do I realise I'd expected the painting to feel like looking in a mirror. What I'd forgotten, of course, is that in a mirror, it's impossible to look at your own eyes without them looking back at you. It's impossible to be dismissed. In the painting, my eyes stare out of the canvas with a gaze that says everything is beneath it.

'You hate me.' The force of my realisation shocks me – a low hollow feeling in my gut, and I'm back at Bree's funeral, Ross turning away from me, Ross saying, *my family's waiting*, and that no longer including me.

'Of course I don't.' Sky comes to stand beside me and I feel an overwhelming need to be comforted, to be told I've done well.

My voice is quiet. It barely makes it out. 'You hate me.'

He stares at the painting, perhaps seeing it properly for the first time. After a long moment, he says, 'Let me show you.'

*

The water, which felt so calm from the deck, is choppy in the X-Ped. It's impossible to talk over the engine roar, the sea spray and the slap of the X-Ped against the waves, and for once I'm grateful. I can't stop thinking about the painting. Is that how Ross saw me at the funeral? Dismissive, the whole world beneath me? No wonder he lives halfway around the world in Abu Dhabi. No wonder he never picks up when I call.

Sharma sits at the tiller, the rifle a dark line across his back, barrel pointing to the sky. At the prow, a second man perches with his body half out of the boat, watching for ice. His bald head is covered by a hat, so it's only when he throws up a darting hand that I realise this is the same birdlike man as before. Something sibilant – a name I don't remember. I watch as he scans our path for danger. Aisi, that's it. Sharma's second-in-command. I know he won't let me try steering this time.

Sky sits on the rim of the boat with one foot on the bench, his grip loose on the loop handles. Out here, his screen-bleached skin looks less drastic, less ill, perhaps because the ice is so much brighter, or perhaps because his spinning fingers are finally still – because for the first time since I met him, he looks as though control is no longer something he has to strive for.

Maretta excused herself after breakfast, said she had things to attend to while we were all on land. It makes it easier to pretend, not having her there, not trying to keep my face smooth, to constantly avoid her eye.

The X-Ped dips into the lee of the bay, out of sight of the ship, where the water smooths. The noise drops. Sky nods towards a rocky beach, clear of ice. 'We'll pull in just up there.'

As we draw closer in, the X-Ped slows. Black and white smudges along the shore sharpen into a group of gentoo penguins, and through the new quiet, I can hear their squawking chatter. We've barely pulled up to the beach when Sky jumps out, splashing into the shallows in his heavy boots. As Sharma cuts the engine, Aisi unfolds the metal steps from the front of the boat. 'Ready?'

I stand and the boat rocks a little. I shuffle to the front, step one foot up onto the rim as the wavelets lap and clack at stones underneath. At the line where water meets rock, Sky holds out his arm. His grip is solid, stronger than expected – a sailor's grip, my hand to his wrist, my wrist to his hand.

I take a breath. I step down from the edge of the boat: first foot, second foot, onto the metal stair. I step down into the shallow water. I step up onto the Antarctic beach.

I want to drop to my knees. I want to run the wave-smoothed pebbles through my fingers, to pick them up and let them fall abundantly like coins, or to press my hands to the ground to remind myself I'm here. Instead, I stand at the bottom of the beach and turn a slow circle.

Sky lets go and spreads both arms wide. This time, the gesture says, 'Look at everything I've built.'

There's a sharp smell of salt and, at the back of my throat, the searing tang of penguin scat. I'd forgotten how marine and faecal it is, how it makes my eyes water. When I breathe in again, I'm back on the expedition with the Foundation, fifty years in the past and so much of my life still unlived. No viral photograph, no Pulitzer, no money, no Ross. Every instant I've ever spent with my son is contained between this moment and the last time I smelled this smell.

I always thought I'd come back sooner. After visiting twice within five years, I'd assumed Antarctica would continue to draw me back. It's easy to think like that when you're young, to not notice your imagined future collapsing until it's all but disappeared.

'Are you OK?' Sky watches, ready to reach out and help. I smile at him and realise I'm crying, and can't remember when I started – when I left the X-Ped? Or have I been crying since I saw the painting?

He takes my elbow and guides me along the shoreline: a satisfying arc, a leading line out towards the deeper blue of the channel. When I stumble, I let myself lean into his support.

We pause. Curious at our arrival, the gentoos crane their necks to look. When they approach, they do it tentatively, one brave leader ahead of the rest, before they all career, squawking, back towards the water. Then they start the approach again. I say, 'It's magnificent.'

'But?'

There must be a waver in my voice. I try to work out where, so I can flush it out.

'See that?' He points to where the edge of the ice shelf winks from across the bay. 'The ice shelf is the nucleus of the whole Plan B project – it's why we chose this site.' *Minimum risk. Performing according to prediction.* He says, 'It's cracked.'

'How?'

'It always has been, from the first moment anyone ever thought to look. A fissure, running right down the middle. I've had scientists, engineers, climatologists, everyone to look at it – and the money we've thrown at trying to fix it . . .' He keeps looking in the direction of the ice shelf, but I see his face fall, his jaw sag the way Ross's used to when the weight of the day grew too much for him to bear. 'None of us are perfect, are we?'

I don't know what to say. I watch the penguins bob like ducks in the surf.

'How long have you been out of favour now? Ten years?'

'Retired,' I say, and feel my voice crack. 'Not quite.' All along the beach, the gentoos click against the stones. I should have come back sooner. Again, I have to remind myself all this is artificial.

Sky stoops to pick up a pebble, rubs it between finger and thumb, and says, 'There are flaws in the system.'

234

'The ice shelf?'

'The IntuTech.' He drops the pebble and it clatters against the beach, setting the gentoos squawking. 'What Maretta said this morning – it's true. I work hard to make myself unpredictable. It's good for business.' He picks up another pebble. 'If I take myself out of the system, I can't predict those directly around me, either. The readings are too inaccurate. So Sharma, Maretta – you, since you came on board . . . I've learned to test people's loyalties the old-fashioned way.'

The painting flashes before me, all fight and hard edges. 'I see,' I say, although I don't. A penguin approaches, cautiously, as the others watch from the shoreline.

'I don't hate you, you know.'

'I know,' I tell him, though I can't tell if I believe it. Besides, why do I care? He's just the rich client commissioning my next feature – it shouldn't matter, not as long as he pays on time. Again, I try not to think of Ross at the funeral. Of their bony and awkward hugs.

The penguin tugs at the bottom of my waterproof trousers with its beak, then gives an unmistakeable shrug, and totters back along the beach. I make to follow it, but Sky grabs at my wrist. 'What I wanted to say . . .' Then he's quiet for a long time. My wrist gives an involuntary twitch under his hand, and he snaps back to himself.

'What I wanted to say is that it wouldn't matter even if I did hate you. You understand that, don't you? Of all people? Success is about loyalty, not like.' He looks tired, heavy, like the solid mahogany desk in his office. For the first time, I think of him not as the richest man in the world but as the man with the most responsibility. 'Do you think I like Maretta? Do you think Sharma doesn't need to lighten up from time to time?'

'It sounds lonely.'

'I can't afford to be lonely.'

I almost laugh, then stop myself. He wasn't always the richest man in the world.

'I trust them. I've tested their loyalty, and it's stood firm. That's what matters.' He holds both my wrists, tenderly, so I face him. 'Can I trust you, Ivy?'

The word falls strangely. Not ma'am. Not Ms Cunningham. *Ivy*. It's the first time I've heard my name in his voice.

In the years since Bree died, it's the first time I've heard my name at all.

'Ivy?' His breath on my cheek is minty, slightly stale. 'I need to know you won't let me down.'

My own name still tumbles through my head – its two liquid vowels, the soft fricative centre. 'Yes,' I say, and it comes out whispered. 'You can trust me.'

*

I expect the X-Ped to take us back to the *Lone Star*, but it bats across the waves in the opposite direction. I catch glimpses between the rocks, but the ice shelf keeps frustrating me. Sky sees where I'm looking and grins. 'We'll pull up on the smaller edge for now.' He has to repeat himself twice before I hear over the roar of the engine.

'Why not the bigger one?' I shout back.

'This afternoon.'

Past a series of low rocky islands, and the *Lone Star* comes back into view. I've lost my bearings and can't be certain, but I think she's moved since we left her. Then I turn and I know she has, because suddenly I can see the edge of the ice shelf. The smaller edge, this must be, though it's still an impenetrable white wall, towering above the X-Ped, above the *Lone Star*, extending out from the land into the sea.

The X-Ped gives the front of the ice shelf a wide berth. Instead, we put in at the bottom of a steep rocky cluster to the left of it, where Sharma moors the boat to a metal pole fixed into the rock.

The pole looks as though it's been there decades, but perhaps it's just that things weather quickly down here. The X-Ped bobs with the water, and the rocky step I'm aiming for rises and falls. Again, Sky gets out first, then reaches in to help me. Again, he holds me with a sailor's grip, hand to wrist, wrist to hand – the idea being that even if one of us lets go, the other can still cling on.

'Ready for a bit of a climb?' he asks.

The rocks form natural steps, slippery and uneven, but manageable in my deep-treaded boots. I keep hold of Sky's hand as he guides me up. When I slip – briefly, for the thinnest second – it's his grip that stops me falling.

Ahead of us, the dark line of the rifle against Sharma's back. Behind, the other man – Aisi – with his steady rolling gait. I hold on more tightly. I concentrate on the climb.

'Welcome to the Station.'

I'm so focused on where I'm placing my boots, at first I don't notice when we reach the top.

Now I'm on a level with it, the ice sheet spreads away from me, bigger, wider than I'd imagined it. Impossibly big. Impossibly wide. Even through my snow-glasses, its edges are obscured by glare. Ahead, set back from the edge of the ice, is a building, if building is the right word. The same dusk-blue as the ship, it looks more like a colossal vehicle, or a robotic caterpillar. There's something about how it hovers above the ice – a series of modules, connected end to end, each one raised on hydraulic stilts – as though it might decide to wander away over the featureless white horizon. Porthole-style windows dot the sides like false eyes, and from the tall central module, the secretive iceberg of the Plan B logo glints silver. A thin metal bridge connects the building's head to the body – the IntuTech's centre of operations to the guest quarters, I will later learn – and even from here, I can see the jewel-crust of ice along the narrow railings, the snowdrift at either end.

Sky notices my surprise and says, 'We needed a permanent

structure to house the central processing unit for the IntuTech. And besides, down here, buildings are the best way of making sure ownership isn't contested.'

I start towards it, but the ice shelf is too bright, too slippery. Even the thick-treaded boots are no match for this. My foot gives out from under me, and Sharma has to grab my arm to hold me steady. His grip is so strong, I can already imagine the five-fingered bruise flowering under my skin. Even through my snow-glasses, the afternoon glare splits my head like an axe. 'I can't.'

Sky tells me, 'You can.'

From his kit bag, Aisi pulls two pairs of extendable walking poles, grip-handled, spiked for sticking in the ice, which he passes to me and Sky. Then he hands each of us a contortion of metal and straps, which I untangle into a pair of foot-shaped rigs – like crampons, but smooth rather than spiked. When I run my fingers over the metal undersides, they hum like a tuning fork. The others have already clipped theirs on over their boots, but I'm wearing too many layers, too cold and stiff and hemmed-in to bend, so Sharma has to kneel on the ice and attach them for me. When he stands, my grip even on the rock is precarious, and I have to hold tight to my walking poles.

Sky digs the spike of his own walking pole into the ice. 'Ready?'

Sharma bends down to touch a switch at the side of each boot, and the metal rigs wake into life: an electric buzz, all the way up my calves, as the straps tighten to my feet, as they grab, claw-like onto the ice. Like crampons, but intuition tech. I can feel them reading my muscle movement, already attempting to predict my gait. I try to shuffle forward, but the claws stick fast and I flail. Then they relinquish their hold so my foot jerks free of the ice, and I stumble, step, land.

'Grippers,' Sharma says. 'Developed for the failed Mars missions, but they didn't take much to adapt to the ice.'

I cling to the walking poles for support, and stumble a couple more steps, feel myself slip. 'I can't.'

The building may as well be a hundred miles away; before it, there is only sun and glare and the treacherous slide of the ice. I try another step, but the grippers hold on and I tumble, Sharma's bruising grasp the only thing keeping me up. Through the thud of my heart in my ears, I hear Sky give a small impatient 'tsk'.

'I'm sorry,' I tell him. I can hear the wailing in my voice.

To his credit, he at least has the grace to look ashamed. But I can feel it emanating from him: the urge to move on, to reach the newest destination, to deal with the next thing. I suppose you don't become the richest man alive by lingering too long at any one juncture. I suppose we have that in common, too.

In the end, it's Sharma who comes to his rescue: 'Why don't you and Aisi go on ahead?'

I can't help but remember Sharma's anger on the ship, at being sent away the night Sky showed me his collection. Sharma's reluctance, then, to be separated from his boss. Perhaps Sky is thinking along the same lines, because he frowns and says, 'Are you sure?'

'Of course.' Sharma's face is as inscrutable as ever. 'I'll take Ms Cunningham through the technology.'

Sky frowns again, but his itch to be moving is palpable – in the rapid weave of his fingers, the juddering of his leg – so when he turns to ask me if I mind, it's impossible to refuse him.

He nods and turns away, Aisi beside him as they head out across the ice towards the Station. I try to study their gait – something rhythmic and deliberate about it, their legs in conversation with the equipment – but before I've figured it out, Sharma has taken hold of my arm again and said, 'So, Ms Cunningham.'

'This is kind of you, Sharma. Thank you.'

'I think it's time we spoke.'

I turn so fast I slip again, and have to steady myself with the poles. So this is why he encouraged Sky to go on ahead – to get me on my own. Away from his boss. Away from other listening ears. Wasn't the floating factory he grew up on owned by Sky? Might that not be as much of a reason as any for Sharma to want to bring him down? *I'll take Ms Cunningham through the technology . . .* I hesitate, then throw all caution to the wind. 'You know something.' When he doesn't answer, I say, 'The Chillers.' I drop the word between us like a stone, watch it fall, count how long it takes to hit.

Sharma's expression remains unrippled. Instead, he lets go of my arm and turns away, out onto the ice sheet. 'Come with me.'

Against the vast spread of white, Sky and Aisi are already distant, diminished. Sound carries strangely down here; already they're too far for me to hear the crunch of their grippers on the ice, too far for them to hear us in return. I look towards Sharma, try another few tentative steps.

There's a lag, between lifting my foot and the grippers relinquishing their hold on the ice. When I place my foot down again, my body slips out from under me before the grippers remember to take hold. I'm constantly on the edge of stumbling. When Sharma says, 'You have to not be afraid of falling,' I try not to think of Bree.

Slowly, shakily, I let him lead me away from the others, perpendicular to the line of the Station. Every step, I have to cling to my precarious balance. It reminds me of the games Keira used to play, walking some imaginary tightrope – a crack in a pavement, or the floorboard join in the kitchen, or the pattern of the living-room rug – trying to keep her balance, to not tilt too far to either side. Keira, or maybe Ross.

When I'm too far out onto the ice to turn back, Sharma places a hand in the small of my spine to guide me. Only then does he say, 'So you've been looking at the Chillers.'

I stop, press the spikes of the walking poles into the ice. Under my feet, the grippers slide against the ice, then grab back on. I can feel my bones humming with the intuition tech. I force myself to wait, to let him speak into the silence.

'What did you find?'

'Nothing much.' I try to look nonchalant, as though the subject is nothing, as though my hunger for information is merely a passing curiosity, but I can't resist glancing back towards the Station, towards the ever-diminishing figures of Sky and Aisi.

'No, I don't imagine you did.' He smiles his eyeless smile as his gaze follows mine. 'Come on.'

The ice crumps under my boots as the grippers re-engage, and I begin to get the hang of it – an off-beat rhythm, *ready–lift, drop–re-engage*, a step of grace notes across the glaring white. My mind churns, and somehow this makes it easier to find a rhythm. The ice stretches out ahead of us, beautiful and inhospitable. It's easy to forget the life teeming below it, a thousand sea creatures killing each other to survive. I say, 'I suppose nobody becomes as successful as he is with their morals intact.'

A shadow passes across Sharma's face. He walks backwards, now, watches as I lurch towards him. I feel like a child taking its first steps, legs always ready to give out from under me. 'Step by step,' he tells me, and he takes first one of the walking poles from me, then the other.

I look down at my feet, try to focus on my rhythm. *Ready–lift, drop–re-engage, ready–lift, drop–re-engage*. I let myself follow him. Without the walking poles, my legs feel too narrow, my pelvis too unsteady to support my weight. *Ready–lift, drop–re-engage* – mechanical, Sharma still out in front, urging me on. I pick up the pace. *Ready–lift, drop–re-engage. Ready–lift, drop–re-engage*.

Sharma is still facing me, still walking backwards, still carrying my walking poles. They scrape across the ice between us. He says, 'I won't let you break Maretta's story, Ms Cunningham.'

His words catch me by surprise, and I don't know how to respond. I hesitate, jolt up through my stomach, my oesophagus, into my head. He walks faster, his eyes on my feet as I try to keep up. *Ready–lift, drop–re-engage, ready–lift, drop–re-engage*. At this speed, the strain between my feet and the grippers and the

241

ice is a three-way wrench, and it's all I can do not to let go as I gasp, 'So it is true?'

He says, 'You know how much he has to lose.'

'You don't owe him anything.' *Ready–lift, drop–re-engage, ready–lift, drop–re-engage.* 'Sky – and people like him, rich white men, they're the ones with the power. They're responsible for every bad thing that's ever happened in your life. In all our lives.'

'I know who's responsible.'

'So why be loyal to him?'

His eyes fix on me as he tilts, backwards, across the ice. 'If you try to destroy him, Ms Cunningham, I'll bring you down in his place.'

I laugh and it comes out hollow. 'I don't have any further to fall.'

'There's always further to fall.'

I'm concentrating on my rhythm. I don't register the threat in his voice. I don't register the walking pole, trailing the ice by my foot. My leg slips out from under me, and I skew – flail – my foot skids across the ice, my knee to the side, and my stomach flips, jolts, up through my chest, my head – flailing and falling. I fling out my arms to catch myself – and something catches me first.

Sharma holds onto me, centimetres from the ground.

For a long moment, I lie there, my breath ragged, adrenaline screaming. I try to calm my heart rate. I try to assess the damage to my body. I let Sharma hold me.

The walking pole knocks against my foot. Against the gripper. Against the switch – and I start to understand how Sharma must have tapped it with the pole, how he switched off the gripper, mid-step, so the mechanical hum died, and I was left sliding on smooth metal across the ice.

I want to lie down on the ice and close my eyes and never get up. I want to get up and away from Sharma's treacherous grip.

'Do you understand?' he says, and his voice is a new hardness, a knife to the skin. It cuts through the rush in my head. 'If you go after this, it'll be you against me. And I will win, Ms Cunningham. I will always win.'

Over his shoulder, the metal gleam of the rifle is inches from my face. He reaches back down towards my ankle and I feel the gripper hum into life. When he lifts me back to standing, I struggle to take my own shaking weight before he lets go. He puts his hand on my elbow to guide me. His touch is a bullet.

I let him lead me towards the Station in silence, and every step is a test of my will against the ice. I try not to think of my bones, of the scans I would have gone for, if only Bree had been there to nag me about them. I try not to think I might be preparing, even now, to shatter.

The ice around the Station is empty, Sky and Aisi long since gone inside. I was so focused on my own balance, I didn't notice them leaving the ice, and like the staff on the deck of the *Lone Star*, it unnerves me how suddenly they can disappear. My whole body rattles. *There's always further to fall.*

Below the Station, a flight of metal steps leads up into the belly of the caterpillar. Sharma reaches down to turn off the grippers, and I resist the temptation to unbuckle them and fling them with all my strength across the ice. I'd only have to wait for him to retrieve them, so he can let us back inside. The quiet is everywhere. In a voice bolder than I feel, I say, 'How did you know?'

He starts, and there's satisfaction in knowing I've taken him by surprise.

I think of Maretta in the purple dusk, the full moon rising above the peak. I remember her constant glances towards the starboard door, as if afraid of discovery. Not checking for Sky, perhaps, but for Sharma. 'Maretta wouldn't have told you – so how did you know?'

'It's my job to protect Sky from threats, Ms Cunningham. I have my own ways of rooting them out.' I turn to climb the steps, but he grabs my wrist, and I imagine my bones crumbling beneath it. In a low voice, he says, 'I mean it. Leave her story alone.'

*

The door into the Station is heavy and round-cornered, with a large metal wheel which Sharma turns. It looks like something from a nuclear fallout shelter or perhaps a submarine, and it unlocks with a clang. We pile into an empty vestibule, where Sharma shuts the outside door behind us, before crossing to open the inside one, like an airlock on a spaceship. Later, I will learn there are two entrances like this, one at each end of the caterpillar, that they fill with snow in a storm, which blows in through miniature cracks and has to be shovelled out by hand. Not for the first time, I remember this is not a continent to which humans ever adapted to survive.

Through the inside door is a mudroom, where we take off our boots and parkas, our fleeces and waterproof trousers. The air inside the Station is a prickling heat, but even through my two pairs of socks, the floor feels cold.

Sharma turns the wheel to lock the inner door behind us. He keys something into the screen beside it, and I see the population of the modules jump from five to seven. So few, and once again, so much space stretching around us. He hands me a pair of slip-on indoor shoes from a locker in the corner – blue, like the parkas and the building and the ship, the Plan B logo embroidered in silver on the vamp. Inside the Station, the logo is everywhere – on the doors of the lockers, in the grip-circles covering the floor, etched into the glass double doors that pass us from section to section of the building.

'Bedrooms,' Sharma says, indicating numbered doors as we pass them. 'Guests only – the crew sleep on the ship. We'll be running on a skeleton team of three, though even that's far more than the Station actually requires.'

I follow him down a long corridor, galleried with huge sepia photos of early Antarctic explorers – all men, all white, all trussed up in fur and sealskin – and I want to ask whether this is how Sky sees himself. I should have asked him to paint a self-portrait instead of one of me. I'm so lost in these thoughts that it's a moment before I realise we've reached the central module, and then my thoughts soar up and away from me.

Now I'm inside, it becomes clear that we approached the Station from the back. Facing forward, a tinted window makes up one whole high wall, tessellated triangular panes of reinforced PlastiGlass, tilted at an angle, so the whole room seems to lean outwards towards the ice shelf. Beyond, everything is white and flat. I find myself staring until I've lost all perspective, till the tilted panes make me feel like I'm falling, and I have to steady myself against the back of a chair.

'Isn't it something?'

I tear my gaze inwards, to where Sky stands, arms outstretched in a now-familiar gesture, turning slowly to show off the lounge with its sparkling bar against the back wall, its art deco staircase spiralling up to a narrow gallery overhead. In pride of place, above a blazing artificial fire, is a photograph of Shackleton, dark-haired and heavy-browed, staring out beyond the camera. He looks relaxed and in control, as though he's just sat down with a drink from the bar across the room. It gives the room an unexpectedly homely, conversational feel.

'It's lovely,' I say. I hear the inadequacy of the word, and try not to think how Bree would have picked me up on it.

Sky waves this aside. 'It's a marvel.'

'Yes.'

'The Station is almost entirely self-sufficient. Renewable energy. Waste recycling. We have to use reconstituted food packs, of course, but we store enough of them on-site to feed twenty people for a full year, if we have to.'

'Or one person for twenty years.'

He picks at his cuticles in that same finger-to-finger pattern, glances towards Sharma. 'I suppose.'

245

I remember the military grade PlastiGlass of the boundary wall, the Station door like the entrance to a nuclear fallout shelter. 'It's your escape plan. Instead of a traditional bunker.'

'Something like that,' he says. Another glance towards Sharma.

'A Plan B.' I shudder at the thought. This Station must be a bleak place to spend a lonely winter, with that ice sheet stretching away into the dark, and your thoughts emptying into it day after day.

'These walls,' he says, as if keen to change the subject, 'even this glass, can withstand any storms Antarctica cares to throw at it. And if the IntuTech decides it's necessary, the entire building can be separated into modules and relocated away across the ice.'

I shudder again at the thought of this many-legged caterpillar, deciding all of a sudden one night to up and leave with all of us still inside it.

'Things are unpredictable down here,' says Maretta, which is the first moment I realise she's there. The *Lone Star* must have another X-Ped to transport the crew.

I'm aware of Sharma's eyes on me, and I try not to think about the cold in his voice, his grip holding me centimetres from the ice. Already I can feel my fear turning to fight. Already I can feel the old defiance kindling inside me. To cover it, I set my shoulders, bristle in Maretta's direction instead. 'Yes,' I tell her. 'I know.'

'Now you've seen it,' she asks, 'what do you think?'

I say, 'It's almost too good to be true.'

Maretta blanches, and I feel a reckless kind of pride in making it happen. Yet again, I have to remind myself that she's a potential ally. Out of the corner of my eye, I see Sharma glance at Sky, but Sky either doesn't notice or deliberately ignores him. The billionaire places a hand on my arm and says, 'Save it. This afternoon, I'll show you more of the site.'

'Save . . .?'

'Your verdict – on all of this.' When I still look confused, he

246

adds, 'For your thinkpiece.' He rubs his hands together, the ener-
getic surge back in the balls of his feet. 'Take some time to freshen
up – then after lunch we can visit the other side of the ice shelf.
Agreed?'

'I can't wait.'

'Excellent.'

Maretta steps forward, back to her bland professional self. 'I'll
show you to your room.'

*

Back along the corridor, with its parade of sepia explorers. We
haven't gone far when Maretta stops in front of a dusk-blue door.
Room Two, this time, and biolocked rather than intuition tech.
She indicates for me to place my thumb pad on the reader, and
the door opens.

'All your things have been brought over and unpacked.'

I'm pretty sure I left my things strewn haphazardly around the
cabin on the ship. I think of Ross's wooden seal on the bedside
table, and wish I'd hidden it in a pocket or in the lining of my
bag. I can't get used to the idea of someone packing up my things
like this, of travelling through the world free of baggage.

Maretta looks at me expectantly. I say a quick thank you, but
still she hovers by the door, and her eyes flit from end to end of
the corridor. When I ask, 'Do you want to come in?' she nods
and follows me inside.

For a moment, I think I'm back on the ship, the room a copy
of the cabin, but with deliberate mistakes: the lush rug on the
other side of the bed, the mirror above the sofa instead of behind
the dressing table, the whisky miniatures full instead of empty.
Above the bed, instead of one of Sky's icescapes, somebody has
hung his portrait of me. It glowers at its own reflection in the
mirror. The room smells of wet paint.

'Well?' Maretta stands opposite me, tapping her heel.

Beyond her, through a triple-glazed porthole, I can see out

towards the edge of the ice shelf, towards the showy blue of the sea. Heat rises from the floor. I prickle and itch in my thermals. 'I thought I was meant to be saving my assessment till I'd seen the rest?'

'I'm not talking about your sightseeing trip with Sky.'

Ross's wooden seal is on the bedside table. Belly-up, exactly the way I left it in the cabin. I hold it for a moment, rub the smooth wood under its chin, wonder why Sky's people didn't take it back for him. I put it back on the table the right way up.

Maretta draws a deep breath, like drawing a full bucket of water from a well. She forces her foot to be still. 'You called your agent.'

'I didn't tell him anything important.' The room is suddenly very bright, very still. Somewhere above us is the distant hum of the intuition tech, taking readings, processing its calculations. I'm aware of my own pulse throbbing in the tips of my fingers. 'How do you know?'

'Sharma.'

'What did he tell you?'

She hesitates. 'Only that you called him.' No mention that he overheard her moonlit confession, then. No mention of my scoop. She hurries on apologetically, as though trying to rush past something. 'Publicity and communications are vital to the success of the Plan B project. It's his job to tell me when somebody's making a call.'

'He doesn't know anything.' How easily the lie drips from my tongue.

Maretta lets out a laugh, barely controlled, a seal-like bark. 'And how are you so sure?'

'Sharma doesn't like me.'

'Of course he doesn't fucking like you!' She's flushed, now, sinew a taut cord at her temple. After Sharma's threats on the ice, every part of me itches to fight, to claw back as much precious control as I can, and this – this is power: to reduce a person to this and feel yourself in control the whole time. This is three dots of coffee staining a pristine tablecloth, and being the one to make it happen. This is a world you can rebuild any way you choose. She says, 'You're the reason he grew up on the floating factories.'

The back of my neck prickles where my portrait gazes dismissively over it. I draw myself up. 'I hardly think— '

'The reason his family are dead – his and countless others – because you did what you always do: turned your back as soon as a bigger story came along.'

Not that simple. Obviously. I was a public figure by that point, not your general strength-in-numbers protestor – and there were always more campaigns to lead, more fights to put my name to. It made sense to step away from them at the right time. To delegate. The details were someone else's job, not mine. Maretta tenses as though she's said too much, so I make her wait till the silence has become uncomfortable, unbearable, till I can feel her desperation for me to break it. Then I say, 'And yet you brought me your story all the same.'

'Isn't that what you've always been about? The next big story?' From her pocket, she pulls the small silver nugget of a data chip – modern and sleek, like everything Maretta does. The Cirrus Holdings logo etched into one side, the word SECURE printed on the other. 'Getting the scoop at all costs?'

Is it? I think of AJ, ignoring me for years. His casual demand for me to lay my past on the line. His desperation for the young and new. 'And that . . .?'

'It's an offline data cache,' she tells me. 'Coded, of course, but all here. All the evidence I have.' She tucks the data chip back into her pocket, gives the smallest of shrugs, doesn't meet my eye. 'All I need.'

'You want me to break the story.'

'Do I?'

'That's why you told me last night – why you're showing me

the evidence.' It all makes sense now; no wonder she's chosen to make herself vulnerable. I think of AJ saying this is my brand. How it's perfect for me. Back in the limelight, rebuilding my name. 'You want to break the story, and you want my help to do it.'

She doesn't answer, just looks at me as though I'm a problem she desperately needs to solve.

'And the consequences? The damage we'd be causing?'

'*That's* why I told you – to see what you would decide.' If Maretta and I were fighting for the upper hand, then this, I think, is the moment I win: a strand of hair comes loose at her temple; a flush of colour across her cheeks; her face taut, like it's been hitched on barbed metal.

'So you're after my advice.'

Unimaginative, that's Maretta's problem. If I'm going to do this, there's no room for a lack of imagination. Not if I'm going to win. My fall to the ice feels distant, now, Sharma's grip on my wrist turned ghostlike compared to the physical possibility of that data chip. Maretta, with her hero worship and history lessons, might think my career has been about uncovering the truth – but it's always the fight that matters, in the end. The ability to butt up against opposing forces and emerge victorious every time.

Almost every time.

Maretta's loose strand of hair sways in the updraught from the heated floor. I tell her, 'Give me time to think.'

HELSINKI

To understand what happened, you have to know that I was in Helsinki for a reason, and that the reason was work. The separation of Church and State – that's how Noah described it on the expedition all those years ago. Bree in Boston and Ross with his family back in Frisco. Me in Helsinki with a job to do.

I sat in the hotel room, sticky in my travel clothes. I kicked off my shoes and spread my toes into the faux-fur rug. I poured myself a drink.

Later, I called Bree.

*

When I landed in Helsinki, it was at a large terminal outside the city – new since the last time I'd visited – where I was met by a greeter and two bored paparazzi. I remember the greeter asked if I was ready to go, or whether there were any calls I needed to make first. No, I said. I'd call when I reached the hotel.

Do I remember the ride into the city? If I make the effort, I can conjure a road, junctions, signs in a language I can't read, industrial lots morphing into houses and flats and jumbled office buildings, into the sleeker constructions of the city proper. I can just about recall the IntuTaxi navigating all of this, while I sat behind the blacked-out windows in the creaking cold of its leather interior and put my trust in its algorithms to get me there safely. But I've ridden in a number of IntuTaxis over the years, through countless cities, and who's to say this memory is the right one? At some point, the taxi must have stopped. At some point, a greeter from the hotel must have held the door as I got out, stiff from the journey, my body already feeling things more than it used to. At some point, I must have checked into the stifle of that rose-scented suite overlooking the city skyline. At some point shortly after that, I made the call.

*

We'd arrived at Boston air terminal together, me and Bree, in another IntuTaxi. An extravagant expense, given the distance from the house, but by this point trains were unreliable, the buses overcrowded – and anyway, it was important to arrive at the airport in style. We would be greeted by a throng of vid-streamers, news reporters, Holo-makers. In Helsinki, the set-up for the summit would be complete, the less important guests beginning to arrive. In the other direction, across the country in Frisco, the rain must already have been falling.

The destination light blinked on the dashboard to show we'd arrived, as reporters crowded the IntuTaxi doors. In the back, I leaned over to kiss Bree goodbye. A slow kiss, sensual, one hand on the door handle, the other on Bree's cheek. A performance, and one we'd been cultivating for years.

'Desire and envy,' Bree once told me, 'are powerful weapons.' When I'd asked how she knew this, she'd said, 'I teach elementary school. No better place in the world to study human behaviour.' In all the years we were together, I never questioned that she always thought of human behaviour as a fight.

I pulled back from the kiss. I told her I'd see her soon. Then I stepped out of the IntuTaxi and away from her for the final time.

As the media crowded around me, as they pressed me with

mics and cameras, Holo-makers and vids, I fixed my gaze on the terminal door, parted them like waves. This was another performance, another thing Bree and I had cultivated through long rehearsal: to walk as if I had never been afraid of falling.

When I reached the terminal door, I finally turned. This, too, was planned: making them wait, making them follow. They asked, 'What will you say to the world, Ms Cunningham?' 'Do you think the leaders will listen, Ms Cunningham?' 'Ms Cunningham, how will you convince the corporations?' I don't remember everything I said. Something about hope. Something about legacy and the future of the planet. I know I mentioned Ross, how I had recently visited him outside Frisco, how it had been a reminder of what the cause was all about. That, I told them, was who I was fighting for: for my son and for my grandchildren; not for my own future, but for theirs.

*

In the air terminal lounge, the state-of-the-art IntuTech system raised the temperature and lowered the music, as I sank back into the purple sofa and tried to memorise my speech. I never gave a speech without having it written out in front of me, just in case, but I liked to be able to make eye contact while I spoke. This was something else I had learned from Bree: as in an elementary school classroom, so at an international summit. They have to believe that *you* believe what you're saying.

Servers brought me champagne, which I sipped, slowly, savouring the one glass I would allow myself before the flight. They brought tiny terracotta pots of spiced olives, anchovies, miniature stacks of crispbread, razor-sliced salmon, caviar, artisanal cheese. My fingers smeared prints on the chrome edge of the table, which I wiped with a napkin. The crumbs I made, I left for others to sweep.

When I stood to board my flight, a server approached, ready to clear the table, and wished me luck in Helsinki – a breach of regulations, but still, I smiled indulgently at her.

'Maybe if you win you could campaign for something other than yourself.'

'Excuse me?'

Her face was hard, her voice low. 'Flood relief, climate refuge, safer housing – or are the rest of us not glamorous enough?'

She breathed quickly, her eyes blazing – which is maybe why I noticed her irises, one brown, one flecked with shades of green and gold. I drew myself up and said, 'You have such beautiful eyes,' then left while she tried to work out how to be offended. I made a mental note to report her later.

Escorted by the security woman the lounge provided, I crossed the air terminal on the raised glass walkway reserved for people like me. Below, scatterings of other travellers ate and browsed and killed time on their vids, while they waited to be called forward, dark-clothed and spidery against the polished floor. My shoes clicked against the tempered glass. When my vid rang, I pulled it from my pocket with the casual flare of someone who knows they're being watched. I smiled apologetically at my escort, then glanced down at the screen. I remember Bree's photo glowing back at me – a younger Bree from before the illness, standing in the soft slanting light of the old Boston apartment, holding Ross as a toddler against her hip.

'Hey! Did you make it home OK?'

Bree's voice came through high-pitched and disjointed. 'Have you been watching the news?'

'Is it the summit?' My stomach flipped. All that planning, all that security – we were so close . . .

She said, 'It's Keira.'

'What?' I reached the steps at the end of the elevated walkway and stopped. Stood.

'There was a flash flood warning, evacuation mandate. Ross's house – the whole block – collapsed from the foundations, they're saying a mudslide.' Bree's voice, real and not real, a smudge against the glass and chrome.

256

'Ross?'

'Safe. He got out, they all got out— '

I felt my shoulders sag. 'Thank god.'

'Ivy, listen. Keira – Keira went back for the dog. They couldn't stop her, you know how quick she is. They've got her to hospital, but it's a bleed on the brain, they're not sure what they can do.'

I stared into the downward pull of the stairwell. 'And the dog?' God knows why I asked that – I didn't care about the dog, never even liked it. I couldn't think straight and it was the first thing that came into my head. 'Sorry.'

'What do you think?' Bree said. 'The dog got out. Course it fucking did.'

'God.'

'Yes.'

I listened to Bree's ragged breathing down the vid, let it fill my head till I became aware of my security escort, waiting. I said, 'They're boarding the flight.'

'Ivy— '

'Keep me posted.'

There was quiet on the other end of the vid.

'Give my love to Ross.' I'd said that so many times before, it fell so easily from my tongue. I said, 'I love you.' Bree hung up without saying it back.

*

Down the steps, the security escort at my elbow as if I might fall. I wouldn't fall. I might. The house crumbling as the ground shifted out from under it, a mess of mud and metal and concrete dust and furniture and polluted water. Through the extended tunnel, across the lipped threshold, onto the plane. Keira on the operating table under the glare of the lights. *Bleed on the brain, not sure what they can do.* Keira just days ago, asleep with her head on the table in the yard, the beloved dog at her feet. *Give my love to Ross.* Ross as a child, the same sleep-filled eyes, the same tired rubbing at their corners. *A mudslide, collapsed from the foundations, the whole block.* On the plane, in my seat, a glass of something on a silver tray. I synced my vid with the flight systems and a map appeared on the screen. *Couldn't stop her . . . They're boarding the flight.* The small icon of a plane hovered over Boston air terminal, at one end of a curving red arc across the northern hemisphere. The flight path, up the North American coast, across the North Atlantic and down into Europe. At its other end, the destination star was a bright pulse over Helsinki.

THE PROBLEM OF THE CHILLERS

I strip off my layers. All this dressing and undressing, over and over – it's exhausting. I leave my thermals in a heap on the floor and change into something more casual. On second thoughts, I pick up my thermals and dump them, unfolded, in a drawer. The air in the Station is stripped so clean I can almost taste the filters – which is ironic, considering outside is probably the freshest air on the planet. I already have the beginnings of a headache, and I can feel the miniatures calling to me. I open one and drink half, then put it back on the shelf. The painting stares past me from above the bed. I knock back the rest of the miniature.

I take a long shower before lunch, to try to wash away the ice shelf and the hum of the grippers. I shut my eyes and tip my head back under the stream. I can't stop shivering. I try to tuck in my shoulders so that every bit of me is under the water, but my body's too much.

I think about getting out and calling Ross, but for the first time, I wonder what the point would be. Then I remember Sharma, monitoring. Sharma, tugging on the threads, reporting my communications – or some of them – back to Maretta. I remember that lag in the connection on the ship, that feeling of pushing through, as though somebody was piggybacking on the signal – though god knows how he managed to break through

261

my vid's security. What else has he seen and heard? Steam billows through the bathroom, but I'm still cold. Perhaps I had it wrong from the start. Perhaps Sharma is the spider, Sky the caught moth.

I get out. I stand for a long time, wrapped in a towel, dripping onto the rug in the middle of the bedroom. I stare through the porthole at the edge of the ice sheet, the glinting sea beyond.

*

Beyond the central lounge, I find a dining room, decorated like the one on the ship: that same grandiose antique style, that same extravagant lighting and heavy table set for lunch. Through the incongruously antique kitchen doors, I can hear murmured voices and the clanging of equipment. The chef, presumably, and at least one of the waiters. They must have come ashore with Maretta. My stomach has started to grumble. Calories burn off quicker in this kind of cold, and it's a good few hours since breakfast, but when I check the time, I'm still early, and the kitchen doors are locked.

The ceiling in the dining room is lower, the window less tilted, but the ice still dominates the room. It's become a bright white siren call, and I turn away from it back towards the lounge – but from here, too, the ice shelf glitters in the midday sun, the spidery shadow of the Station stretching away across it like a summons.

While I wait for lunch to be called, I climb the twisting stair-case at the back of the room, up to the metal-railinged gallery. There are four doors up here, two on either side. The first leads to a snug, filled with books on natural history and polar explorers. Shackleton, I notice, has a whole section to himself, and I'm starting to wonder if it's just hero worship, or if Sky has a bit of a thing for him. Beside the snug, in a room facing out towards the sea, is a domed observatory, with a heavy telescope for exploring the unpolluted night sky, and star maps to guide its users to basic constellations: Ursa Major; upside-down Orion; the

262

Southern Cross. Across the gallery, a small gym overlooks the ice shelf.

The fourth door leads to an office, where an array of vid screens shows the Station's corridors and mudroom and lounge. Behind them, a wall of dials and blinking lights relays the wider site readings from the centre of operations in the caterpillar's head. The room is so busy, it's a moment before I notice the man, and when I do, I jump. Then my brain catches up with my instincts, and I realise it's Sharma. I hold my head aloft, root my weight through the balls of my feet, solid now, no ice to slip out from under me. I ignore my racing heart, make an effort to fill my lungs, languorously and with great appetite, to stake a claim on the purified air. It feels good, standing over him like this. I allow myself to revel in it. 'So this is where you hide yourself.'

'Ms Cunningham.' He leans back in his chair as snatches of other rooms flicker in and out of shot around him. I have a sudden flashback to the night of the storm, the cubby in the bowels of the ship and all the pieces of my life projected around me on the walls – and right then, certain as breathing, I know it was Sharma. A spider weaving a web of my past – but why?

'Don't let me keep you from . . . whatever it is you do when you're not threatening people.'

'So you can go back to prowling?' He says this with raised eyebrows and his usual flat smile. One of the screens flashes up the corridor outside my room. He shuts it off.

'Exploring.' I over-pronounce every consonant. I turn to leave.

'Ms Cunningham, wait.' He taps one finger against the arm of his chair as his gaze travels over me. On the largest screen is a view of the external staircase, leading down onto the ice. As I watch, it flickers, then transforms into the deck of the *Lone Star*. On another wall, a livestream display shows there are seven people in the building. Me, Sharma, Sky and Maretta. Three of the crew. 'Let me escort you back down to lunch.'

I feel like a specimen pinned to a board. I shrug my shoulders, like trying to shake out trapped wings. 'I can find it myself.'

He smiles, makes a show of shutting off the screens and logging out of the systems. He makes another show of unlocking a cupboard under the desk and taking out his rifle. Then he says, 'Nevertheless.'

He doesn't wait for an answer. He leads me out onto the gallery, then places a hand in the small of my back to hold me there, teetering at the top of the spiral staircase, gripping the railing to stop myself plummeting to the siren call of the ice. A gunshot touch – but my head is still held high. Taut, like rigor mortis.

'What do you think?'

My whole body is caught between fighting him, and the flight towards that beckoning view. From somewhere, I hear myself say, 'Stunning.'

'I'm glad you like it.' And he's smiling again, all bite, all tunnel-deep eyes. But then his hand is gone from my back, and I'm carrying myself in state down the stairs, Maretta's data chip knocking against my chest through my breast pocket, and Sharma is just a man. Just another obstacle. Another fight, put there for me to win.

LEARNED
BEHAVIOUR

It was the side room of a local church, at an advice session recommended by Bree's doctor. This was in the early days of her illness, back when we still attended these things together, so we sat in a circle with people much older than us, all on rickety plastic chairs that trembled whenever we moved. Into the middle of the circle, a HoloPlayer cast its repeating footage of an elderly woman carrying a cup of tea, stumbling, going slack as she hit the floor. Then the clip looped back and she was standing, ready to begin the whole process again. A young man (a boy, really – I wanted to ask if he was qualified for this) twiddled his lanyard around his finger as he spoke: 'You're all getting older now, ladies.'

There were a couple of men in the group, too, but apparently he had learned his script by heart and was determined to carry on regardless.

'Your bodies aren't as resilient as they used to be. What this means,' he said, 'is that you're going to break more easily.'

I wanted to throw one of the heavy-duty coffee cups at his head, to see how resilient the younger generation really were, but the rest of the group were nodding. The woman on the HoloPlayer stumbled, collapsed to the ground.

'The trick,' he said, 'is not to brace. That's how those poor bones end up cracking. You put out your hand to stop yourself, and snap! There goes your wrist. The trick,' he went on, 'is simply to let it happen. If you feel yourself falling, go slack. Offer no resistance, and let gravity take you. OK?'

He gestured towards the HoloPlayer, and we watched the holographic woman trip and fall like a rag doll. I remember thinking: this is bullshit. I remember thinking that resistance was written through me like a stick of rock, and if I ever reached this stage, I would keep on fighting even if it shattered every bone in my body.

'Good,' he said. 'Now, we're going to practise relaxing in our chairs. That's right. Close your eyes, and let's imagine the way our bodies feel when we fall asleep.'

It was only later, when Bree was in the home, that I understood the difference: how, if she fell, she had people who would care enough to pick her back up. For me, alone in the big house outside Boston – and, later, in the Edinburgh flat – there was no one.

*

I don't say much over lunch. His meetings done for the morning, Sky is cresting a wave of enthusiasm. So I let him talk – about technology, the future, his plans for the expansion of the site. Along the table, Maretta eats in silence. Sharma stands guard beside the swing doors, through which the piercing-scarred waiter, Kip, delivers us our food – today a fiery Thai curry, another country's cuisine laid claim to by Sky's chef. I try to eat as though Sharma isn't there, to focus on the grain of the reconstituted rice. When that fails, I try to imagine increasingly unlikely ways of making him disappear.

Into the silence, Sky enthuses to nobody in particular about the upstairs observatory. On a clear night, he says, the stars down here are like nothing else. 'We tend not to think of polar explorers in the dark like that – probably because historically, night time was so much harder to photograph – but imagine how it must have been, in the days before satellite comms, alone with your team in the middle of the ice and the whole sky alive overhead. The Milky Way,' he says. 'Down here it's like you could fall into it and swim.'

*

After lunch, we layer up and descend the metal staircase. As I take Sky's offered hand to guide me across the ice, to help me down towards the X-Ped, I try to ignore Sharma, stepping out ahead of us. Clouds have rolled in, and the ice this afternoon is grey and heavy under the covered sky. I focus on the rhythm of the grippers. *Ready–lift, drop–re-engage, ready–lift, drop–re-engage.* I take them off as soon as we reach the edge of the ice.

The speed and spray of the boat revive me. Sharma steers us around the promontory, Aisi perched at the front again, scanning for ice. I glance at Maretta, her blank stare, her refusal to let herself be awed. Out in the open, the waves jolt and slap at the prow, a last-ditch reminder that this place does not belong to us, before we turn back into the shelter of another bay.

Here, the landscape is a world of sharp distinctions. At the head of the bay, the ice shelf butts up against the edge of a glacier, and the grubby grey stripe of a moraine forms a dark ridge between them. The water is littered with breakaway: a sprawling city of ice floes, which the X-Ped has to slow to navigate.

Sky turns to shout over the engine, 'The entire ice shelf is within Plan B boundaries. We have Chillers all along the edges, and underwater – but the centre is kept frozen by the volume of the thing itself. It's the first step towards being self-sustaining.'

His gesture takes in the broad sweep of the bay, and I have to remind myself that this is just another item in his collection, like the scrimshaw and Shackleton's boot. A showpiece. Between the ice floes, the water is flat and dark as oil. When the X-Ped slows, I can see tiny discs of ice suspended like frozen jellyfish in the dark, waiting to freeze into a single mass. It looks so certain of itself that it's hard to believe any of it could ever disappear. I scan for wildlife: a couple of penguins on a distant floe – Adélies, maybe, though it's hard to tell at this distance – and closer in, a darker vortex that might be a seal turning below the surface. I watch the patch of water, but nothing appears.

We bump against a rocky shore, which rises into a steep ridge, packed with snow and ice, the white algae-tinged to delicate pink. The beach is littered with frozen spheres – from marbles to glittering globes – where the wind and sun and sea have carved away the ice's sharp edges. When we clamber out of the X-Ped, Sky places a foot on one, like a painting of a conquistador with the world at his feet. The hollow sphere cracks and his foot crashes through to the stones below.

Sharma helps Aisi draw the X-Ped up onto the beach. As they unload shovels and set about clearing a path, Maretta asks, 'Do you think you might make it to the top of that ridge?'

'Yes,' I tell her. Again, I want to ask how old she thinks I am. 'I think I can just about make it.'

'Wonderful.' And she goes to direct the two men shovelling the ice. As though they need any direction. They work efficiently, drawing a dark line up the beach towards the snow.

On land, Aisi's movements are less darting and birdlike. Instead, he walks like the rest of the crew, his body rolling and pitching as though riding out a storm: bend to shovel, straighten to throw the ice aside. Aisi and Sharma, the same listing gait, the same low centre of gravity. It's only now, seeing them work together, that I realise why: because these are both men who have spent their lives on ships. Men whose every movement has been defined by the tug and swell of the ocean. No wonder they walk as though the ground beneath their feet is uncertain.

Out of the corner of my eye, I catch Sky watching me. 'Maretta's very solicitous,' he says. 'Towards you.'

We walk along the water's edge. I smash icy golf balls under my boots. At the edge of my vision is the pitching movement of the men, clearing the path. 'I don't need her to be solicitous.'

'We all need help sometimes.'

I try to pick my way between the littered baubles, but my boots are too big, too clunky, and I end up crushing them all the same. The scrape of shovels carries towards us along the beach.

'You know, it was Maretta who suggested bringing you here?'

I pull up short. Right from the start, I've had the impression she resented my presence. 'Why?'

'Those articles, those *opinion pieces* – you were becoming a nuisance. I hope you don't mind me saying.'

'I'm flattered you noticed.'

'Don't be.' He bends to pick up an apple-sized ball of ice. 'They were more annoying than damaging. A fly in the ointment. Maretta wanted to give you a second chance – an opportunity to get you on-side. I suppose we both did.' He cups the ice in his gloved hands, inspects it as though looking into a crystal ball. When I take it from him, it sits cloudy and delicate in my palm. 'I didn't understand it at first.'

'You know she used to have my photo on her vid screen?' I try to keep the pride from my voice, but it creeps in. The icy globe is a chill ache through my gloves. When I drop it, it smashes spectacularly against the stones. 'I was a spokesperson for the barrio regeneration project – something of a hero for her, apparently.'

'Until you weren't.'

I shrug, toe at another icy bauble with my thick-treaded boots. 'We all have phases we grow out of.'

'Did she tell you she wrote to you?'

'About Plan B?'

'As a child.' He glances up the beach to where she stands, all efficiency and poise, watching the two men work. 'After you bowed out, the barrio rebuilds were done on the cheap – you know how it is, governments awarding expensive contracts to their friends and their friends pocketing the difference.' He speaks as though he has personal experience of this kind of transaction. 'It was a disaster in the making. When she was twelve, maybe thirteen, there was an electrical fire. They lost half the neighbourhood –

271

school, community centre, almost everyone she knew – and she wrote to you. Her hero. She wrote and asked you for help.'

Despite the cold, I feel hot and itchy, claustrophobic in all my layers. 'I used to get a lot of begging letters,' I say, then wish I hadn't used the word *begging*. Further up the beach, the scrape of shovels pauses. The men have reached the snow line now, and their work is slower. Sharma leans against his shovel, deep in conversation with Maretta. I take a deep breath that sears the inside of my throat. 'What happened?'

'I did.' Sky says this matter-of-factly, not boastful, just narrating events. 'Cirrus was barely more than a start-up back then – we needed a site big enough to test and develop the IntuTech. We funded the rebuild on the condition we could install intuition tech throughout the barrio and harvest the data.' He presses his heel against the ice until fault lines appear, then pulls back. 'So really I ought to thank you.'

'Opportunistic,' I want to say. 'Manipulative. Unethical.' I don't say any of this.

Sky places a hand against my elbow, grips hard as though to hold me back from danger. His face clouds, fills with something hidden and tense as he teeters on the edge of speaking. 'Ivy, listen . . .'

From above comes the continuous scraping of shovels, loud against the quiet of the bay. It strikes me that they're probably doing this for me, that this path-clearing is another example of Maretta's over-attentiveness and that there are any number of reasons why I should object – but after this morning, I'm in no hurry to walk across bare ice again. When I turn back to face Sky, the clouds are gone from his face, and in their place is a locked door.

A thin mewing leaks into the air, small and sad, like an abandoned cat.

'What were you about to tell me?'

'You hear that?' he asks. The mewing stops, then starts again, louder and more plaintive, It makes me think of Ross, crying in the night. Sky looks along the beach, to where a cluster of ice

272

floes have jammed themselves against the rocks. 'Want to go see?'

Before I can answer, he's picking a route along the beach, between the ice. I follow more cautiously, pushing my feet into the sliding stones till I feel them anchor. Ice and shingle tumble against my boots, almost loud enough to cover the small animal cry, the scrape of shovels.

I'm only two steps behind Sky when he turns and whispers, 'Look!'

Ahead of us, rafts of ice have gathered in the shelter of the rocks and jammed up against the shallowing breach. Out on the floes, a few metres from the rocky beach, is a small mound of mottled grey fur, white underbelly bright against the ice. A seal pup. When it opens its mouth to mew, I can see the tender pink gums, the plaintive tongue.

Sky pulls out his vid and trains it on the pup. 'It's a leopard seal,' he tells me. 'Analyse.'

A string of diagnostics flashes up on screen: LOW RISK. UNWEANED. MINIMUM CHANCE OF SURVIVAL.

The seal mews again. Away up the beach, the shovels keep scraping. Sky takes a tentative step.

'Don't— '

The ice creaks under his weight, then holds firm. He looks from me to the seal, weighing us up. I see the decision form behind his eyes. 'It must have been abandoned,' he says, and he takes another step. The seal pup pleads with its oil-deep eyes.

'Let's wait for the others.'

'I want to see.' He shuffles out towards the pup. The ice creaks, settles, creaks again, tests its limits against his weight.

'Careful— '

He turns and grins at me. Beneath the usual calculating eyes, his expression is wild and joyful. So easy, in this moment, to picture him as a young boy, bright-eyed in his bedsheet tent, lost in the thrill of adventure stories. Or splashing through the shallows in the beach dome – glitter of the water, skinny yellow trunks, the surf dragging him under. He turns to me and grins.

And the mother seal pushes from the water, sleek grey head and scream of teeth.

'Sky!'

Is that what I shout? The seal must be three metres long, her wide jaw snapping, her breath furious on the frozen air – and I'm running, ready to throw my body between him and the seal – running – as the ice cracks like a gunshot and the seal falls back. Long enough for me to get to Sky, to grab at his sleeve as if my touch might save him. The whole world hangs in the balance as I wait for the seal to launch herself at us again.

But the seal is still. Her eyes start to film, to grey into the colour of her mottled body. A thin red stain leaks from her neck onto the ice.

My hand is still on Sky's sleeve, still holding him back from her steel-trap jaw. I become aware of the silence. An enormous, ringing silence.

The path-clearing scrape has stopped. Halfway up the ridge, Sharma's rifle is still raised. Behind him, Aisi leans on his shovel, Maretta's arms hang slack by her side, and the shape of the cry still reverberating in my mouth is not Sky's name at all. 'Ross!' I screamed, as I threw myself towards him. 'Ross.'

*

Some facts about the leopard seal:

The leopard seal looks as though she's smiling – but this is only the way her mouth has evolved, to allow wider opening of her jaws.

The female leopard seal is more powerful than the male. While the pup is young, she will protect it, fiercely, until the pup is able to protect itself. Then she will leave.

Unlike the other principal Antarctic hunter, the orca, the leopard seal is not found in packs or family groups, and generally prefers her own company to the company of others. When she becomes lonely, she will call out across the vast icy distance. She

274

will call, and then she will listen through the quiet for a response. If no response is heard, she will call and call and call again.

*

Sky kneels on the ice, one glove off, his bone-white hand on the mother's mottled underbelly. The seal shudders, then goes still. His lips are moving, but no sound comes out. When I place my hand on his shoulder, he reaches up to take it: one hand on mine, the other on the body of the seal.

'I'm so sorry.'

'It's not your fault.'

Later, I won't remember which of us said what. Behind us, the seal pup mews.

*

When the others arrive, I snatch my hand away. Maretta's face is loose as she stares at the seal, flung back against the ice. Sharma has slung the rifle back across his body. He reaches out to help Sky to his feet.

'I'm OK. Thank you.'

With half a glance at me, Sharma says, 'I never miss.'

There's no sound but the sound of our own breathing, the creak of ice under our boots. We should move. I say, 'What about the pup?'

The pup is quiet now, eyes closed as it rests its head on the ice. I wonder why it didn't take to the sea when it heard the shot, but perhaps it's too young. Sharma looks at it, then looks away. When Sky speaks, his voice comes thick and quiet. 'Can we save it?'

Maretta's face still hangs loose, and suddenly, it's all too easy to picture her as a frightened child, her home destroyed, community gutted by fire. Sky never said whether that included her own family. Aisi glances at Sharma, then gives a small shake of his head.

'Maretta?'

She starts, stands taller. I watch her fit herself back into the role of overly efficient project director. 'There's nothing we can

275

do for it,' she says. She holds her voice tightly, like a sharpened knife. 'I'm sorry.'

Shaking, Sky points his vid at the pup again. Then he slips it back into his pocket and looks away. I can't stop thinking about the words he showed me on the screen. *Alone. Unweaned. Minimum chance of survival.*

'We don't have the facilities to care for it,' Maretta says. 'Our interference would do the project more harm than good.'

It's Sharma who suggests putting it out of its misery. The rifle barrel must still be warm. The mother seal's blood still seeps across the white.

There's a long silence. The ice under our boots threatens and creaks. Eventually, Sky says, 'Leopard seal pups wean at just a few weeks old, right? There's a chance it might still survive in the wild?' He glances at me. 'Even without its mother.'

'Yes, of course.' I watch the way Maretta's face glasses over as she says this, and I know she's lying.

Aisi says, 'We need to step back onto the beach.'

'What?' Sky's gaze skips over the body of the mother, and Aisi looks again towards Sharma.

'He's right. This ice isn't stable, and we need to get back to the Station.'

'But we've just got here.'

Aisi shakes his head at me. 'We need to get you both treated. For shock.'

Am I in shock? I don't think so – though I can hear my heart beating inside my skull and I can't remember if that's normal. 'Couldn't a couple of us stay?' I ask, 'To keep watch on the pup?' I'm not sure how long I expect us to wait. Maretta's right: there's nothing we can do for it.

Maretta shakes her head. 'We stick together for safety. Weather can change suddenly out here.'

I know, I want to scream at her. I know about the bloody weather.

But Sky's face is still tight, and maybe he is in shock. Maybe he does need to go back to the Station. So I let Aisi guide me off the ice, let Sky be led meekly by Sharma behind. We head back along the beach. No longer careful how we pick our way, we shatter icy baubles under our boots. As we board the X-Ped, I hear the seal pup start to mew again. Then Sharma pulls the cord to start the engine, and the sound is lost.

DID YOU HEAR THE ONE ABOUT THE SILENCE?

I sink a miniature and let myself fall back onto the pillows.

I close my eyes and try counting back from one hundred. I try to become aware of the weight of each of my limbs in turn. I try to visualise a candle flame and meditate. Nothing works.

When we arrived back in the mudroom of the Station, a crew member was waiting with a medical bag, ready to check us for shock, concussion, hypothermia – anything that might have befallen us on our trip across the bay. A quiet man, with another rolling gait from a life spent at sea. Brawny. A dusting of stubble along his jawline. It was a moment before I could place him: the cleaner outside the lounge in the sailor outfit; the crew member cleaning the ice on deck, the morning after the pass-chip disappeared. Two days ago, although already it feels like a lifetime. Cleaner, handyman – and now doctor? I suppose I shouldn't be surprised. It was the same on the expedition with the Foundation, everyone doubling up on roles; it's always paid to be efficient down here, even with people. Still, it was unnerving, the way the crew shifted from one role to another, morphing into new roles whenever they arrived at the Station, before vanishing back to the ship. Like kneeling on an ice floe, feeling what you thought was solid ground shift and disintegrate beneath you.

The crew member pronounced me fine – nothing a rest

wouldn't improve – and handed me a pack of sleeping tabs. Then he moved on to Sky, while Maretta helped me with my outdoor layers. 'I can do it myself,' I wanted to tell her – but I let her fix the stuck zip on my parka, let her hand me my Plan B-branded slippers as though I was incapable of performing basic tasks alone. In return, I took her indoor suit jacket from its locker – slower than necessary, perhaps, but why not play into her expectations – and carefully and solicitously helped her into it.

I open my eyes and catch sight of my staring portrait, and roll the other way. I'm too hot for sleep. My skin itches from switching between bitter cold and dry artificial heat. I take a crystal glass from the shelf at the back of the desk and pour in another of the miniatures. The icebox underneath is empty – so I sip the whisky without. One of these days, I tell myself, I'll learn to ration. The data chip I took from Maretta's jacket pocket is a small silver nugget in my palm.

Such an easy thing, so small to take and slip into my own pocket, so big an impact if I make its data public. *When* I make it public. I'm tempted to unlock it now, to sync it up to my vid and start decoding, but Sharma will be perched once more in his web of screens above the lounge, and I can't risk him seeing. Better just to sit with it for now, let it niggle at the corner of my brain till I get back to Edinburgh.

I put the data chip back in my pocket. I won't leave this one lying around. I won't make the same mistake twice.

While I finish the whisky, I send a message to Ross: a close-up of the bedroom ceiling, so close it could be a blank page, or an aerial shot of an ice sheet. I don't speak. I let the brightness speak for itself. Halfway through recording, the vid beeps twice and the message cuts out. A signal glitch, maybe, or a technical error. I try not to think about Sharma, watching, interfering from the room at the top of the metal staircase.

I sit on the edge of the bed and try to picture all the messages I've ever sent to Ross: a glass of ice; the Beagle Channel at night;

the rusting red bridge across the Firth. They stack up against each other, jostle for space on the vid I know he no longer uses – stuffed at the back of a kitchen drawer, maybe, or in the pocket of an old coat, the messages accumulating, unwatched, as he and his family sleep through the humid Abu Dhabi night.

*

I find Sky in the lounge, his feet tucked under him on one of the easy chairs facing the window. His body is an empty food packet stranded on a beach, and he cradles a bowl-sized coffee. I can smell the whisky in it from across the room.

'How are you doing?'

At my voice, he looks up. His face is wan in the washed-out light, and dark smudges drag at his eyes. I sit opposite him, my back to where the wind flurries snowflakes from the roof, dances them down to the ice. There's no steam coming from his coffee, no way to know how long he's been sitting here.

'I'm sorry,' I say. 'About what happened.'

He shrugs.

I tell him, 'You weren't to know.'

For a long time, I think he isn't going to speak. When he does, his voice is hollow. 'All I want is one little corner of the world.' He sits low in the chair. Where the light from the fire catches his face, he looks dirty, his cheeks stained with old tear tracks. He looks as though someone has pulled the ground out from underneath him. *There's always further to fall.* He says, 'Sharma told me you still leave vid messages for your son.'

The change of topic makes me start. 'Sharma shouldn't spy on people.'

'It's why I let you take the seal. It's why I showed it to you in the first place.'

At first, I think he's talking about the seal pup, keening from the ice floe beside the body of its mother, and I don't understand.

283

Then I realise the seal he means is Ross's wooden carving, and my heart is a glacier crumbling. *If you feel yourself falling, go slack.*

'What you said the other night,' he says, 'about redemption.'

That night was the night we drank and talked about the expedition. The night I woke up clutching the seal so tightly, it left purple grooves across my palm. The night I barely remember. 'What did I say?'

'It's why this place is called Plan B. A chance to acknowledge our mistakes and make things right. I let you take the seal because I had to know if you felt guilty.'

'A guilting?'

'No.' Without looking at me, he says, 'When my dad first disowned me, I thought one day he would make amends, or I would. I thought eventually the money would matter less than all those years we were still family.' His knuckles are white around the coffee cup, and he presses into his thumbpad with his fingernail. 'But the longer it's gone on, the less I believe it.'

'He's still alive?' All this time, Sky's spoken as though his father is already dead. My stomach clenches as I imagine Ross talking the same way about me.

'You're not the only parent to have abandoned your son.'

'I didn't abandon him.' I want to tell him about Bree's funeral, how Ross was the one who turned away from me, how I've been trying to get back through to him ever since – but then I see his face, expression collapsing in on itself, and something clicks. 'That's why you were cold to me. When I first came aboard – it wasn't the articles. It was about your father.' The painting, hanging in my room: brutal, unforgiving, Sky's hatred and resentment bleeding through with every brushstroke. 'It was about my son.'

'All I've ever wanted from him is an apology.' For a second, I think he's talking about Ross, and my heart skips. Then I realise he's barely registered what I've said, that he's still thinking about his father. 'One apology, and all these unspeaking years would be forgotten.'

284

The wind picks up and the snow from the roof dazzles in the artificial light. 'There's still time.' Even as the words come out, I know they're empty.

He says, 'Maybe we shouldn't have been there,' and it's a moment before I realise he's back to talking about this afternoon on the ice floe, and the seal pup abandoned to the elements. Once again I have that image of him as a small boy, clinging to his forbidden ambitions in his father's high-rise flat. He says, 'I used to love all those stories, explorers battling nature to survive. Accomplishing great feats. Testing themselves in environments not safe for human habitation.'

'Shackleton,' I say, with a nod to the portrait above the fire. 'The Boss.'

Sky ignores me, stares down into his undrunk coffee. 'I shouldn't have pushed it.'

I reach out and touch his elbow. He ignores this as well. Through my pocket, the data chip digs into my leg. Again, I say, 'You weren't to know.'

'Wasn't I?' He navigates his vid to show me the rest of the reading from this afternoon. LEOPARD SEAL PUP. HEALTHY. MOTHER LIKELY CLOSE BY. He taps his thumb against the side and the screen goes blank. 'I wanted to see how you would react.'

What was it he said this morning on the beach – already a world away – how he needed to be certain he could trust me? 'A test.'

He shrugs. 'I'm sorry it had to end the way it did. That wasn't what I intended.'

I have to stop myself from laughing. 'But if it was a test, then I passed!' When he looks at me, I have to force myself to look back without flinching. 'I saved you. Maternal instinct, maybe.' Though I remember the beach dome and know there were times I didn't do the same for Ross.

'Sharma saved me.'

'It's his job,' I say, then try to shrug off the bitterness in my voice. No good involving Sky in any of that, not if I want to keep his favour, not if I still want the chance to break my story.

'Yes, it is.' He considers me for a long time, then sets the undrunk coffee aside. He says, 'I'm glad we went out today, Ivy.'

My name again. I shiver. He gets up to leave, and it isn't till he's at the door that I think to ask, 'Even though the seal died?'

'Yes,' he says, and his eyes are bright and metallic. 'Yes, it was worth it.'

*

I wake in the night to the sound of mewing and wonder whose turn it is to settle the baby. Then I remember the baby is eight thousand miles away and almost fifty years past needing to be settled, and the mewing is just the seal pup, repeating itself into my dreams.

My breath is sour against the pillow, the way Bree's often was, towards the end. The sleeping tabs have left my mind anxious, my limbs stiff and heavy. My bladder presses for attention. I push myself onto the edge of the mattress and uncrook my back. Something clicks. It's so easy to imagine my skeleton chipping away at itself, till there's nothing left and I collapse from within.

I stand up and the light sears on, so bright I have to hold my hand to my eyes and say, 'Dim,' which is slightly better. In the softer glow, the jumbled shapes on the desk cast sinister shadows. Through the porthole window, the ice and sea and rocky bay are subsumed by the dark.

Sharma's words keep playing in my head. *There's always further to fall.*

In the unlit bathroom, my face looms from the mirror like an ice floe in lightless water, as I splash the fug from my head.

*

Moments like this, I catch myself thinking about the photo. Not the first photo – the saviour photo with the seals and the drill ship and the ice – but the second. The one in the bar in Helsinki, with its seductive lighting and glittering other woman.

Except that she was never just 'some woman'. She was the Climate Responsibility Officer for PacifiCorp.

The next day, this sparkling woman would vote on behalf of her CEO, and her vote would be a deciding factor in the ratification of the Antarctic Industry Cap. If the vote was successful, the Industry Cap would all but stop trawling and mining and manufacturing in Antarctica. If I could win her over, this woman's support would keep the corporations out of Antarctica for decades to come. The continent would be protected, and I would be praised as a hero.

Which is why I had come off the vid to Bree the night before, had gone in search of her, had let her lay herself out on my bed like a cadaver, watched her come undone. Because I was committed. Because I was ruthless. Because I would do what it took to win.

*

Me, standing on the table in the bar. Glass in hand, two bottles deep at least. The shots lined up behind me. Wild. Already celebrating.

Someone says, 'You've not won yet, Cunningham.'

The woman's head between my legs. I open my mouth to speak.

*

There's always further to fall.

*

The tap pours itself into the sink and away, and for once I don't even think about conserving water. I think of Sharma, watching everything from his web above the lounge – think of the cubby on the ship, with the screens and the HoloPlayer and all the IntuTech data running through it, my own cabin's readings conspicuously absent. Maretta, knowing exactly what I'd said to AJ, and all because Sharma had told her. Sky earlier in the lounge: *Sharma told me you still leave vid messages for your son.* I think of his bone-tight grip on my wrist. The slide of my feet across the ice. *You know how much he has to lose. If you try to destroy him, I'll bring you down in his place.*

You know how much he has to lose . . .

How much of Sky's life had I tried to find on the IntuNet back in Edinburgh? As I'd filtered through information at my kitchen table, how wild had the speculations been – and wasn't that the point? To keep people guessing? Eat the rich, maybe, but not if you can't judge the size of the buffet.

But I know exactly how much he's worth. I know it from the information I accessed through the pass-chip I found behind the painting in my cabin.

And Sharma knows that I know.

I remember what he told me about the floating factory, making tech parts. Like the grippers, adapted from the Mars missions to suit Antarctic ice. Like an old-school pass-chip, modified to fit a modern vid.

Sharma knows, I realise, because the pass-chip belonged to him.

Back in the bedroom, the bleak eyes of my portrait stare overhead. My legs are still heavy from the sleep tabs. I pace the room: bed to sofa to chest of drawers to bathroom door, back to the bed again.

But if the pass-chip belonged to Sharma, why was it behind the painting in my cabin? My heartbeat still feels jerky from the sleeping tabs. *There's always further to fall.* No reason at all for him to hide the pass-chip in my cabin. Not unless he wanted me to find it.

I remember when I first discovered it, how I'd worried about scams that might infiltrate my vid. And I remember that feeling of resistance when I searched for the Chillers, as though something was piggybacking on my connection. Monitoring. Feeding all my searches back to Sharma, and all because I'd taken the bait. Because I'd been unable to resist plugging it into my vid.

Knowledge is power, isn't that the old maxim? Knowledge is power, and Sharma has both in abundance.

I try to call AJ but the connection keeps on cutting out – no way to tell if this is from the weather or because of Sharma. I hang up and type him a message instead: *I'm being tested.* I delete it and write: *I'm being trapped.* I delete this, too. I take out the other data chip, the one from Maretta. Sharma out on the ice, his grip on my wrist. His every threat challenging me to take him on. What was it he said in the lounge, the night of the storm? *We both know you revel in doing the opposite.* So he threatened me because he knew I was wavering, because he had heard my conversation with AJ and knew I hadn't yet decided to break the story, because he knew threatening me not to break it would push me to do the opposite. Sharma, for whatever reason, wants me to break Maretta's story, and so far I've let him manipulate me like a puppet.

From above the bed, my painting glares. No sense in playing into Sharma's hands any more than I have done already. I set Maretta's data chip on the bedside table.

In the end, I type: *Don't worry – I have everything I need.* I send my message to AJ out into the void.

From beside the data chip, Ross's wooden seal watches me with its paint-dot eyes. When Ross was young, I used to tell him, 'Hold onto this.' Every time I went away for work, I would say, 'You've got your seal. Keep hold of it, and it'll bring me right back to you.' What kind of parenting was that? To suggest my return was in some way conditional?

I navigate my vid until I get to Ross's name. I close my eyes and try to picture him in Abu Dhabi, in an oversized bed with bleached white sheets. I don't even know what time it is in Abu Dhabi – it could be the middle of the day, and he's staring out of his office window at the streets and public squares below. Except his office could be a windowless basement. His bed sheets might not be white. I hold the wooden seal so tight, I can feel my own pulse through it, giving it life.

Ross will come around eventually. I've told myself this every time I've left him a message. I've told myself at the bottom of every glass. My boy. The only family I have left. The last remnant of a life turned sour. Eventually, he'll come around.

I hover with my thumb over his name. From above the bed, the portrait sneers.

SORRY, THE MAILBOX YOU'RE ATTEMPTING TO REACH IS FULL

Those two beeps again. Then nothing.

Stop.

Redial.

Sorry, the mailbox you're attempting to reach is full.

Stop.

Redial.

Sorry, the mailbox you're attempting—

Stop. Redial.

Sorry, the mailbox—

Stop. Redial.

Sorry—

Stop.

Sorry—

Stop.

Sorry – sorry – sorry—

Stop.

A gale against the window – a katabatic wind – or, no, the fury is inside my head, it batters at my skull. Hurricane howl. It strips away thought – gasping – short, shallow – gasping, grabbing at the air.

Pick up, Ross. Pick up pick up pick up.

Sorry, the mailbox you're attempting to reach is full.

I throw the vid down on the bed. Blank screen marble-eye to the ceiling.

The air is thin.

I snatch in small parcels, bites of it – struggle. Breathe, Ivy. Breathe. I throw back my head, gasp, heave, struggle for my lungs as I swallow, swallow, swallow. I reach for a miniature. Empty. I reach for another, and the next one, the next one, the next – empty. I knock back the glass and there's not a slip, not a single stale drop. Check the icebox under the desk. Empty.

The cabin is small. The walls are shrinking. I struggle to breathe, and the portrait fixes her heartless gaze overhead. No, not heartless – *ruthless*. 'Look at me,' I yell, but I can't get the breath and I just wheeze 'me', and the portrait holds her own hard gaze in the mirror. 'Fucking look at me!' I hurl the empty glass at the painting – so hard, my intercostals shriek, the painting rips across the cheekbone, the glass smashes against the wall behind: three fat shards, crack, then onto the bed. My breath snags at the air. I have to get out.

Thermals – where are my thermals? I fling open drawers, haphazard, till I find them, try to pull them on. The bottoms won't fit over the sleepsuit so I abandon them. Under the top, the sleepsuit rubs at my ribs. I pull on a jumper. Trousers, two pairs of socks. The porthole is blue-back, an empty dark. I pick up the broken glass from the bed, slice the side of my thumb – shit – straight white ridge, then blood, a thin red score, a border on a map, a fattening leak. Shit.

I try to stem it with tissue but it bleeds through. There are bandages in the cupboard in the bathroom. One-handed, I tug one out – an avalanche of tab packets and plasters and gauze – and wrap it around. Then another, and another, tight, my thumb fat and throbbing.

This isn't how you dress a wound. A voice in my head. Maybe from the expedition training. Maybe Bree's. I try to stuff things

back into the bathroom cupboard, but they won't go. It's difficult with just one hand, and that hand bandaged and bleeding.
(Why am I not using my good hand? I look down at my good
hand and it's holding Ross's wooden seal. I don't remember
picking it up.)

I'm sorry, the mailbox you're attempting to reach is full.

My hand throbs. Up into my throat, my skull. I check the
miniatures for whisky. Empty. I look at the bed and wonder why
there's broken glass. I gasp for air and it comes as a sob.

Out. I have to get out.

Through the door, now, into the corridor – mausoleum of dead
white men – empty, the crew retreated to the ship for the night,
Sky and Sharma and Maretta god knows where. I grasp at the
air and the air pushes me out, through the glass double doors,
iceberg logo splitting and reforming. In the mudroom, in the
locker, I find my parka. I pull it out and it drops to the floor.
When I pick it up I can't find the sleeve, then it's there but my
hand won't fit – Ross's seal, caught in the cuff. Didn't I leave it
in the room? I remember seeing it on the bedside table – when?
– belly-up in the lamplight beside Maretta's data chip. I push
through, stuff the seal in my pocket.

Overtrousers. Boots, hat, scarf. First pair of gloves, second pair
of gloves. In the locker are the grippers, all strap and metal,
expectant hum. Fuck it. I put them on.

My neck prickles, now, sweats, the parka a band around my
chest. I have to get out. Up at my left temple, a light flashes like
a migraine. No. Not a migraine. Greener. Smaller. A light on a
machine, a waiting message. Ross.

No. The quiet pulse of Sharma's security log, to register who's
in or out of the building. Monitoring. Regulating. Controlling.
Not a message, then, but an expectation – and damned if I'm
going to fulfil any more of Sharma's expectations. I turn the wheel
to unlock the inside door. My cut thumb throbs.

Through the door, into the interim space, close the door behind me. Throb. Has it bled through the bandages? I grip the outside door. The wheel won't budge.

Push now. Grip – difficult in gloves. Strain – muscle, brain, breath. Push – but the wheel is stuck and I'm trapped, frozen, neither in nor out, and I'm not strong enough, but I push and I strain and I push – until suddenly, a slip. A fraction of give, and the wheel budges, then eases, then slides, and I turn it, and then the door is open and the cold is in and I'm out. Finally, out.

My head is a weather balloon, rising. I can't feel my arms. I can't feel my legs. But I can feel the data chip, niggling through my pocket. I can feel the small wooden weight of Ross's seal.

Down the steps, then, one two three, counting the clang of grippered boots, four five, the cold metal ring, six, the photo of Keira in the park below the red metal bridge, seven, Keira on the splashpad, eight nine, Keira laughing at the unexpected chill.

Ten. Crunch underfoot as I reach the ice. Only then do I look up, and see the world lit blue, ocean blue, the blue of night forgetting itself. For a second I'm back in the tunnel in the Frisco aquarium, the whale shark elegant and mournful overhead. Keira's small finger traces the krill tattoo at my wrist. I try to breathe.

The air stings at my face, flenses the inside of my throat. I cough and my eyes stream. I wipe them on the back of my glove.

This isn't a human landscape – nothing here to measure myself against. No fucking perspective, Kay would have said.

Except I've never had much grip on perspective, never been good at distinguishing big from small.

*

Helsinki winks at me through the picture window, all streetlamps pinging on and gunmetal light off the water.

A bead of condensation gathers, grows heavy, runs down the chill bowl of the wine glass. On the thick pink of the bed, I sit and call Bree. I tell her, 'All checked in and in my sleepsuit.'

Bree with her video turned off. Bree nothing but a blank screen. Bree saying, 'Ivy, Keira's dead.'

*

No point in trying to go back. Only forward. Only out onto the ice.

I flick the switches and the grippers hum into life. They stretch, contract, adjust to the shape of my feet. I feel them strengthen their grip.

I remember my training with the Foundation, fifty years ago. Never leave shelter without a clear route back. Never go out without a map and compass, without GPS, without some way to navigate home. Never go without communications equipment, without backup communications equipment, without letting someone know where you're going and how long you expect to be gone. Never go without telling people when and where to search for your body. Never go out onto the ice alone.

I step out of the shadow of the building, into the frozen world beyond.

I STEP OUT

I step out and there's yellow on the ice. Did you hear the one about the yellow snow? Funny, yes – something about eating, something about waste. Never consume again what you've already exorcised from your own body.

But anyway it isn't yellow, more gold. A yellow-gold glow, a light-bath like sunrise, except it can't be, not yet, not even this far south. Light-spill from the Station, then, from the big window in the central module. Always gold, always achingly lit.

Turn away from it.

To the left, a thin pink wash spreads from behind the mountains. At this time of year, the night can't last forever. There will be a dawn soon.

I turn away from that, too.

The grippers release and I stumble, catch myself, feel them grip the ice again. *Ready–lift, drop–re-engage, ready–lift, drop–re-engage.* I keep moving forward, the ice sheet blue and innocuous ahead. A winking blue. Beckoning. Impossible to see the join of ice and sky – only a haze I could let myself fall into, like swimming in an artificial pool, like drowning among the small blue tiles.

*

Ivy, Keira's dead. I remember the small image of myself in the corner of the vid screen. I remember Bree saying something about flights.

I told her, 'I already have one.'

Pause.

'Bree?'

'You're coming home?'

I remember saying, *I have a speech.*

*

My thumb throbs up through my wrist. Isn't ice good for wounds? Or is it water? My legs are cold where I left off my thermals. I keep walking.

I should have run my thumb under the tap. Or – isn't alcohol also good for disinfecting? No. Remember, there was no alcohol. I should have used something other than just a bandage. I remember that now. The bandage is the binder, not the dressing. I picture the fibres knitting into the cut.

I should have tied it tighter. Or looser. Probably I should have pressed a fingernail into my skin afterwards to check the circulation. Probably I should have found somebody else to tie it for me.

Probably I should have done a lot of things.

*

I have a speech.

*

Bree saying, 'Can't you vid it in?'

The floral curtains. The dusky pink carpet. Everything perfumed, cloying, thick at the back of my throat. 'It's going to a vote.'

'Damn it, Ivy, it's your fucking grandchild.'

'She isn't, technically.'

302

The wrong thing to say.

Obviously.

*

The ice is denser now. Compacted. The grippers work harder with every step. *Ready–lift, drop–re-engage.* I feel the jolt of each contact in my pelvis, in my stomach, up through my head.

When my eyes water, I dig in with the heel of my hand. Sniff. The cuffs are rough on my cheeks, glitter of frozen condensation. I stuff my hands in my pockets for warmth. Stupid. What if I fall and need to catch myself? What if I shatter?

*

'She isn't, technically.'

'So is Ross not your son?'

*

In my pocket, through the gloves, I nudge the wooden seal. If I tripped, would I bother to stop myself falling? If I fell onto the ice, would I get back up?

The floral curtains. The dusky carpet. My voice already hoarse: 'I'm sorry – I love you – I'll be on the first flight back. As soon as the voting's done.'

Pause.

'Three days.'

Another pause. Another bead of condensation gathers, starts to fall.

'I promise, I'll be straight back home.'

Bree, quiet from the blacked-out screen. 'Don't bother.'

*

I drank my third glass of wine and told myself I needed to stop. Outside the window, the lights of Helsinki flickered out as I sat on the bed. I told myself I ought to call Ross. I went in search of the woman who could swing us the vote.

*

'I'll be straight back home.'
　　'Don't bother.'

*

I walk towards the horizon that isn't a horizon, but a blue haze between ice and sky. The world folds in on itself and disappears.

BREAK

I can see my breath, now, and the ice is a shallower blue, the dawn threatening to spill. Against the blue everything, the edge is a dark diagonal scar across the ice. It takes a moment for my eyes to register. Then the scar drops away to become a void.

I stop but the grippers predict my patterns and release me from the ice, so suddenly I'm sliding, the chasm in front – until I stamp my foot and the grippers re-engage and I'm still.

The crack in the ice shelf.

Impossible to tell how wide it is, how far I am from the edge. Impossible, down here, to get any sort of perspective.

The ice here is unstable. I tell myself it is a cliff edge, a network of cracks and fissures on the verge of collapse. I remember the stories from our training, of explorers who tumbled into crevasses, who clung on for days with no hope of rescue, who had to cut themselves loose to save their partners, who had to cut their partners loose to save themselves. It would be stupid to approach the edge.

*

Ross in the hospital in Frisco – the same hospital where Keira was born, a different room, a different ward – sits beside her small body, holds her paling hand.

Ross at the too-empty house – no, the house is no longer

307

there, the house was washed away. The house they rented from PacifiCorp. Built on bad foundations.

Ross checked into a hotel, somewhere functional, impersonal, bland.

I go in search of the glittering woman, bring her back to the too-soft mattress in the thick-pink room. Help her lose control.

*

I get down on my knees. It's difficult, with the cold and the bulk of my layers, to lower myself to this level. The grippers hum and grasp at the air for purchase. I stretch back and turn them off.

Behind me, the ice is paling. In front, the chasm is an unplanned depth. I crawl forward, hands and knees, closer, closer to the edge. The ice burns through my overtrousers and my lack of thermals. I lie flat out and pull myself along. The edge crawls closer. The wooden seal shifts in my pocket, knuckles against my stomach.

My face is so close to the ice I can smell my own body through it – sharp, metallic, desperation at the back of my throat like burnt toast. I drag myself forward, look out over the edge.

*

And remember the photo in the bar.

*

The ice makes my head swim. The ice plunges my head into an ocean and drags it further down. The ice is a current I struggle against; it taunts me with the urge to draw breath.

It would be so much easier to let myself fall.

*

And remember the photo in the bar – all decadence and flint. And the woman. The Climate Responsibility Officer for PacifiCorp, her glittering head. And on the other side of the

308

world, the mudslide has let slip the house on its bad foundations, and hers is the company responsible. And me on the table, celebrating the almost-certain ratification of the Antarctic Industry Cap. And the room is spinning, the crowd is glittering, guilting, glinting in the low seductive light. And when someone says, 'You've not won yet, Cunningham,' I push the woman's head deep between my legs, and when she laughs, I fling out my arms like I'm back in the Ross Sea, the gesture of the movement – glittering arc of spilled wine – look straight at the camera and say, 'Who the fuck will vote against me now?'

And somewhere in Frisco, Keira lies cooling in a hospital morgue. And after a sleepless night, Ross stares at the hotel carpet, doesn't find the strength to move.

And later, after the press have shared that photo of Keira at the splashpad under the red bridge, after they've shared the photo of the bar in Helsinki, the PacifiCorp woman's head between my legs and my arms outstretched like I'm invincible, after the woman has emphatically denounced me, has voted against the Industry Cap just to prove to her board that she isn't under my control, and after all the subsidiary corporations have rallied around her, and everything I've ever worked towards has failed, I will finally call Ross.

'I was doing this for you,' I will tell him. 'Trying to make the world a better place. I've always been doing this for you.'

And there will be silence at the other end. And the screen will go dark. And that will be it.

*

'Who the fuck will vote against me now?'
There's always further to fall.

*

I stare down into the chasm, all jagged edges, all deepening blue. Bluer and bluer, down to where the oldest ice hardens, where it strains and strengthens under the weight of what it carries.

309

I lean out over the edge. The deeper into the chasm I look, the further it takes me back into the past.

I lean out more and the ice beneath me shifts.

Unlocks.

The world unlocks and I'm falling, arms and legs out of control, my feet all metal and slide, and there's nothing but blue, rushing up and over me, a tidal wave – until suddenly I'm still. Frozen.

I splay my fingers against the ice, hold myself low to the surface. The chasm is still open in front of me.

The smallest shift. Only the ice resettling, finding a new balance. My body is loud inside my skull.

Breathe, Ivy.

Breathe.

Gradually, I become aware of my stomach. It burns cold where my parka has shifted up around my chest. The wooden seal digs like a thorn into the space between my ribs.

Carefully, so carefully, I reach round, struggle it from my pocket with my too-fat gloves. When I place the seal on the ice – flippers spread, worry-smoothed head staring up at me – it could almost be the real thing.

I drop it over the edge. It clatters off the side, then tumbles away into the dark. For a moment, I watch the space where it disappeared, as though something else might rise up from the blue to take its place. Nothing does.

LOOK FORWARD/ LOOK UP

By the time I look up from the void, the other side is brighter. The line between ice and sky has narrowed to swallow less of the world. Inch by shuffling inch, I pull myself back from the edge. Only when I'm the length of my own body back from the chasm do I let myself kneel up. Only then do I realise how little I can feel my stomach, my legs. Only then do I realise how sore my skin sings against the ice. Isn't there IntuTech in the parka – a switch on the inside of the inside pocket? I fumble with the zip, but my fingers are too raw. I can barely even switch on the grippers.

I turn away from the fissure, focus on placing my feet. My movements are erratic, now. The grippers have no regularity to latch onto, which makes walking in them easier. Unable to find a rhythm, they respond to each individual step, and I can look up instead of at my feet.

The golden light from the Station is a distant beacon, and above it, the dawn's pink beginning has lifted into something brighter, something alive. A rare phenomenon: the sun still unrisen, but from below the horizon, its light catches in the highest clouds. They swirl with streaks of pink and orange and silver. The light strikes against a million ice crystals and makes them sing: a chorus of colours; ghosts departing the night on a high note.

I'd forgotten, in the dark of the blue night, how brightly other colours can shine.

I want to throw back my head and laugh, to spread my arms, to spin circles to the music of the colours. The throb in my hand is smaller, now, easy to close the door on. Easy to close the door on my whole body, if I want to. Or to let myself rise, iridescent as a ghost. To sing myself into the choir.

My training calls to me, softly, across half a century: *when you start to feel euphoric, seek shelter.*

I make for the light from the Station, but there's nothing to measure myself against – who knows if I'm even moving? Like I'm on a walking sim and the ice is just turning and turning under my feet. I giggle, and then I can't stop. I clutch at my throat as I walk, going nowhere, and the sky still warbling its chorus overhead. I keep on towards the winking gold – except now the Station is moving. Not the light, but the spindly dark shape around it. The caterpillar building has finally got up and is wandering away across the ice, leaving its glowing heart behind. I wave as though I'm waving a ship from the dock. 'Goodbye!' I shout across the ice, and for a second I think the building hears me, because it pauses, then carries on crawling away. 'Goodbye, goodbye!'

Except the building is still there, so it isn't the Station moving, but something in front of it. Tall. Puffed up. Coming closer, a rolling gait, winking the light in and out of existence. A creature, out on the ice.

A Plan B parka, branded blue against the gold.

The figure in the parka is running, calling something I can't hear, and I try to wave again, but now my arm won't lift, and my feet have stopped, and the grippers are the only thing holding me to the ice, the only thing stopping me from floating up to join the song.

And then the figure is here – is folding its arms around me, except I can't tell if this is a choke hold or a hug.

The figure says, 'Thank god.'

Urgent. I realise this and then think someone else is realising it inside my head, and I giggle again. Urgent and familiar. Ross. Ross is here – summoned by the falling wooden seal, the old Ross, called up out of the past.

'It's alright, Ms Cunningham, I've got you.'

And then the voice is someone else's.

The man from the X-Ped. The birdlike man. Aisi. His name swims up from the depths as he hugs me into the insulated down of his parka.

For the first time since Helsinki, I let myself go slack. Let myself be held. Aisi tries to rub warmth into my arms, and my face presses against the cold shine of the Plan B logo on his chest, the iceberg hiding so much of itself below the surface. Overhead, the choir begins to fade to white and the clouds let go their ghosts. The sun lifts its first rays above the horizon.

WILD ABANDON

The mudroom of the Station is bright and painfully warm. As Aisi unfastens the grippers from my feet, Sky says something about data. I don't answer. I sit like a dead fish. Aisi unzips my coat, the way I used to do for Ross.

Sharma turns the wheel on the inner door, shutting out the cold and the burgeoning dawn, as Sky pulls aside Aisi to ask where he found me. 'I'm right here,' I want to say, and don't. In the warmth of the mudroom, my fingers and toes tingle so violently they hurt, and I can feel the blood throbbing in my head. Easier just to sit here among them. Isn't this what I wanted? To be back at the centre of things? To remain still and let others come into my orbit. To move and feel the world shift with me.

The door closed – the light locked out – Sharma stands sentry beside it. As if any of us could make a break for it. As if there would be anywhere to go. My feet are blocks of unchiselled stone, and the warmth is sharper now, a thousand needles up my calves and along my arms, a heavy throb emanating from my hands and feet. My mind wanders along the too-clean corridor with its portraits of dead explorers, through the cavernous lounge towards the kitchen. I let myself picture the chef in his ridiculous toque, rustling up breakfast for Kip to deliver to the pretentious wooden table – something hearty and smelling of

319

long-lost childhood; crispy bacon, or sausages still sizzling from the pan – but it's too early, and Kip and the chef and the rest of the crew must still be on the ship, sleeping to the gentle rocking of the bay. I allow myself to close my eyes, just for a moment.

'Ms Cunningham.' Maretta's voice. I ignore it.

'Ivy.' Sky's voice is harder, an unexpected accusation. When I open my eyes, a shadow steals, slow, across his face. 'Is there something you'd like to tell us?'

He sounds so much like a disapproving schoolteacher – so much like Bree – that I can't help but laugh. There's an army rising up inside my head, clamouring, every thought a landmine sending searing pain into my temples.

'When he realised you were missing, Sharma checked your room.' Sky holds up the sleek silver data chip, and like a magnet it draws my gaze. The Plan B logo gleams from the side like an accusation, and I can't help myself, can't keep the surprise from my face. His voice is flint. 'Tell us about it.'

'It's Maretta's.' I spit it out like something caught between my teeth.

When Maretta makes to speak, Sky holds up a hand to silence her. 'She's told me what it is. The question is why Sharma discovered it in your room.'

I try to stand, to put myself on a level with them, but my knees are locked shut and there's no strength left in my calves. Instead, I try to find that hardness I felt on the first night onboard ship: that resistance lingering just below the surface. I can still win this. When I saved Sky from the seal – or at least, *would* have saved him, if Sharma hadn't beaten me to it – I proved to Sky that he can trust me. Time to put that trust to the test. 'They're in it together,' I tell him. 'Sharma and Maretta.' Out of the corner of my eye, I see Sharma's instinctive twitch, before he stills himself. 'They want our project to fail.'

'Our project?'

'Plan B. I want to write your thinkpiece – sell this place to the world. They want me to do the opposite.'

'Go on.'

'They want to tell the world how it was built on stolen technology. They want to destroy it.'

'But not you.'

'No.'

'You want to help me, yes?' The fidget has returned to Sky's fingers, weaving their anxious pattern, finger to thumb to finger to thumb. 'And yet you took this.' The disapproving tone again. A Victorian master in a prestigious school.

'Or it was planted.' I say the words without thinking, but once they're out, I don't want to take them back. This, I think then, is how I beat Sharma. Bringing him down, raising myself up in his place – and if Maretta has to tumble with him, then so be it. *There's always further to fall.*

'Someone planted it in your room?'

'Sharma,' I spit out. 'Sharma or Maretta.'

'I see.'

Quiet. The world stands still. I nod and my skull feels heavy, my movements over-exaggerated and slow-motion.

Over the thud of my heart in my head, he says, 'I was willing to give you a chance, to see if Maretta could get you on-side. An amicable solution.'

Then he looks to Sharma, who nods and says, 'The Cunningham problem.'

'Yes.' Sky closes his eyes as though the weight of the world has dragged them shut. When he opens them, his face is clear. He smiles his smile from the first night I met him, all spider, all bite. His eyes slide off me like oil. 'All yours,' he says to Sharma. Then he hands the data chip back to Maretta, and turns away.

SHARMA

And so now here I am: in the lounge in the middle of the Station, in the middle of the conservation site, in the middle of absolutely nowhere, staring out at the endless white glitter of the ice. There are narrow grooves in my hand from gripping so tightly to the data chip.

I thumb my vid as I pour myself a drink – still early, but nobody's going to stop me. My last message to AJ flashes up on the screen: *Don't worry – I have everything I need.* There's no connection anymore – just a loading wheel, turning.

Like I told you from the start, this book is a guilting. A physical manifestation of guilt.

*

In the bustle of bags being packed and loaded into the vestibule, Maretta was taut-faced, as though her words were stuck like communion wafers to the roof of her mouth. I sidled over to her. 'Sorry I sold you out,' I told her, even though I would have done it again in a heartbeat.

'I'm sorry you took it.' She pressed the data chip's vulnerable weight into my palm. Even here, accused at the edge of the world, she managed to look crisp, unruffled. As she pulled back her hand, I noticed she'd fixed the notch in her polished nail. 'I really did hope you wouldn't.'

Around us, the men were busy organising our departure.

'It was a test, Ms Cunningham.' The corners of her mouth turned down as she smiled. 'The technology was never stolen; Sky oversaw its development himself.'

'But I did it for the cause.'

'What cause?' She looked the full length of me, gave a small shake of her head, then removed my hand from her arm. 'You know, I used to buy into all of that.'

'I think you still do.' I pictured the fingerprint-smeared frame in her cabin, how she must cling to the past, that connection to her younger, more optimistic self. To the person she was when she wrote me that letter. A small flame inside her, which cynical professionalism could never quite extinguish. 'Sky told me – even after all the things I wrote about him – how you invited me down here. When he wanted to silence me, this was your idea.'

'That isn't exactly— '

'The *Cunningham Problem*, right? You wanted to give me a second chance.'

She glanced again at Sky, at Sharma lugging bags into the vestibule for Aisi to carry back across the ice, to where the X-Ped must have been waiting, hidden from view at the bottom of the rocky steps. Then she looked at me with the air of a parent, about to destroy delusions their child should long have grown out of. 'Sharma's idea, not mine.'

Sharma? I couldn't think of anyone who so clearly wanted me here less – but then I remembered him in the room above the lounge, at the centre of his web of monitors, the impression of him tugging on the strings.

'When Sky asked me to – what was your phrase? *Silence* you? – I didn't know what to do.' She paused, and for a second she looked as surprised as I was by this admission of her own inadequacy. Then she smoothed the front of her jacket, unruffled her face, and continued: 'I worried my emotions might be clouding my judgement – all those years I hated you for casting us aside.' I started to explain, but she carried on as though I hadn't spoken: 'That's why I went to Sharma – he understands people, he's good at solving problems – only to discover he'd spent as many years hating you as I had. More, in fact.'

'If he hates me so much, why would he want me here?'

'I told you, you altered the course of his whole life. This whole expedition, it's . . .' She paused. Her eyes slid off me, and for the first time since I met her, she looked embarrassed – so awkward and real that I wondered how I could ever have been fooled by that whole performance with the moonrise and the data chip. A *test*. When she looked towards Sharma, he paused in the act of zipping up his parka to nod back at her, reassuring and victorious. She told me, 'You'll have to ask him.'

*

Maretta: *I'm sorry you took it.*

Me: *You wanted to give me a second chance.*

*

'I wonder if you can imagine it yet, Ms Cunningham. A rusting hull out in the middle of the ocean. Total abandonment by the people who promised to protect you.' Sharma stood in the too-bright mudroom, one hand on the door to the vestibule, the outer door shut. 'I want you to understand how that feels.'

Through the porthole, I could just see the miniature figures of Sky and Maretta, walking away across the ice. Aisi striding out ahead, no longer birdlike, but heavy. A metal hull navigating deep waters. All three of them so small by then, that if I raised my hand, I could have blocked them out entirely. I had been so preoccupied with Maretta's data chip, I hadn't even noticed them leave. On the screen by the entrance, the occupancy showed only Sharma and myself.

Every part of me screamed to back away from him, to seek out the warm safety of my room with its view out across the ice – but even there, there would be no refuge from his prying. His web of monitors. His seeking out of Maretta's data chip. No option, then, but to plant my feet. To stand my ground – except how do you tell solid ground from what's only ice pretending, ready to crack and give way beneath you?

My heart was a drumbeat against the inside of my head. I forced myself to breathe deep. 'You brought me here.'

'Yes.'

'Maretta told me.' I held my head high, as though this news might catch him off guard. 'The floating factories. You know none of that was ever really my responsibility?'

I expected him to argue back, but he just smiled. Wolfish, not meeting his eyes. 'Maretta thought you could change. It was her one condition, that I let her give you that chance.'

I wanted to ask: her condition on what? But I pictured her sharp suit, her officiousness on that first evening, betraying her desire to be at the centre of all of Sky's operations, and I knew what: letting Sharma take control. Letting him call the shots.

The excitement built in his voice as he nodded to the data chip in my hand. 'She genuinely believed you might pass her test, that you might be capable of putting others before your own ambition.'

I am, I wanted to tell him – I have. But my heart was a wet rag in my throat and the words refused to form around it. Through the porthole, the others were already out of sight, dropped below the top of the rocky steps to where the X-Ped must have been waiting.

'But you've had dozens of second chances, haven't you?' His voice trembled, his whole body rigid with the force of keeping it steady. How long had he been building towards this moment? How long waiting to meet me, to blame me for the course of his

328

entire life? 'I know you, Ivy Cunningham. I've studied you for years. Every time, you've made the same mistake.'

I've studied you for years . . . The cubby in the belly of the ship. The HoloPlayer scattering my career – my life – across its four small walls. Every speech, every photograph. Every feature as I leapt from project to project, patching up the world and moving on.

Laid out like that, I can see how it might have looked callous, ambitious. Especially to someone like Sharma, only seeing his own side of the story.

But it wasn't like that. I'm sure it wasn't like that.

'People are patterns, Ms Cunningham. I told you, I learned early how to judge the direction of the tide, when to let it carry me, when to turn and fight against it. I waited a long time to get to you.'

The words forced themselves past the clagging lump in my throat: 'And now you're leaving.'

'Yes.' His chest heaved, breath shallow as though he'd just pushed up from underwater. On the screen, he clicked the occupancy down to one, then moved into the vestibule.

Inside me, everything clamoured, but I held my head high, refused to give in. Besides, hadn't Maretta worshipped me when she was younger? And hadn't I saved Sky from the leopard seal? Hadn't he told me himself what it proved: that he could trust me? Connections like that, they mean something. Umbilical bonds it's impossible just to walk away from. Sharma's gaze kept on pinning me like a rare moth, but I was damned if I was going to squirm beneath it.

Let him have his long-fought-for moment. Let him think he's won. I've been playing the game far longer than he has, and there is always another chance. There is always a way to make things new, always a Plan B.

I remembered what Bree taught me, about feeling my vertebrae stack one on top of the other, employing my full height. With all the superiority I could muster, I told him, 'I'll wait.'

He closed the door, and I listened to the slow metallic grind as the wheel locked fast. Then, fainter, the sound of the outer door being opened, then closed. I imagined I could hear the clang of boots on metal steps, the crunch away across the ice. Then nothing. Only my own breath.

FRISCO

There's one more moment I want to tell you about. It was that last summer evening outside Ross's house on the outskirts of Frisco – the PacifiCorp complex they moved to after Keira was born, which clung so precariously to the loose earth on the side of the hill.

Through the smog, the sunset mingled with the glow from distant wildfires. Heat lingered in the air, whispered to the sweat and sunburn still on our bodies, and the patio radiated with the warmth it had spent the day collecting. From other yards across the concrete wall came drifting laughter and the rapid chatter of a parrot, as Hanna spread sheets of brown packing paper across the wooden table, as Ross carried the big metal pot from the kitchen, flat-footed with the weight of it, as he tipped the food out onto the table to eat with our hands: chunks of sausage; crab; shrimp, pale in the thin light; ghosting onions; cobs of corn like rolls of golden teeth; fat buttery hunks of potato; the smells of oregano and paprika; the gentle must of sage.

The food burst and melted and scalded and squashed in our mouths, and we caught each other's eyes and smiled, spice-drunk and woozy. The dog lay in wait at our feet, breath hot on our ankles as we picked pieces from the pile, as we licked and slurped the flavour from our fingers. When she thought nobody was watching, Keira dropped bits of sausage through the gaps in the table, stifled giggles as he snuffled them up.

The paper ran semi-transparent under the warm grease and our fingers left smeary prints on the beer bottles. The yard was full of the scent of stone-dust giving way to dewing earth, as the sky faded to purple and the lamps flickered on.

I remember Ross leaning on his tired elbows, wiping a drop of butter from the corner of his lips. I remember his eyes-closed sigh, his lazy smile. When the baby woke from his nap and hiffled, I remember Ross picking him up and rocking him calm again.

My stomach settled against my waistband. Beside me, Bree's breathing came deep and quiet, the anxious tucks around her eyes loosened for the moment. Somewhere from a neighbour's upstairs window, a vid speaker churned out slow folk, and I found my head swaying to it. When the bats flitted from their daytime hiding places to unstitch the sky, the dog watched them with half-raised eyes, too sleepy and fat on scraps to bother barking. Keira pushed back the paper and dozed on the warm spice-smelling slats of the tabletop. Hanna hummed as she breast-fed the baby.

On the other side of the world, at a hotel on reclaimed land in Helsinki, preparations for the summit were already underway. Security forces had been staking out the site for weeks, and every room redecorated to within an inch of its life. Soon the photographers and vid-makers and correspondents would begin to gather, poised and electric as an oncoming storm. The politicians and their aides. The representatives of CEOs – everyone who had or wanted power over the world – the statisticians, the economists, the activists flown in to make our case, to argue against the continued industrialisation of the Southern Ocean, to try to ratify the Antarctic Industry Cap.

The agenda had been set. My speech had been written. The vote was tabled and the eyes of the fickle world were already starting to turn.

I pulled the last beers, dripping, from the melted ice bucket and passed them around. I remember Ross clinking his bottle against mine across the table, above the remnants of the meal. When I drank, it tasted hoppy, rich with the remains of the summer. I swilled each mouthful, held each chilled gulp for as long as I could bear to, before letting go.

THE END OF THE WORLD/
THE BEGINNING OF EVERYTHING

Some nights, I have this dream where everything is underwater. Where it blocks my ears, where every movement is a struggle and I have to push against it with each of my limbs in turn.

As I load Maretta's data chip into my vid, everything slows, then stops.

Outside, the day is bright but not yet broken, two halves waiting to be torn apart. Beyond it, the waves hold themselves in stasis above the beach, and all the ocean's currents pause their circumnavigation of the globe.

A guilting is not a confession. It is not a bargain for forgiveness. It is simply an acknowledgement: this is what I've done; this is how I've hurt people; this is where I made the wrong choice.

The words swim up from the screen, swim back to me across the years. Starlings in the trees outside the window of the Boston flat. Ross in his pram, his sleep-breath shallow, full of hope, while I sat, snatching short moments at my desk, writing the article that would win me the Pulitzer, that would shape environmental discourse for decades to come.

This is how I've hurt people; this is where I made the wrong choice.

I stare at the screen as though something else might rise up from between the familiar words. There is always a Plan B. And perhaps my own words, left for me to rediscover, here at the end of the world, are a reminder of that. *This is how I've hurt people; this is where I made the wrong choice.* Outside, the waves crash, the currents push, and the day resumes its breaking.

What was it Sky said about his father? After I tried to save him from the seal? *All I've ever wanted from him is an apology, and all these unspeaking years would be forgotten.*

Isn't that what my Pulitzer article was all about? A chance to take credit for past mistakes, and then to set them aside? An apology, and everything is forgotten. A chance to move on.

An acknowledgement. A guilting. A Plan B.

I send a message out into the void: *I'm sorry.*

*

I pour myself another drink. And a third, and a fourth. I check my vid again.

After I've drunk my fifth, I will raid the kitchen for whatever reconstituted food packet looks most appealing, and I will eat it here, in the armchair beside the artificial fire, with Shackleton's conversational smile for company.

When I've finished, or perhaps this afternoon, Sky and Sharma and Maretta will return, to accept my apology in person, and everything else will be forgotten. My guilting. My own Plan B. I will acknowledge my taking of the data chip. I will acknowledge the electrical fire that gutted Maretta's neighbourhood. I will acknowledge the conditions on the floating factories, Sharma's feeling of abandonment.

An acknowledgement – a guilting – and everything can be made good.

The words said, the past stepped over, we will sit by the fire and tell each other stories of long-dead explorers, and it will be just like the ship on the night of the storm. Tomorrow, when we make for Ushuaia, it will be together, as a team. The *Lone Star* will slip back along the Beagle Channel with her sails unfurled, all wide and white and billowing. All of the skeleton crew will

340

have come out on deck for our arrival, but this time, there will be voices as they work the ship, calling instructions to one another to navigate the narrow channel, their shouts lifted by the joy of a full sail, and it will feel like coming home from war.

And I will stand in my customary spot, right at the *Lone Star*'s prow, with the crew bustling behind me, the whole world ahead. And there will be whales, mother and calf, and they will slip ahead to guide us home.

And when we disembark in Ushuaia, there will be an IntuTaxi to deliver us from the dockside to the tiny airport, where Sky's private jet will be waiting to carry us north, back into the world. I will send AJ my thinkpiece on the miracle of Plan B, and AJ will find it a home in whichever publication scraps for it the hardest. It will be read. It will be quoted. The world will be hooked on Antarctica again – and when people are eager for more information, I will be the one to give it to them.

Because really, isn't that what people want? To believe the world – like any of us – can be made new? Can be brought back from the brink at the eleventh hour? To live in beautiful denial?

*

I'm sorry you took it.
You wanted to give me a second chance.

*

Or perhaps: *You wanted to give me a second chance.*
I'm sorry you didn't take it.

*

If I blur my eyes, the Station around me slips away. If I close my ears, there is only the soft rush of blood in my head.

I stand by the window in the lounge, right up against it, my body pressed to the view. For once, I let myself lean forward into the window's tilt, until my whole weight rests on the reinforced glass, and all I can see ahead and below me is ice, stretching on and on forever, to the haze where it bleeds into the sky.

I hover above the ice shelf, caught in the act of falling. The glass is cold against my forehead. I spread out my arms against it and imagine this might be how it feels to fly. Beneath me, the world simply spins: still ungrieving, still resolute and hopeful on its path.

*

My words come slowly now, up from the gut, where all language begins, each one winched on its own taut string.

I write as a way to exorcise the past. I write as a way to kill time before the future.

I write while I wait for someone to return.

I pour myself another drink and check my vid. A purple dark begins to creep across the ice, the moon rising like a buoy untethered from its mooring, no longer quite full. I listen to the soft whirring of the Station, its mechanical heart.

I balance the drink on the arm of the chair, where at any moment the glass could tip and shatter.

On the screen, the loading wheel turns. Searching, searching for a connection.

Acknowledgements

Enormous thanks are due to Lucy Luck and Saida Azizova for all their encouragement and support. Without them, this book would still be a hopeful document on a tired laptop. Also thank you to Aa'Ishah Hawton, Leah Woodburn, Rali Chorbadzhiyska, Leila Cruickshank, Helen Bleck, Caitriona Horne, Anna Frame, Amaani Banharally, Valeri Rangelov and everyone at Canongate responsible for bringing the novel into being. We did it!

For the writing that wasn't done at my kitchen table, I am grateful for residencies at Gladstone's Library, Moniack Mhor, and Heinrich Böll Cottage (funded by Mayo County Council and the Arts Council of Ireland). I'd also like to acknowledge the financial support of: a Northern Writers' Award from New Writing North, supported by Northumbria University and Arts Council England; an Authors' Foundation Grant from the Society of Authors; and a Gulliver Grant from the Speculative Literature Foundation.

Huge thanks as well to the British Antarctic Survey, the Scott Polar Institute, and the Hurtigruten team on board the *Fram* for their help in researching the book, and to the Intrepids (Frankie, Sarah, Ian, Mike, Nadja and Helene) for their constant inspiration and sense of adventure. Also thank you to Sarah Davy and Northern Writers' Studio, and to Polly Atkin, Will Smith and

Ange Harker, for letting me bounce ideas off them, and for keeping me writing during lockdown – as well as to the neighbour's cat Monty, without whose daily affections the novel might have been completed much sooner.

Lastly, the most heartfelt of thank yous to Mum and Dad, for always encouraging me to work towards a better future – and to Loren, with whom I plan to share it.